NEW DETROIT

(Cris De Niro, Book 6)

ALSO BY GERARD de MARIGNY

What readers are saying of ...
THE WATCHMAN OF EPHRAIM (Cris De Niro, Book 1)

"For a real page-turning thriller with twists and one which keeps the reader hooked, read this book."
beckvalleybooks

"The Watchman of Ephraim was a ride. I loved every minute I spent with the story and characters. I found myself getting choked up with the description of the events of 9/11. I was totally drawn into the story and couldn't put the book down."
Daniel N. Wallace

"Just finished reading The Watchman of Ephraim and I must give a very enthusiastic WOW! Gerard de Marigny has crafted a very exciting and engrossing story of international espionage with vibrant, fully-developed characters who the reader connects with. Throw in a few exotic locales and you have a totally worthy successor to either James Bond or Jack Ryan. Read it – you won't be disappointed."
Musicman

What readers are saying of …
RISE TO THE CALL (Cris De Niro, Book 3)

"The corporate nature of The Watchman Agency calls to mind the Clive Cussler "Oregon Files" series with Juan Cabrillo, and I was pleased to see that de Marigny allows his main character to take a back seat from time to time … With action that spans the globe from the United States to Iran, and considerable high-tech gadgets, the story certainly appeals to techno-thriller fans, with a world that is peopled with principled spooks, mafia, Russian deep-cover agents, and Iranian leaders."
Stephen England (Author of PANDORA'S GRAVE)

"Another jaw-dropping political suspense novel from Gerard de Marigny … I'm always amazed at the amount of facts that Gerard puts into the novels to make (them) as accurate as possible."
Tim Proctor

"One blockbuster novel filled with betrayals, deceits, lies and a high degree of realism and research into the storyline and plot. Read the ending. You decide who wins."
Samfreene (Amazon Review)

What readers are saying of …
PROJECT 111 (Cris De Niro, Book 4)

"Another home run on a well-executed story that has plenty of suspense, action, thrilling moments. The story unfolds in a well-paced storyline that at the end, you are left wanting the story to continue. I am a big fan of de Marigny novels and look forward for more to come."
Robert "Robear" (Amazon Review)

"If you enjoy Thor, Flynn, Siva, Coes, or any books in this genre, you'll love this series! The depth of the characters is so well done you get hooked from the first page on. I'd recommend reading the books in order. Not that they don't stand on their own, they do, but the way the author builds upon each character really engages you in their lives. Love the patriotism, attention to detail and storylines. Keep 'em coming!!!"
Barb (Amazon Review)

"This book was a delight to read … The development of the main characters is great and believable. I like how everyone that is connected to Cris becomes family to him, even the Russian prisoner. I enjoyed the little bits of humor every now and then … I like how the author references actual events that happened in the real world in this book … This was a great book."
Bobmandingo (Amazon Review)

What readers are saying of …
NOTHING SO GLORIOUS (Cris De Niro, Book 5)

NEW DETROIT

GERARD DE MARIGNY

(Cris De Niro, Book 6)

JarRyJorNo Publishing

HENDERSON

JarRyJorNo
Publishing

Published by JarRyJorNo Publishing
Henderson, Nevada

Edited by Lisa de Marigny

ISBN: 197642772X
ISBN-13: 978-1976427725

Library of Congress Control Number: 2017914537

1 3 5 9 10 8 6 4 2

AUTHOR'S NOTE

Narcotics and alcohol addiction are responsible for taking the lives of too many of our loved ones. My wife and I have lost so many family and friends in just the last couple of years. If you are suffering from addiction or know someone that is, please reach out for help. A Narcotics or Alcohol Anonymous Chapter is standing by. Just pick up the phone and ask for help ... before it's too late.

Well … It's been a while since the last CRIS DE NIRO novel! First and always, all thanks and praise goes to our heavenly Father for bringing Cris De Niro into my life!!!

Eternal thanks to my wife Lisa and sons Jared, Ryan, Jordan, and Noah. Your faith and support are my greatest blessings.

Continued thanks to my ever-growing group of friends on my website, Twitter, Goodreads, Facebook, and LinkedIn … I'm very grateful for your friendship and support!

Very special thanks and everlasting gratitude to my mentor, writing partner, and amigo-for-life, legendary producer Mike Greenburg who is not only dedicated to bringing CRIS DE NIRO to screen, but has taught me all I know about screenwriting!!

Special mention and continued gratitude to dear friends, Executive Producer Phil Norbert, DP to the stars Jay Nemeth of Flightline Films, Master of all things Audio John McClain of Dog and Pony Studios, and screen and stage actor extraordinaire Elijah Alexander for the superb audiobook narration to the first three CDN novels.

All my hopes … All praise to Him!
g

NEW DETROIT

(Cris De Niro, Book 6)

CHAPTER 1

"Holy crap, do you see the size of those guys?" John "Johnny-F' Francis announced as he thumbed over his shoulder. The über-geek Chief Information Officer of The Watchman Agency was oblivious to the fact that he interrupted the President of Detroit's largest investment bank, as the man was introducing himself to Cris De Niro and his brother-in-law Louis "Mugsy" Ricci, President of The Watchman Agency.

Mugsy glanced over Johnny-F's shoulder, "Offensive linemen for the Lions."

To the obvious annoyance of the investment bank President, Johnny-F whispered into Mugsy's ear loud enough for the other two to hear, "Well, they parked themselves in front of the buffet table like they're protecting the quarterback."

Winking at De Niro, Mugsy whispered back, "Maybe you should call a blitz?"

"I did. I bull-rushed the one in the middle, but I bounced right off him. He didn't even notice." Francis rubbed his head, "His back felt like it was made of granite."

Mugsy held in his laugher, "Why don't you get a drink instead?"

Johnny-F thumbed over his other shoulder, "'Cause the bar is protected by those other freaks-of-nature!"

Mugsy looked over, "You mean those basketball players ... they're members of the Detroit Pistons—"

"Would you gentlemen like to meet them?" The President of the investment bank interrupted.

"I would, indeed," replied Mugsy.

"Then, maybe I can get something to eat and drink," Johnny-F chimed in.

The bank president traded nods with De Niro as the three headed to the bar.

Cris De Niro saw Karla Matthews, The Watchman Agency's Vice President of Government Affairs standing with the Mayor of Detroit, near the entrance to the room. He could see the look of pride beaming from Karla's face as her younger brother Kevin stepped up to the podium, in front of the small group of invited guests.

Wearing an electric blue gown, Karla was a tall, stately, well-educated, African American woman. Karla was beautiful and could be a force-to-be-reckoned with when it came to a cause in which she believed.

Karla's personal passion was twofold – fighting poverty and drug addiction. So, it came as no surprise to De Niro that Karla jumped at the opportunity to help her brother when he informed her he was heading a new community-improvement project in their hometown of Detroit, Michigan. She knew this project would do battle with both.

Kevin Matthews was the youngest sibling of Karla's six brothers and sisters, and he was the only one to remain in Detroit. Kevin earned his law degree at The University of Michigan, and as soon as he passed the bar exam, he went to work for Detroit's Public Defender's office (PDO).

Ultimately, Kevin's objective was to spend a decade with the city's PDO and then run for mayor of Detroit. He thought, as mayor, he could make the biggest difference. His goal was to make Detroit great again. Yet, after almost two decades representing Detroit's poorest, and seeing the roots of so many of their problems, Matthews came up with what he thought would be an even better way to rebuild his hometown. The idea came to him after visiting Las Vegas, at the invitation of billionaire Cris De Niro.

De Niro walked Matthews through how Las Vegas was developed as master-planned communities. He was impressed with how each master required a balance of housing, retail and commercial establishments, professional and health services, police, fire departments, schools, libraries, places of worship, and parks.

He was also intrigued with how each residential neighborhood was managed by a community association, comprised of residents who interfaced with the city administrators, who oversaw the maintenance of its roads, landscaping, and building permits. The former Public Defender liked how the community association also organized social events, and managed the budget funded by fees paid by every resident.

Matthews saw how intertwined the residents were in the master-planned communities. Since they were managing their own communities, financed by their own fees, they had "skin in the game" and a reason to care. He knew that kind of integrity was something badly needed in Detroit. For too long, the city's politicians and business leaders were considered among the most corrupt in the nation, while the city's residents were criminal and violent.

Kevin Matthews was now convinced he had to change everything from the bottom up. Entire generations of Detroiters, predominantly black, were being raised in one-parent homes, and were either considerably under-skilled, or uneducated. And since the close of the big-three automakers there simply weren't enough jobs to go around.

Thus, the population of Detroit dwindled, but not enough. Some people couldn't leave, while others had no place else to go. With no other sources of income, other than welfare and subsidies, Matthews saw too many people turn to crime – many selling drugs. The irony was, while half the population of the city was selling drugs, the other half no longer had the money to buy them. Eventually, the city's largest drug gangs were going broke, which led to the emergence of smaller, more violent gangs.

Matthews watched helplessly as too many of his friends were either murdered or imprisoned in the 80's and 90's, while the rest, over the last 16 years, were barely surviving in crumbling, burned-out neighborhoods.

Like a man on a mission, Matthews came home from his trip to Las Vegas convinced what he learned from Cris De Niro was the solution Detroit needed to stage a turn-around. Instead of running for mayor, he would find a way to bring the master-planned community concept to Detroit. The idea would have to be tweaked to work in Detroit, but after spending his entire life in the Motor City he knew the right people to help realize his dream.

Matthews looked out from the podium. Scattered around the small ballroom in front of him were those very people – local bankers, city engineers, real estate executives, business owners, and members of the clergy from all the major religions. And to help finance the project, Matthews invited athletes from the Detroit's sports teams, the Tigers, Lions, Pistons, and Red Wings, along with other celebrities who had grown up in the Motor City. Yet, it was his sister Karla who had invited the whale in the room, Cris De Niro.

Kevin caught Karla's eye and winked, as he addressed the room, "I want to thank y'all for coming this evening, and a special shout-out to my big sister Karla, for bringing some incredible people with her. Some of you may have already recognized him … Mr. Cris De Niro is with us tonight, all the way from Las Vegas."

The room erupted in applause.

Matthews joined in clapping then continued, "Mr. De Niro and the President and CIO of my sister's firm, Captain Louis Ricci, and Mr. John Francis have taken the time to join us tonight. And by us, I mean the Detroiters in the room. This is our city we intend to rebuild and our people we intend to help."

There was more applause.

"And now, without further ado … the reason why we are all here … ladies and gentlemen, our initiative to create master-planned communities throughout our city now has a name …,"

Matthews removed the drape to reveal a scale model of the first master-planned community, "… Project New Detroit!"

Everyone in the room applauded enthusiastically, and a few whistled. To De Niro's amusement, Karla was one of the whistlers.

Everyone in the room crowded around the model, as Matthews continued, "Located in the northeastern section of the city, New Detroit will measure two miles, by one mile, and encompass thirty-one residential neighborhoods, seven commercial complexes, four parks, three schools, two spiritual centers, a public library, and a police substation.

"It'll stretch, west to east, from St. Aubin Street, to Van Dyke

Avenue. The northern border will run along the ninety-four and stretch south to East Canfield Street until it intersects with Gratiot Avenue, then follow Gratiot up to Van Dyke."

One of bankers raised his hand, "What about a fire station and hospital?"

"There are two fire stations that presently cover the area, and Henry Ford Hospital is only five minutes west of the westernmost perimeter of New Detroit."

One of the football players spoke up, "So, you plan to level that whole area? What about the people living there now, and the businesses?"

A small grin appeared on Matthews' face, "Brother, I can tell, you haven't been in this area lately. There are hardly any businesses or people living there right now. The entire area is composed of burned out and gutted buildings. However, for the few people and businesses that are currently there, we'll work with them to minimize any inconvenience, while we build them new homes and facilities. Our intention isn't to displace, but instead, to incorporate them."

The football player scratched his chin and nodded, impressed. The room filled with chatter. Matthews raised his arms over his head to get back everyone's attention, "It takes more than sound buildings to create a community … it takes sound people. And unlike other cities where an influx of bright people became the foundation of their revitalization, Detroit is gonna do what we do best … we're gonna grow our own!"

Laughter erupted in the room.

"What I mean to say is … we're gonna educate our children, while giving them safe parks in which to play. We're gonna train our adults, while giving them places to work and earn a fair living wage. And we're gonna give everyone places of worship with which to pray and congregate."

The room quieted down. Matthews could see the reserved looks on the faces of many.

"The whole thing begins with jobs for a percentage of the adults. To that, Project New Detroit is very pleased to announce an agreement with Mr. Cris De Niro and Mr. John Francis. Upon groundbreaking, Mr. De Niro and Mr. Francis have agreed to base Mr. Francis's new high-tech component manufacturing facility in our New Detroit community!"

Applause broke out in the room to the joy of Johnny-F, while De Niro nodded graciously to Matthews.

Matthews raised his arms again, "The facility will employ over 1,500 people. Even before that facility is completed, the construction companies interested in building New Detroit have all agreed to hire exclusively from within the community. That means thousands will have full-time employment for the next few years.

"The neighborhoods of New Detroit will offer everything, from apartments, to town homes, to single-family homes. As it becomes populated, the residents will need restaurants, dry cleaners, grocery stores, clothing stores, dentists, barber shops, and hairdressers, locksmiths, bakeries, plumbers, electricians, gyms, law offices, eye glass stores … you name it! And every one of those establishments will also hire from within the community."

A member of the Detroit Tigers raised his hand, "How can a high-tech component company hire uneducated workers?"

Matthews looked at Johnny-F. It took a moment before he realized Matthews wanted him to reply.

"We can't. So, as the plant is being built, we'll begin hiring folks we feel have the ability, integrity, and discipline to be taught the needed skill sets, and we'll pay them as we train them. We'll also pay for them to complete their formal education.

"To do that, we'll have to start with skilled managers from the outside until we train local replacements for them. In time, perhaps within two years, we believe we can attain a workforce, including executives and management upwards of 90% locals."

Matthews allowed for the positive reaction of the crowd before continuing, "Thank you, John."

Another voice rang out that Matthews couldn't identify, "What about crime?"

"Our streets will be safe and clean, maintained by association assessments paid by every resident and business. And we won't just be relying on Detroit Metro. We will hire our own private security force. On top of that, many of the neighborhoods inside New Detroit will be gated communities with 24-hour security and video surveillance."

Matthews smiled at the skeptics, "Listen to me ... this can be done! It has been done in other places and we can do it here.

"And best of all, residents and business owners in New Detroit will receive common-interest community ownership shares, which means the success of the area will directly benefit every occupant."

Matthews' smile broadened as the volume of chatter increased. He let a minute pass before holding his hands up to quiet the room again, "I didn't say it'll be easy, and it damn-well won't be cheap, but it is possible. We'll need investment, bank support, and the moral support and effort of many, many people, but it CAN be done."

Matthews let his serious stare melt into a smile, "Thank you all very much for coming. Now, get your checkbooks out. I'll supply the pen!"

The room filled with laughter and applause.

Matthews walked off the podium and into his big sister's arms. Karla hugged him then kissed his cheek, "You were pretty good up there."

"We'll see how good, with how many checks we collect."

De Niro, Mugsy, and Johnny-F joined them. De Niro offered his hand. Matthews shook it and kept it in his.

"I thought we agreed to leave my name out," said De Niro.

"I did … well, at least I didn't tell them about the $50 million you're going to invest. Mr. De Niro, there would simply be no New Detroit, without you."

De Niro patted Matthews' hand, "I'm just writing a check. You're the one that has to make it happen."

"Me and a lot of others—"

A stocky, dark-skinned man wearing horn-rimmed glasses interrupted him, "Excuse me …."

A look of annoyance crossed Matthews' face, "Mr. De Niro … gentlemen, this is my executive assistant, soon-to-be Director of Project New Detroit, Clifton Hays."

The men nodded to him. Hays returned their nods then continued, "Sir, Shah just walked in."

"Tell him to wait for me in the lobby."

"I did, but he wouldn't."

The men followed Matthews' eyes to a well-dressed, bald, African American man heading their way, donning gold-rimmed sunglasses. The man was wearing a black leather suit with a dark purple mock, and De Niro noticed he was sporting a $20,000 Cartier Tank Anglaise Roman white gold watch. De Niro also noticed how tense Kevin Matthews had suddenly become at the sight of him.

The man walked up to Matthews with a grin, ignoring the others. Hays spoke first, "Shah, I thought I told you to wait outside."

The man shot Hays an evil stare, but spoke in a soft tone, "I don't go by that name anymore … Clifton."

The man turned back to Matthews, "Well, homeboy, you gonna introduce me to your friends, or shall I?"

The man didn't wait for a reply. Instead, he turned to De Niro, "Mr. De Niro, it's an honor to meet you, sir. My name is Antonio Brown. But y'all can call me Tonio. My friends do. Kevin and I are—"

"Were," Matthews corrected him.

Brown raised his brow and smiled, "Were … childhood friends. Ain't that right, Kevin?"

"We were. Tonio … I thought I told you I was busy tonight."

"I can see that. And I told you it was important. Besides, what I got to say has to do with your New Detroit project."

Matthews couldn't conceal his surprise, "How do you know about Project New—"

"Homeboy, you know better than that. Anything that goes down in the hood I know about. What I'd like to know is, why I wasn't invited to this little shindig of yours? From what I hear, you lookin' for investment dollars. My money no good?"

"Is that why you came, to make an investment?"

Tonio turned from Matthews and walked over to the New Detroit model. He ran his fingers playfully across the tops of the miniature buildings, "Actually, I might like to … but not until you hear what I got to say. Ya see … the area where you want to build ain't safe."

Hays snickered sarcastically, "Ain't nowhere in Detroit that's safe, brother."

Matthews ignored his executive assistant's jibe, "You're talking about the drug gangs?"

Tonio took his glasses off and tucked them into his breast pocket, "Oh, they're not the problem, homes. The gangs can't wait for you to start packing in hard-working folks, with money to spend on their product."

Matthews realized De Niro and the others were still there, "I'm so sorry, Mr. De Niro. I should speak with my friend now. I can catch up with all of you a little later."

"Actually, I'd like to hear what your friend has to say. I'd like my friends to hear it too … if that's okay with you and Mr. Brown."

Tonio grinned, shrugging lightly, "Like I said, I would be honored, Mr. De Niro."

After a stern gaze at Tonio, Matthews also shrugged, "More than anyone else, you have a right to hear, Mr. De Niro."

Matthews turned to his sister, "Karla, would you and Clifton escort the rest of our guests out, so we can have the room? If I do it, it'll take all night. Don't worry, we won't continue until you rejoin us."

Karla and Clifton began escorting the rest of the people into the lobby, as Tonio headed over to the bar. He grabbed a magnum of champagne and a tray of champagne flutes and started pouring, "We might as well finish this DP. But after I tell y'all what I have to say, you might want something stronger."

CHAPTER 2

DIRECTOR'S ROOM
THE HENRY, AUTOGRAPH COLLECTION
DEARBORN, MICHIGAN
8:30 PM (LOCAL), SATURDAY, JULY 02, 2016

Clifton closed the doors to the conference room then escorted Karla over to the men standing around the scale-model on the table. Tonio took his place on the far side, with Kevin Matthews, while De Niro, Mugsy, Johnny-F, Karla, and Clifton stood opposite them.

Tonio winked at Matthews, making his nostrils flare in anger, and then took a moment to study the model. Everyone waited in silence. Tonio finally chuckled, "Impressive, if I must say so myself, very impressive, brother."

"Say what you came here to say … brother."

Tonio's smirk disappeared, "I get the feeling I'm not welcome here, homes."

"You're not. If you were, you would've been invited."

Tonio stepped up to Matthews, leaving only an inch between their noses, "I shudda been invited. I got more right to be here than any of y'all people. This is more my hood than any of y'all's!"

Matthews sneered, "All you ever did for this hood is peddle poison in it!

Tonio's eyes flared. Neither man broke their stare until Tonio reached into his jacket. As a reflex, Clifton also reached into his, as did Mugsy, hands grasping their pistols.

Matthews looked over Tonio's shoulder. Following his eyes, Tonio turned then raised one arm over his head as a sign of surrender, as he withdrew his other hand revealing the photo that was in it. Mugsy released his hand from his jacket. Clifton's grip remained on his gun.

Turning back to Matthews, Tonio winked at Clifton, as he held the photo up for all to see.

Matthews glanced at it almost dismissively, before examining it closer, "Is that your son?"

Tonio nodded, "Teddy … the last and the youngest of my six sons."

Matthews took the photo from him, "He got big. How old is he now?"

Tonio's eyes welled with tears, "He's dead K … Teddy was murdered."

Tonio looked at the others, "I buried three of my sons. They died in drug-related gun battles. Another two are doing life for murder and selling drugs … but young Teddy was supposed to be the one, you know! He was a star halfback in high school. Hell, he was the only one of my sons who ever went to high school … the only one who didn't try to emulate what I was."

No one spoke, but Tonio could feel the contempt in the room. He nodded, "Yeah … that's right. Kevin here is right about me. I sold drugs and I did a lot of other things I ain't proud of … but I also served my time and rebuilt my life the best I could.

"I ain't gonna bore y'all with the whole story of my life. Hell, it ain't much different than anybody who grew up in Northeast Detroit. No father ... my mother was an addict and a whore. Kevin and me became friends in grade school. We were the two best basketball players in our church's league. Ain't that right, brother?"

Matthews nodded, "You were a better shooter than me, but you would foul out all the time. You never could follow the rules."

Tonio flashed a smile then let it melt away, "Nah ... not back then, anyhow.

"My grandmother tried her best to raise me and my brothers and sisters, but the lure of fast money selling drugs was just too much for me. By the time I was nineteen, I was driving a Benz, drinking DP and blowin' fifty large in Vegas on a weekend. I had six sons with six different baby mamas by the time I was twenty-five. But, by the age of twenty-six, I was sitting in prison serving twenty to life."

Matthews handed the photo back, "You were one of the reasons I became a lawyer."

Tonio laughed to himself, "Yeah, you was gonna be my Perry Mason, but you were too fresh and I was too ... guilty."

Tonio turned back to the others, "With their overcrowding problems, I ended up doing only fifteen years. They let me out on good behavior, and I was gonna keep it straight.

"Teddy's mom visited me my whole stay. She'd always bring Teddy. I watched that boy grow up from behind bars. In my last year, Teddy would spend his visits telling me all about Islam. Some mosque in the hood was recruiting right in front of the park Teddy and his friends would hang out at.

"By the time I got out, I didn't even know it, but Teddy had quit his high school football team ... in his senior year! He took a Muslim name, Tariq Ali. I tried to spend more time with him, but he was never around. I tried to call him, but he wouldn't take my calls.

All I wanted to do was make it up to him … all the time I wasn't there!"

Tonio took a moment to regain his composure, "Two weeks ago, his mama rang me up and told me Teddy wasn't coming home anymore."

Tonio shook his head, "That boy could've played college ball on scholarship. Instead, his mama said all he did was go to this mosque. She was frantic, so I went up over there to find him." Tonio wet his lips, "Let me tell you something, those boys don't play. Inside, I gave the Nation of Islam boys a wide berth. They mostly stuck to themselves and weren't looking for trouble, but the ones I ran up on at the mosque were different."

"Different how?" asked De Niro.

"Different, as in I asked the ones at the door if I could enter the mosque to see if anyone knew where my son was, and their reply was to show me their hardware … one had an AK under his robe and the other had a brand-new US government-issue M16A4."

"You know your weapons," replied Mugsy.

Tonio winked at him, "Mostly, from video games, brother. As soon as I got out, I used what was left of my stash to open a video game store. I own three now."

"I didn't know that," Matthews said almost in a whisper. Tonio's eyes met his.

"Forgive my sublime ignorance," Johnny-F broke in, "but why didn't you call the police? Carrying concealed automatic weapons is a crime, even in Detroit … isn't it?"

Tonio grinned, "Let's just say, folks around here are hesitant about calling 5-0 for any reason. Besides, they don't respond to much on this side of town."

"You said your son was murdered, replied De Niro. "You think members of that mosque murdered him?"

"I didn't see or hear any mention of Teddy's murder in the papers or on the news?" added Matthews.

Tonio looked incredulous, "People are murdered in the hood every day, my brother, and no one takes notice. The police don't investigate and the media only reports when they find a body, but there are lots of bodies that are never found."

"What about Teddy's?" asked Matthews.

Tonio's back stiffened, "They ain't never gonna find my son's body."

"Then how do you know he was murdered, or even dead, for that matter?" asked Karla.

Tonio reached into his jacket again and handed Kevin Matthews another photo sealed inside a plastic baggie.

Matthews stared at it in horror.

Tonio took it back and placed it on the table. Everyone crowded in to look. They saw a beheaded corpse with the head placed on the corpse's stomach. The face on the head was a disfigured version of the one in the first photo.

Karla gasped, "That's Teddy …? Does his mama know?"

Tonio wiped a tear and nodded, "I wouldn't let her see the photo. I just told her he was a victim of a drive-by."

"How did you get that photo?" asked De Niro.

Someone delivered it to me, at one of my stores, last week."

Tonio picked the photo up and held it out to De Niro, "As far I know, other than by courier, the photo hasn't been touched. I made sure of that, with the baggie.

"Like I said, I can't trust the police. Hell, they might arrest me …. Mr. De Niro, I was thinking that maybe you …."

De Niro took the photo and handed it to Mugsy, "Have the

Watchman investigate it. Tell Michelle to check it for prints, and if there are any—"

"She'll let us know," replied Mugsy.

Tonio tapped his chest with the side of his fist, "Thank you, Mr. D."

De Niro nodded then turned to Francis, "Johnny, why don't you go to the front desk and tell them we'll be keeping our suites for a few more days. We're not leaving, at least not until we hear back from Michelle."

Francis headed for the door, "On it."

Kevin Matthews joined them, "Since, you'll be staying on, why don't you gentlemen let me buy you breakfast and show you the area tomorrow? It'll give you an idea of the scope of Project New Detroit."

De Niro looked over at Tonio, drawing Matthews' eyes to him. Matthews patted Tonio's back, "You're invited too, old friend."

Tonio smiled, "Thank you, brother."

"Meet us for breakfast, here," Matthews looked at De Niro, "… say 9 AM?"

"Sounds good," replied De Niro. "Now, how about you gentlemen joining me for a nightcap?"

* * * * *

Tonio and the others spent an hour in De Niro's Presidential Suite before the men called it a night. Tonio stretched as he walked out the front entrance and handed his ticket to the young, African-American valet who took off running.

Tonio checked messages on his phone until the valet drove up with his car, a blacked-out 2016 Cadillac Escalade Platinum. He handed the valet a twenty-dollar bill for keeping it up front then jumped in and sped off.

The valet smiled as he took out a small wad of cash from his pocket and added the twenty to it. His smile was short-lived as a late model sedan roared past, almost hitting him.

The valet recognized the man in the passenger seat from his long beard. He was the same man that entered the hotel earlier that evening, a moment after Tonio arrived.

CHAPTER 3

The doorman held the door for Cris De Niro, Karla Matthews, John Francis, Kevin Matthews, Antonio Brown, and Clifton Hays.

Mugsy appeared a moment later and headed over to De Niro, "The photo is on its way, same day service. Michelle said she should have an answer for us, one way or the other, by this evening."

De Niro nodded, "Hopefully, we'll get a match. I wonder if the courier is friend or foe."

"I would think foe, no? It's a grizzly photo, and Tonio received it after getting the cold shoulder from the men at the mosque. It could've been one of them."

De Niro rubbed his chin, "Maybe … but if they were the ones responsible, they took a big chance hand delivering it. I mean, why not just drop it into the mail?"

It was Mugsy's turn to rub his chin, "Why do you think?"

"I think whoever delivered that photo might have meant to hand it to Tonio … maybe even knew him or his son. I don't know … showing up at the store just seems like it was personal."

Tonio handed his ticket to the valet, a different young man than the night before, "We can all go in my SUV, if you want."

It took only a minute for the shiny black Escalade to pull up. De Niro held the door open for Karla to get in the front. She passed on the invitation, "If you don't mind, I'll get in back with my brother. I don't get to see him enough. You ride up front."

De Niro jumped in the front passenger seat as the others piled in back. The radio was tuned to a hip-hop station. Tonio lowered the volume a bit, shrugged and winked at De Niro.

De Niro grinned, "Nice ride."

Tonio turned back to Kevin, "Where we goin'?"

"Let's start near the northwestern perimeter of New Detroit. Take us to Chene and Palmer."

Tonio put the SUV in gear and took off, speaking to De Niro, "I'll blast the AC. I advise you to keep your windows up."

Mugsy leaned forward, "Tonio, how far is where you're taking us, to that mosque you went to?

"The mosque is only about a mile north. You know the one, Kevin, off Mt. Elliot."

"There's a few in that area, I think," replied Matthews.

* * * * *

The bearded men in the dark sedan from the night before drove past the hotel entrance, this time a bit slower, being more careful not to draw attention. The passenger took his cell phone out and made a call.

(In Arabic) "Syed, we stayed with the black one since last night. He came back to the same hotel. This time he left with six others. I snapped photos of them. We are following them. We just turned east on Ford Rd. They might be heading for the highway."

* * * * *

Syed Malik, a 28-year-old Pakistani, born in Chicago, traced the route on the laptop screen with his index finger, as he spoke into his cellphone, "They're heading in our direction. Send me the photos, and let me know when they reach their destination."

Ending the call, he leaned back in the battered wooden chair, and ran his fingers through his jet-black hair. The underground compound he sat in was a group of basements along Chene Street that were interconnected by tunnels, dug by Malik, and his fighters.

A slender woman in her early thirties, wearing a burqa, walked into the makeshift office. Except for the Islamic headdress, everything about the woman's appearance was Anglo, from her bright blue eyes, light, freckled skin, and blonde hair, to her ruddy, rounded cheeks, and British accent. Her real name was Samantha, though she hadn't been called by that name in over a decade. Everyone in the underground compound knew her only by her latest alias, Naheed.

Since converting to Islam at seventeen, British-born Islamic-extremist convert had used several Islamic aliases, as well as one other Anglo-sounding name. Yet, Samantha, known now as Naheed was branded by the global counter-terrorism world by a much more infamous name ... the White Widow, a play on words given to her by the news media. It alluded to her race; the death of her first so-called "husband," a suicide bomber; and the practice of referring to Chechen female suicide bombers as "black widows."

Naheed took a moment to look at the man seated before her. Malik stood just over six-foot tall and was a toned 170 lbs. The two were attracted to one another from the moment they met, at a hotel in Islamabad five years before, yet Naheed rarely smiled at Malik, regardless of whether she was angry or aroused. The only time she smiled, it seemed to him, was when he showed stress. He knew she didn't smile to comfort him, but to mock him.

She was smiling now.

Naheed raised her chin, her favorite arrogant expression when asking a question, "What's wrong?"

Malik closed his eyes and stretched back in the chair, "Nothing."

Naheed shot him a skeptical grin, "You only stroke your hair when you're worried about something. Is it that black man again … the one who said he was Tariq's father?"

Malik nodded without opening his eyes.

"Where is he now?"

Malik opened his eyes, sat up straight, and exhaled audibly, "Khan and Bilal are following him …"

She raised her chin again for him to go on.

"He is with several other people, and they are heading in this direction."

Naheed knit her eyebrows as she leaned over the dirty wooden desk, "They know our location?"

"I don't think so."

"You don't think so?"

Malik slapped the desk, "I don't know!"

Touching his fingertips together, he paused in thought, "How could they know."

Malik brought up the photos Khan sent him, and handed Naheed his phone. She swiped the screen with her finger to look at each photo as he continued, "The black one would not come with that group of people if he knew of this location. You recognize the other black man?"

Naheed scrolled back and stared at the photo of Kevin Matthews, "He is the one that was running for mayor not long ago."

Malik nodded and took his phone back, "He used to be with the public defender's office. He's a lawyer. When we checked Tariq's father out, we found out that he was only recently released from prison. He was in one of the gangs here in Detroit. It is possible he knows Matthews from the past?"

Naheed shrugged her shoulders, "But where are they going?"

Malik stared at the map on his laptop screen for a moment then leaned back in the chair again, "I have no idea. I told Khan to contact us as soon as they arrive at their destination."

Naheed leaned in again, "Syed, what if they know about this location? We cannot just sit here with fifty fighters ready to embark tomorrow!"

Malik stared at the infamous Anglo convert. Her eyes blazed with hate. He realized that while his hate was learned, hers came from the womb. Malik believed Naheed was born with hatred in her heart for infidels. It was an aspect of her he admired.

Malik's phone rang again. He answered, and after a moment hung up without saying a word to the caller.

Naheed raised her chin again.

"It was Khan," Malik glanced up, "those people … they just stopped on Chene and Palmer."

Naheed's eyes opened wide, "We must find out why they are here!"

Malik's eyes, filled with anger of a different sort, met hers. Though she technically outranked him, like most Muslims, he did not take kindly to being ordered by a woman.

"We … no, it is much too dangerous for you to be seen."

Naheed frowned knowing he was right, "I'll conceal my face and remain behind you, while you go out and inquire of them."

"I said it is too dangerous! I am in charge here!"

Naheed rested her knuckles on the desk and leaned over it, "You oversee the operation, but I am the one who raised the financing and I am the one who trained the fighters."

"That is why it is too dangerous for you to show your face to anyone in this country. You are too important. It was risky enough sneaking you into the United States over the Mexican border and transporting you here. If you are recognized, more than our operation will be blown."

Naheed smiled then walked over to a dented metal locker in the corner where she retrieved a black burqa. Once the head-scarf was on, only her bright, blue eyes were visible.

She softened her stance, "Syed, I've been able to fool authorities on two continents. These people will be no different. You will do the talking, but I need to see and hear first-hand. The fact is, in these situations, I have more practical experience than you."

He stood and stared back at her for a moment, before nodding, "Go tell the others that we are going up to the street and for no one to go out until we return."

A grin appeared on his face, "It's time for me and my wife to take a stroll. After all, we need to find the next location for our little restaurant chain."

CHAPTER 4

CORNER OF CHENE & EAST PALMER STREET
DETROIT, MICHIGAN
11:00 AM (LOCAL), SUNDAY, JULY 03, 2016

Tonio came to a stop across the street from a dilapidated white brick building with the name, 'W. SMUCZYNSKI' etched just below the roof's crown. Built in the 1950s, the building was named for a once-successful furniture company whose prominence long since faded. The building's coined front was constructed of white brick to add grandeur. In its day, the W. Smuczynski building was known for its impressive street presence. Now, half of the second floor had completely collapsed, while the first floor was still encased in a rusted security fence.

Everyone exited the SUV and looked around. Almost every building still standing was a burned-out shell. They were separated by barren overgrown fields and littered with trash where buildings used to stand.

Mugsy Ricci use his hand as a visor to block the sun as he stared at the remnants of the once prominent building across the street, "What the hell happened here? This whole area looks like it was hit by a nuke."

Johnny-F stood next to him looking south down Chene Street, "I can't believe this is in the United States, let alone a major city. It's a friggin' ghost town."

Kevin Matthews stepped up to them, "Welcome to old Detroit, gentlemen."

De Niro put his hands on his hips and looked around, "And this is where you want to build New Detroit?"

"Cris and I are from a poor neighborhood in Brooklyn, New York," said Francis, "but I've never seen so many abandoned, burned-out buildings in one place in my life ... outside of black-n-white photos of Hiroshima and Nagasaki in 1945."

Karla put her arm around her brother's shoulder, "At least you won't have to evict anyone."

"You may've spoken too soon," said Tonio, nodding down the street.

A young man of obvious Far-eastern decent, and a woman wearing a burqa, appeared from an overgrown lot between two burned-out buildings. The couple was heading in their direction.

Mugsy stood next to Cris, both watching the couple approach, "Now, where would they be coming from?"

Johnny-F shook his shirt, "It's so friggin' hot and humid out here ... maybe they were making whoopee in the shade behind the buildings."

De Niro looked up and down the street, "So, where's their car?"

Everyone looked around. Before anyone could reply, the couple reached them.

The man held his hand out in greeting, "Would any of you be the owners of some of the properties on this street?"

Matthews shook Malik's hand, "I'm Kevin Matthews. Who might you be?"

"My name is Syed," Malik turned, "and that is my wife, Naheed."

Matthews nodded to the woman standing a few feet behind the man. She remained stoic and motionless, with her arms crossed.

Malik flashed a toothy smile, "You are the one who ran for mayor, yes?"

"That would be me. How can we help you?"

"My wife and I own and operate a chain of fast-food pita restaurants. We are always on the lookout for new locations."

"And you're looking here?" replied Tonio. He had circled behind the couple until he was standing in the middle of the street with his back to them.

Surprised, Naheed's training kicked in. Her arms came up in a fighting posture. She tried to relax as quickly as she could, but not before De Niro and Mugsy noticed the defensive stance she had taken.

Naheed noticed that they noticed.

Deflecting attention from her, Malik walked over to Tonio, "Many believe this area will someday be rebuilt. My wife and I continue to come here to see if there are any signs of that, so we can be among the first restaurants. So, you can understand our curiosity when we spotted your vehicle."

"Speaking of vehicles, where is yours?" asked Mugsy.

De Niro noticed a slight glance, from the wife to her husband.

After a moment, a grin emerged on Malik's face, "We parked it many blocks away, on the other side of the ninety-four. This area is not particularly safe. Besides, my wife and I like to walk."

Malik turned back to Matthews, "But, you have not answered my question."

Matthews winked at De Niro, before handing Malik his New Detroit business card, "If you're serious about opening your restaurant here, give us a call."

Naheed stepped next to Malik and examined the card in his hand. Though her face remained emotionless, her eyes gave away her shock.

Malik stared at the card for a moment before replying, "So, you do own property here?"

Before Matthews could respond, Tonio grabbed Malik around his shoulder and turned him slowly, while pointing in front of them, "As far as your eyes can see, my man. Now, you be sure and call us. We can't talk business here and now, but we'll be glad to sit down with you sometime soon. Ya dig?"

Malik knew he was being dismissed. He nodded to Naheed who began walking back in the direction whence they came then turned to Matthews again, "We shall be in touch."

Tonio elbowed Matthews side, "You and I can split the commission on that one. I do believe we have our first resident of New Detroit."

De Niro walked over to Mugsy, "What do you make of them?"

"He's got all the personality in the relationship and she's got all the temper."

"I caught that too. That and pretty blue eyes."

Johnny-F joined them, "Personally, I couldn't be happier. With all the time I'm gonna have to spend at our new factory, at least now I'll have somewhere healthy to eat. I love lamb pitas with hummus and Israeli salad."

"Something tells me those two won't be serving anything with the word Israeli in it," replied Mugsy.

Matthews waved them to follow, "Come on, gentleman let me show you around."

* * * * *

Back in their underground bunker, Malik and Naheed walked up behind one of their men who was sitting in front of a bank of large monitors. Having removed the head-scarf, Naheed was speaking on her cell, "Khan, I want you to continue to follow those people. If they split up, stay with the white men. I want to know everywhere they go, understood? Good."

She put her phone away and scanned the monitors. On a few of the screens were various angles of the people they had just met. Naheed tapped the seated man on his shoulder. She pointed to Kevin Matthews and Antonio Brown, "Nabil, forget these two men, zoom in on the rest and snap headshots, then run them through our recognition software. I want to know exactly who they are and I want to know quickly."

Malik stood with his arms folded, "Why the urgency with these people? With such little time remaining, we have other more important matters to attend to. I did not detect any need for concern—"

"Which is why it was so important for me to see and hear them firsthand. Those men, not the blacks, the others … they concern me."

"Why? I tell you, I saw and heard no reason—"

"It is not in what they said or what you saw, but in how they observed."

Malik's tone filled with reservation, "And how did they observe?"

"Keenly … apparently, more keenly than you did." Naheed held out her hand, "Let me have that business card."

Malik handed it over and she gave it to Nabil who was already working on the headshots, "Check into this company also, and let me know all you can. And Nabil … quickly!"

Naheed walked to the door then turned to Malik, "I need to get back to our fighters. I must keep them motivated in these final hours. You better warn the Imam."

Malik waited for Naheed to leave the room before placing the call. He didn't like being ordered around, though he did not doubt her abilities or her intuitions.

"Imam, it is Syed. The father of Tariq Ali just arrived on the street near our bunker. He was accompanied by several others.

"No, no police, at least not ones in uniform. We are checking on the identities of the rest now, but they might be heading for your mosque.

"No, they did not ask about Tariq Ali. I am not sure why they came here, but it could be that they own property here. In any case, Imam, make sure you say nothing that will send them back here. Time is short now. Our victory is upon us, Allah be praised."

CHAPTER 5

PRESIDENTIAL SUITE
THE HENRY, AUTOGRAPH COLLECTION
DEARBORN, MICHIGAN
3:00 PM (LOCAL), SUNDAY, JULY 03, 2016

Johnny-F tinkered on the grand piano, while Cris De Niro sat across the room with his eyes on the muted plasma TV reading the scrolling text underneath the local newscast. A female reporter was standing in the foreground. Visible behind her were two large barges.

While the reporter's mouth moved, the text that crawled on the bottom of the screen read, "... This year's Fourth festivities include spectacular fireworks shows at no less than 10 locations in the Detroit area, like here at White Lake. The largest event, of course, will be the four-day celebration, dubbed the 23rd Annual Salute to America at Greenfield Village at The Henry Ford."

De Niro noticed Johnny-F had started tapping out "Yankee Doodle Dandy" with one hand, while chugging down a Stella Artois tall neck with the other.

Mugsy Ricci emerged from the dining room with his cell phone to his ear, headed for a small table with a laptop on it, opposite the piano. De Niro glanced at him as he scratched onto a pad with a hotel pen before replying, "Got it, thanks Michelle."

Mugsy began typing on the laptop keyboard, as De Niro stood and walked over to a window. De Niro took in the cloudless bright-blue sky overhead. In one direction, the Detroit skyline sparkled in the sunlight, and in the other, De Niro could see the Ambassador Bridge, which connected Detroit with Windsor, Ontario, Canada.

Mugsy finished typing and walked over, "That was Michelle. They finally found a match for the prints."

Johnny-F got up from the piano and joined him at the window, "What took them so long?"

"Michelle said the prints belong to a Terrell Briggs, eighteen-years-old. He has no criminal record and no driver's license, so the only way to find his prints was to use Big-Brutha™ to search every database in the city. That's what took so long."

Johnny-F grimaced, "That's not Big-Brutha's fault. That's this city's archaic database system."

Mugsy winked at Francis and continued, "They finally found this young man's prints on file with the Detroit Public School system. Apparently, he applied to become a volunteer tutor for their Reading Corps program. The application requires a background check."

The doorbell rang. Johnny-F answered the door. It was Karla and Kevin Matthews, and Antonio Brown. Tonio pointed to the beer in Francis's hand, "You got any more of those? It's as hot as hell out there."

Francis retrieved bottles for everyone and handed them out, while the three took seats on the couches.

De Niro sat next to Karla, "How did it go at the Mosque?"

Karla shook her head, "It didn't. They gave us the same welcome they gave Tonio the first time he went there."

Kevin Matthews continued, "It was weird. I noticed from the

time we pulled up they seemed to be expecting us."

"If anything, they were even more aggressive this time," added Tonio.

Karla pressed the ice-cold bottle to her brow, "One thing's for sure … they have no intention of answering our questions."

Mugsy joined them, "They don't have to. We finally heard back from Michelle. Watchman was able to match the print from the photo to an eighteen-year-old teen named Terrell Briggs."

"Terrell Briggs?" Tonio downed half of his bottle, before continuing, "Terrell was the cornerback on the high school team with Teddy. They were best friends until Teddy quit school."

Tonio furled his brows in thought. A moment passed before he noticed all eyes were on him, "I don't believe Terrell could have anything to do with Teddy's murder. I just wonder … how he got that photo."

Mugsy motioned everyone over to his laptop. On the screen, was a map with a mark, over an address in northeast Detroit, "Why don't we go ask him? I traced his address. He lives with his maternal grandmother not far from the Project New Detroit area."

Kevin Matthews looked closely at the screen, "Hey … that address is literally around the corner from the Mosque. Coincidence …?"

"Coincidences happen every day, but I don't trust them," replied Mugsy.

"Neither, do I," De Niro took a final pull from his beer, got up and headed for the door, "Let's go pay a call on young, Mr. Briggs."

CHAPTER 6

UNDERGROUND COMPOUND
BASEMENTS ALONG CHENE STREET
DETROIT, MICHIGAN
4:00 PM (LOCAL), SUNDAY, JULY 03, 2016

Naheed stood in front of ten nervous black men, each wearing vests with special pockets sewn into them. The pockets contained canisters of highly-explosive triacetone triperoxide (TATP) and bits of shrapnel. Naheed knew that essentially everything, from their wristwatches to their bones, would become shrapnel when the vests were detonated.

The primary reason Syed Malik reached out to Naheed was because he wanted his cell of fighters to carry out, if not the most destructive terrorist attack on American soil, the most dishonorable and demoralizing one. For that, he needed a trainer who was an expert with suicide bomber attacks, could infiltrate the U.S., and could speak English. He knew of only one person who could fulfill those requirements – the White Widow.

Malik knew the type of terror acts he desired – simultaneous attacks on the ten most popular Fourth of July events in and around Detroit. He was impressed with the amount of horror the Boston Marathon bombers produced with only two explosives. The multiple blasts in Paris were also impressive to him, as were the famous attacks carried out on 9/11. Yet, none of them would compare in quantity to what he intended to initiate. Ten blasts at ten different locations, all simultaneously, as the crowds, and the rest of the U.S. celebrated their birthday as a nation.

After arriving in Detroit, Naheed spent a year planning the attack. Photos from last year's events at each location were collected and examined in detail, along with photos of the routes to and from each venue. Naheed also expanded and re-designed Malik's underground compound to accommodate living quarters and training facilities, while working with the Imam of the nearby mosque to radicalize as many young locals as possible.

When Malik learned of the number of fighters called for by Naheed's plan, he lobbied for her to incorporate a percentage of Islamic fanatics from overseas. But, Naheed explained to Malik that local fighters would help them infiltrate each location, with minimum suspicion.

Naheed's original plan was to utilize a total of sixty young men and women, six per location. Each location would have assigned to it: two bombers – the primary and a replacement; two bomb-vest makers, one driver, and one handler. The handler would accompany the bomber as insurance. The handler could also trigger the explosive remotely by use of a cell phone, if the bomber had second thoughts about triggering it him/herself.

Naheed soon came to realize that sixty male and female fighters wouldn't be possible. First, the Imam explained there simply weren't enough young Muslim women that attended his mosque, and the few that did were not the type to be radicalized. They were mostly reformed crack-addicted single moms who had converted to Islam to try to better their lives. The young men, on the other hand, were mostly ex-convicts converted to Islam in jail, and pointed to the mosque by their cell mates. The Imam regularly spoke to the local prison inmates, specifically to recruit them, so they were already familiar with him, but there just weren't enough devout followers who returned on a regular basis.

By June, Naheed realized she'd have to make do with only forty radicalized converts, and they would all have to be male, which meant only one bomb maker per location. That usually wouldn't pose a problem with experienced bomb makers, but Naheed was teaching the young black men from scratch. She selected the ten brightest and considered it fortunate that, while they had virtually no formal education, they were all adept at learning the intricacies of constructing suicide vests.

Naheed appointed the ten oldest to be drivers. There could be no getting stopped by the police on the road to each location. The older ones could be trusted not to speed or run stop signs. That left her with ten of the angriest converts and ten of the most frightened.

From decades of experience, Naheed knew that angry young men attracted more attention than scared ones, so she trained the angry ones to be handlers. Their anger also made them best at intimidating the bombers and remotely detonating the bombs if necessary, leaving the ten most frightened ones to be the bombers.

Naheed had to accept the difference between the radicalized believers she trained in Europe, the Middle East, and Africa, and the young, black Detroit miscreants standing before her. While she could tap into, and even amplify the zealous religious convictions of all the others, the Americans had virtually no religious upbringing of any kind. Their hate stemmed from the futility of their surroundings. They were unemployed and for the most part, unemployable, with no skills except to sell drugs and play video games.

Naheed knew of only two effective motivators to train young men to become suicide bombers – reward and fear, and both had to be dramatic to get someone to willingly commit suicide.

She knew it was easiest to tempt males outside the U.S. with something spoken about in their religious texts. Something they craved, but never had - sex. Naheed knew the notion of sexual reward was grounded in Qur'anic text, which describes a carnal Paradise where believing men are rewarded by being wed to big-breasted virgins. And like other terrorist leaders, Naheed added to the erotic dogma by promoting the concept of not one, but seventy-two virgins (houri) waiting for martyrs in Paradise.

The fact that the authenticity of the seventy-two-virgin concept was only supported by weak references outside the Qur'an mattered little to Naheed, or to the men she brainwashed. The visual image was just too powerful for the sex starved male population outside America.

The reality was, most of the youth in the Middle East and abroad had little opportunity with the opposite sex. Islam prohibited pre-marital and extramarital sex, and homosexuality. Their name for all unlawful sexual relations was "zina," and zina was forbidden.

Most of these impoverished, uneducated men knew they would probably never attract a wife, which meant they would never in-dulge in the pleasures of the flesh. So, being given the opportunity to "earn" their way into a paradise where they could spend eternity having any kind of kinky sex with seventy-two nubile vixens--who would come to them as virgins--was all the incentive they needed. All they had to do to earn their way into Paradise was strap a bomb to their bodies and pull the trigger. Naheed knew that, to many of them, that was a fair bargain.

Yet, Naheed learned when it came to sex, the black youth of Detroit differed profoundly from the Islamic youth outside the United States. While they were poor and uneducated, they certainly were not sex-starved.

In fact, to Naheed, all American males seemed to do was have sex, play video games, and sell drugs, in that order. That meant the reward of sex in Paradise wouldn't entice them to give up their lives for Islam. Fear would have to be the key motivator, which led to her realization that the young black youth of Detroit weren't afraid of much, because they didn't care about much. In fact, the only thing they seemed to care about were the people that raised them – their grandmothers.

These boys had converted to Islam partially because they hated white people, and partially to become better men for their families, namely, their grandmothers and siblings. They also felt being associated with a mosque offered them some protection from the drug gangs.

With that in mind, Naheed decided to employ the two strategies on the Detroit recruits: Reward - Obedience would lead to financial compensation for their families; and Fear - disobedience would lead to violent retribution toward their families, with primary focus on their grandmothers.

The strategies worked.

When the virtue of obedience and the penalty for disobedience were explained, virtually all the men fell in line. All but two, Teddy Brown, aka Tariq Ali, and his friend Terrell Briggs who adopted the Muslim name, Hooman Halim. The Imam and Naheed realized they misinterpreted the two outliers' quiet dispositions for obedience and radicalism. It wasn't until their training was completed that they discovered their rebellious natures.

On the very night Naheed informed them they were chosen

to become bombers, both were caught trying to escape. Escape was betrayal and betrayal needed to be punished in the harshest way. Though they were already low in manpower, Naheed knew she needed to make an example of at least one of the boys to keep everyone else in line.

The more rebellious of the two was Tariq. He would be the one to pay the ultimate price for disobedience, while she could show compassion to Hooman. That would set an example to all the others that while she was harsh in her punishment, she was also capable of mercy. Mercy built trust and she needed their trust for the plan to succeed. The remaining boys needed to trust that their families would be compensated. Their trust in being rewarded in heaven while their families were rewarded on Earth would be their entire focus, right up until their bombs were detonated.

Tariq would suffer the death deserving of all infidels, a beheading. As for Hooman, he would be offered a choice. To be spared Tariq's fate and to regain Naheed's, Malik's, and the rest of the fighters' trust, he would have to carry out his friend's execution, as a form of repentance.

Naheed was sure Hooman would never again disobey her commands after he beheaded his friend. To make sure he would carry out the act, Naheed told Hooman that either he beheaded Tariq, or she would behead Hooman's grandmother. And to add to the fear, the others would learn this ultimate lesson of disobedience by having to watch.

Teddy was brought out from the meal room and forced to his knees by two of Khan's men who remained on each side of him. Terrell tried to make eye contact with Teddy, but his friend never raised his eyes from the floor.

He looks drugged up!

Khan handed Terrell a 10" serrated dagger with a black, wooden handle, then drew his hand across his own throat, to mimic what Terrell was to do.

Tears rolled down Terrell's cheeks as he turned to his friend and moved the blade toward Teddy's neck. His arm began shaking uncontrollably.

Terrell dropped the dagger and cried out, "I can't do this! I won't! You can kill my Grandmom and me, but I ain't doin' this!"

Naheed nodded to Khan. The powerful man picked up the dagger then hooked his forearm around Terrell's throat and dragged him behind Teddy.

Terrell struggled as Khan choked his airway. Terrell's vision became dim as he blacked out from lack of oxygen. He came to as Khan was forcing the dagger into his hand. Terrell tried to break away, but he was too weak. Squeezing his hand over the young man's, Khan pressed the serrated end against Teddy's throat, just under his chin, while holding Teddy's head still.

Terrell wanted to scream out, but all he could manage was a throaty howl, as he felt the blade sink deeply into his friend's throat. Terrell's heart and mind shut down as shock overwhelmed him.

When the gruesome deed was done, Khan lifted Teddy's severed head like a basketball and plopped it down, unceremoniously, on the chest of the corpse. Malik took a photograph of the grisly aftermath and pinned it to the wall of their training area. It was to act as a constant reminder of the penalty for disobedience.

Only a day later, Naheed noticed the photo had disappeared. She decided not to look for who was responsible because Tariq's death already left her one bomber short. It was too close to July Fourth to subject any others to the punishment she would have to carry out for the infraction. Besides, the witnessing of Tariq's punishment and the photo had done their job. Naheed could tell, from the looks of terror on the faces of the young men standing before her now, including Hooman, they were all properly motivated.

Naheed pointed to Terrell, "Tell me your mission."

Terrell wet his lips before speaking, "I'll travel to the target location and walk to an area with the largest crowd. When I get there, I'll glance at my watch and when it reads 9:06 PM exactly … I'll detonate my vest."

Naheed walked over to Terrell until she was standing nose-to-nose with him. She looked deeply into his eyes, "Will you fail me again, Hooman?"

Terrell blinked several times, continuing to wet his lips, "No, ma'am."

"If you do," Naheed stepped back and raised her voice to address the rest, "if any of you do, your families will pay the price. Is that understood?"

Almost in unison, they answered, "Yes, ma'am."

Naheed smiled, "Success is life for your families. Success is riches for your families. And success allows you to enter Paradise. Yes?"

Again, the reply was in unison, "Yes ma'am!"

Terrell waited for Naheed to leave the room before vomiting. Being called by his Muslim name made him sick and the smell of that British bitch made him sicker, but he couldn't let her see him puke.

Terrell had been vomiting every day since Teddy's murder. He could only control it by not eating, but Naheed noticed and forced him to eat. She said he might attract attention looking emaciated and sick. She also warned him about vomiting, because of the effect on morale it was having.

Terrell couldn't help himself though.

Smelling that white bitch when she got in my face … her scent will forever remind me of what she made me do to Teddy.

The only thing that made Terrell feel better was taking the photo. He took a big chance taking the photo down and even a bigger one sneaking out and delivering it to Teddy's dad's store.

Terrell noticed as soon as the photo was missing, around-the-clock guards were posted at all entrances and exits. That meant he'd no longer be able to escape. The only thing Terrell could hope for now was that Teddy's dad … "Shah" used to be his street name … would find them and come pay a call before it was too late.

Tears welled in Terrell's eyes.

I might not get out of this alive, but I'd love to see Teddy's dad cap that sorry-bitch's ass! I don't deserve to live anyway, after what I did to Teddy. I'd blow that bitch up myself, but they won't arm the vests until we're in the cars.

Terrell walked back to his bunk and fell back onto it, his eyes staring blankly at the ceiling. Come on, Shah!

CHAPTER 7

One by one, they stepped out of Tonio's SUV – Mugsy Ricci, John "Johnny-F" Francis, Karla and Kevin Matthews, Tonio and finally, Cris De Niro.

De Niro stretched as he glanced over at the small grey, two-story home of Rita Briggs. The house was edged by a small patch of over-grown lawn, and the front was capped by a cement-block-enclosed porch and stoop. For its spartan appearance, De Niro could see that it was well-maintained.

Someone cares.

De Niro nodded in the direction of the door, "Kevin, why don't you knock on the door, while the rest of us wait. We don't want to scare the boy's grandmother. But, tell her we'd all like to talk to Terrell, if it's okay."

The tall, dapper Matthews ascended the stoop, opened the screen door, and rapped his knuckles three times on the wooden door. A minute went by before he noticed the blinds move near the corner of the bay window. Eyes were all he saw, first scanning the crowd on the sidewalk, then shifting over to him. Another minute passed, before the front door cracked open, as far as the small chain lock would allow.

"Who you ...?" came the rough, old, cigarette-dried female voice from inside.

"Ma'am, my name is—"

"Don't you ma'am me, young man. I asked who you is ... po-lice or you tryin' to sell me something?"

"Ma'am ... I mean, Ms. Briggs—"

"How you know my name? So, you the po-lice then. Who they by that fancy truck? They don't look like po-lice."

Tonio hopped up the stoop wearing a smug grin. After Matthews invited him to take the lead, with the wave of his arm, Tonio stepped in front of him, "Allow me ... Mrs. Briggs, my name is—"

"I know who you is ... trouble! You ain't no po-lice. You the other. Take yourself outta here!"

"Ma'am, you don't understand—"

The long muzzle end of a double-barrel shotgun poked out of the door crack, aiming right at Tonio's head, "I ain't your ma'am neither. You best walk off, young man, 'fore I let the Almighty deal wit' you!"

Tonio tilted his head back and raised his hands.

De Niro whispered into Karla's ear, "You better go save them before someone gets hurt."

Karla shook her head in disbelief as she walked up the stairs. Gently, she moved in-between her brother and Tonio, "Hello Ms. Briggs, my name is Karla Matthews. Are my brother and his friend bothering you?" Karla turned and faced them, "Get off this stoop, and don't come back unless you're invited. Ya hear?"

Her brother descended the cement stairs first. Tonio slowly

stepped back with his hands still in the air.

"Put your fool hands down, and watch where you're walking!" cried Karla.

The long barrels retreated into the crack and the door was shut, followed by the sound of the chain rattling, before the door was cracked open again. Standing before Karla was a white-haired, heavily-wrinkled woman wearing glasses and a stern face.

Karla offered her hand, "Ms. Briggs, like I said, my name is Karla Matthews." Karla pointed behind her, "That's my younger brother Kevin and his friend Tonio."

"That Shah," replied the old woman. "That boy trouble."

Karla went on, "Yes, he was, for sure. And those men by the truck are my boss, Mr. Cris De Niro, and two of my co-workers, Captain Ricci and Mr. Francis."

"Captain …, you sure none of you po-lice?"

"No Ma'am, we just want to speak with your grandson Terrell for a few minutes. Is he here?"

Karla could see the old woman's face get stern again, "T ain't here. What you want with him?"

"We just … Terrell was friends with Shah's son, Teddy."

The old woman's continence changed when she heard Teddy's name. Tears welled in her eyes.

"Teddy dead. My grandson told me. He was cryin' … those boys were close."

Karla looked back at the men for a moment, "Ms. Briggs, Terrell told you Teddy was dead? When did he tell you this?"

The old woman opened the door wider, stepped aside, and made an inviting wave with her arm, "I'm called Mother Briggs. Come in, Sweetie."

Karla took a step inside, "Mother Briggs, would you mind terribly if everyone came in just for a moment. It would be very helpful if all of them heard what you had to say."

Mother Briggs stepped out onto her porch and waved them in, "Come on up and wipe your feet before you come in."

One by one, each man filed past Karla and Mother Briggs, finding places to stand inside the small living room. Karla led the old woman to her rocking chair and took a seat next to her, on a worn sofa. Karla glanced at De Niro, who motioned with his chin for her to continue.

Karla noticed an empty forty-ounce bottle of Olde English 800 on the end table, "Mother Briggs, may I get you something cold from your fridge?"

"That would be nice, child."

Karla fetched another bottle of the malt liquor, poured a tall glass, and handed it to Mother Briggs.

"Thank you, child." Mother Briggs downed half of it, before coming up for air.

Karla glared at the men who were suppressing smiles before continuing, "Mother Briggs, you said that Terrell told you Teddy was dead ... when did he tell you that?"

The old woman sipped from her glass and thought for a moment, "Must be a week ago, Friday."

"Have you seen your grandson since then?"

Mother Briggs shook her head. Her voice weakened, "No, I sure ain't. Boy don't even have called his grandmamma."

Tonio leaned down to make eye contact, "Mother Briggs, exactly what did Terrell say happened to Teddy?"

The old woman scowled at Tonio with mistrusting eyes, "He said, 'Grandmamma, Teddy dead. I gots to tell his daddy.' He tell you?"

Tonio looked over at Karla then backed away.

De Niro took his place, kneeling on one knee, "Mother Briggs, we think Terrell could be in trouble. We want to help him. Do you know if Terrell was attending the mosque up the street with Teddy?"

Mother Briggs looked from De Niro to Karla, who gently nodded that it was okay to reply.

"They both tried gettin' me calling them their Muslim names, but I'd have none of dat. No sir! That boy named Terrell by my son, may he rest in peace. Ain't no way I was gonna call my grandson that …," she picked up a crumpled piece of paper and handed it to De Niro.

De Niro read it out loud, "Hooman Halim."

"He gave me that when he and Teddy first joined that church. Tryin' to show me how to pronounce it and what it meant. 'Good natured and wise' … he said. They'd come here wearin' those beanie caps … both of 'em trying to grow beards …."

Mother Briggs wiped a tear away and laughed at the memory. After a moment, they could see a painful memory replaced it. She stopped laughing and emptied her glass.

"Then last week he come home lookin' white as death, all sweaty and upset. He tell me Teddy dead and he gots to go tell you," she pointed at Tonio. Her voice broke down, "That boy ran out as fast as he came in, and I ain't seen or heard from him since."

De Niro got her attention back, "Mother Briggs, have you tried to call him?"

"Hell yeah, I tried to call him. I've been callin' and callin' his cellphone all times of day and night since he be gone. I even tried to call Teddy, but all I gets is their messages."

Johnny-F leaned down next to De Niro, "Mother Briggs, may I

have Terrell's cell number?"

She handed Francis another crumpled piece of paper, "He wrote it down for me."

Francis tried the number. The call went directly to voice mail without ringing. He whispered into De Niro's ear, "His phone is either turned off or isn't receiving a signal."

De Niro took the old woman's hand in his, "Thank you, Mother Briggs."

She covered his hand with her other hand, "You tell my grandson to call his grandmamma when you find him. Ya hear."

De Niro straightened up, "I will. And Mother Briggs, let us know if Terrell calls you or comes here."

Karla handed her a business card, "That has my cellphone number. You call me if you need anything."

Another tear fell from the tough, old woman's eye. Her voice sounded tired, "I just need my grandson back."

De Niro was first to exit the house. The rest followed without saying a word until they were in Tonio's SUV.

Mugsy was the first to speak, "You think the kid is still alive?"

De Niro strapped himself into the front passenger seat, "I bet the folks in that mosque know."

Johnny-F leaned forward, "Something tells me they ain't gonna be very neighborly if we just go knock on their door."

Tonio pushed the ignition button, "I was thinkin' … I could call some of my old crew. I was gonna call 'em before I reached out to Kevin, but I figured I'd try it up-and-up, for once."

Kevin Matthews leaned forward, from the third row, "You mean your gangsta friends. I would think the ones that aren't dead are in jail."

"Not all of them. Some got out and got straight."

"Like who?"

"Like Jimbo, Frankie Parker, Timmy Means …."

"Jimbo … you mean the one that used to carry that machete everywhere he went and kiss it all the time?"

Tonio looked back at Matthews, "Yeah, well … he still got that machete, and he knows how to use it, too."

De Niro put his hand on Tonio's forearm, "We don't want to hack our way into that mosque in case Terrell is still alive and being held in there. We have someone we can call."

Tonio nodded.

De Niro turned to Mugsy, "Call Scipio. Tell him to tell Duke to fly him here tonight in one of the Lears."

A grin widened on Tonio's face as he pulled from the curb, "One of the Lears? I like your style Mr. De Niro."

CHAPTER 8

UNDERGROUND COMPOUND
BASEMENTS ALONG CHENE STREET
DETROIT, MICHIGAN
5:00 PM (LOCAL), SUNDAY, JULY 03, 2016

Samantha, aka Naheed, sat in front of a large computer monitor. On it was a photo and article on Cris De Niro and his counter-terrorism firm, The Watchman Agency. Next to her sat Nabil who had been the White Widow's computer tech for the last five years. In that time, Nabil had never failed her before. Technically, he didn't fail her this time either, although he didn't completely succeed. He was only able to identify one of the men, the one on the screen, Cris De Niro.

Nabil used proprietary face recognition software he developed with the help and financial support of the Chinese government. The software interfaced with and could scan, among others, virtually all the Departments of Motor Vehicles (DMV) databases in the United States, as well as those of the FBI, CIA, British MI6, Russian SVR, Interpol, and private corporations. It even tapped into various nations' military and civilian police department systems, and scanned many global news and media broadcasts, as well as all of the major social media sites.

It only took seconds for the software to identify Cris De Niro, and the reason was obvious. De Niro had a high profile in the media. News articles about him began to pop up, even before his Nevada driver's license photo. The software's early success didn't hold for the others. Nabil was amazed that literally nothing came back on the other two white men, or the black woman. The software found neither news articles nor photos from anywhere – employment, social media, even the country's DMVs.

Nabil was convinced it was virtually impossible to keep one's likeness completely off the internet. The fact that the software was unable to find a trace of these three meant only one thing. Someone, somehow, had deleted their photos from everywhere.

Nabil didn't think that was possible, yet the proof was evident. His robust face recognition program had been searching for over five hours. It had never taken that long, ever, to identify someone.

Nabil sat quietly next to Naheed hoping the woman would overlook his failure identifying the three, for his success identifying the one. He watched as she sat quietly reading each article on Cris De Niro.

Naheed's cell phone rang. She answered it while still reading, "Yes Khan …." She sat back in her chair, "She is the grandmother of Hooman Halim? All of them went into the house …?"

Naheed paused a moment to think. "Where are you now? Yes, I remember the hotel. Remain out of sight in the parking lot. I will join you there, soon."

Malik walked into the room as she was still talking, "That was Khan?"

Naheed ignored the question and pulled up Google Maps on the monitor. She typed in "The Henry Hotel, Detroit" and The Henry, Autograph Collection appeared on the map.

Naheed stood and headed for the door, but Malik stepped in front of her, "Where are you going?"

"Follow me."

She led Malik to the room where the explosive vests were kept, grabbing a carrier bag and placed one of the vests in it.

Malik grabbed her arm. She pulled away holding the bag up, "Don't ever grab someone who has explosives in their hand!"

Malik held his hands up, "I want to know what you are doing? What did Khan tell you? It was Khan who called, was it not?"

Naheed took one of the electronic detonators and carefully added it to the bag, then put one of the cell phone triggers in her pocket.

"It was Khan. He said those people just talked to Hooman Halim's grandmother."

Naheed zipped the bag then walked to a locker and removed a pistol from it. She checked the clip then chambered a round before slipping it into her belt.

"Wait … I do not understand. What difference does it make? We know all about Hooman's grandmother. That drunk, old woman knows nothing about us. But why would those people speak to her? I thought they were interested in real estate?"

Naheed put a jacket on, making sure to conceal the pistol, then carefully lifted the bag and headed for the door. Again, Malik stepped in front of her.

Naheed looked up at him, "Syed, go ask Nabil to let you read the information he found on the one named Cris De Niro."

Naheed waited for Malik to step out of her way. He didn't, "Naheed, what are you going to do with that vest? You can't use it or you will blow our entire operation!"

The British woman's blue eyes sparkled, as a grin formed on her face, "If all goes well, I won't be detonating it, but we'll have prisoners here tonight, so prepare one of the rooms."

She stepped around him and turned, "Monitor the news tonight. If you see a story about an explosion or fire at The Henry Hotel, it means our operation has been compromised. You know what to do then.

"Don't wait for me. You and Nabil, gather everyone together in the large room, the bombers, handlers, drivers, everyone. Have the bombers don their vests then lock them in, get in your car, and detonate all of the vests. After that, head immediately to our rendezvous across the border. Understood?"

Malik, dazed by what she just told him, didn't reply.

Naheed stepped face-to-face with him, "Syed, do you understand?"

Malik hesitated then nodded.

Naheed saw the fear on his face. She put her hands on his shoulders, "Don't worry, I worked too long and hard to mess this up now. Secure one of the rooms as a jail and then do what I said."

Malik watched her disappear down the corridor before looking up, "Allah be with us."

CHAPTER 9

The food ordered from room service was set up buffet style. On the large dining room table, silver trays were lined up next to one another. On one side of the table – Lake Superior whitefish tacos and dry, aged angus sliders, arugula salad, Caesar salad, butternut squash ravioli, mushroom lasagna, roast cauliflower, garlic mashed potatoes, poached asparagus, mushroom gratin, pillow tator tots, and house fries. On the other side of the table – butter-basted farm chicken, local Peking duck, maple-soy beef short ribs, and double-bone lamb chops. There were also small tureens of onion and creamy tomato soups set up on one room service cart, and on another were bottles of various Michigan local brews, cider, and bottled water.

Standing around the table filling their plates were John Johnny-F, Mugsy, Kevin and Karla Matthews, Tonio, and Cris De Niro.

De Niro scanned the array shaking his head, "John, you remind me of my sons … did you order everything on the menu?"

Francis was busy piling sliders on top of his tacos and ravioli,

"You know how it is Cris, your eyes are bigger than your stomach when you order room service."

De Niro smiled but clenched his brows, "Who's paying for all this?"

"Not to worry brother-in-law," Mugsy Ricci replied while adding tator tots to his plate of lamb and duck, "I'll be sure to charge this to John's tech department. Their budget is big enough to handle it."

De Niro stood there holding an empty plate, "So, it doesn't come out of my right pocket, it comes out of my left ... and that's supposed to make me feel better?"

Francis walked over with a rack of beef ribs he carried with tongs and placed them on De Niro's plate, "Quoting Napoleon, 'An army travels on its stomach.'"

Mugsy walked over and swiped a slider off of Francis's plate, "Actually, Napoleon never said that."

Francis shrugged and took another slider from the tray, "Well then, quote me on that one."

"I, for one, haven't eaten this good since Thanksgiving," said Kevin Matthews, as he ate a forkful of chicken.

Karla walked over with a steaming cup of soup, "Our mother hosts the best Thanksgivings. She makes enough food for an army. John, even our mother would be impressed with this spread."

"Why, thank you."

"You only forgot one thing," replied Karla, as she winked at De Niro, "dessert."

"For your information, I didn't forget it. I told them to wait awhile before bringing it up. In Brooklyn, every good meal must end with cake and coffee, am I right Cris?"

De Niro just smiled at his old friend. De Niro and Francis both grew up in Ridgewood, New York, an immigrant neighborhood that bordered both Brooklyn and Queens.

The chime of a video call came from the living room area. Mugsy Ricci responded first, "That must be Scipio. I told him to contact us once they reached cruising altitude."

Tonio followed him over to the laptop, "He can video call us from the air?"

Mugsy tapped a button on the keyboard. Within seconds, the large screen monitor filled with the rugged face of the Vice President of Operations for The Watchman Agency and head of paramilitary force ARCHANGEL. He was a man known only by his clandestine operations codename, Scipio.

Tonio nodded with satisfaction, "Impressive."

Tonio's cell phone rang. He answered it then pointed to one of the bedrooms, "It's Teddy's mom. She's upset. I'll take it in there." Tonio closed the door behind him.

De Niro joined Mugsy and Tonio, "How's my sons?"

"Not happy," replied Scipio. "First, I had to tell them that their dad and uncle wouldn't be home for the Fourth party, and then I had to tell them that Duke and I weren't gonna be there either."

Francis came up behind De Niro and spoke with a mouthful of food, "And wha ... what about their Uncle Johnny?"

"Oh yeah," replied Scipio, "they wanted to know the password you used for the fireworks controls."

Francis nodded proudly, "See, I knew they'd miss their Uncle Johnny!"

Mugsy tapped another button, "Scip ... I just uploaded all the info we have so far into Big-Brutha. You can access it in the folder named Project New Detroit."

They watched as Scipio typed on a keyboard, "Got it. Not using our data protocol, I see."

Scipio enjoyed teasing the President of The Watchman Agency, Ricci about the proper naming of folders and files within their massive, proprietary Big-Brutha data and communications system. The system was designed by tech genius Francis, but it was the former Navy SEALs Captain Louis "Mugsy" Ricci who was anal about utilizing a standard file and folder-naming criteria, within the database. Not inputting a folder with the proper six-number prefix signifying the date, followed by the folder name, and ending with a hyphen and abbreviation, for the type of operation (i.e. "sv" for surveillance, "fg" for fact gathering, "in" infiltration, etc.) would usually lead to a dressing-down from Ricci himself.

The tease didn't get past Ricci, "Technically, this isn't a Watchman Agency op. So, the rules don't necessarily apply."

"The rules don't necessarily apply ... hmm," replied Scipio, "I gotta remember that."

The doorbell to the suite rang.

Kevin Matthews hollered from the dining room, "I'll get it."

"That's got to be the dessert," added Francis, "told you I didn't forget it."

Kevin and Karla Matthews led the way. Behind them a blond-haired woman wearing the familiar room-service white jacket rolled in a cart.

Francis walked over to her, pointing to the dining room, "It goes in ... there." His voice trailed off.

Francis raised his hands and stepped back, from a 9mm Glock pistol being pressed against his forehead by the woman.

Naheed barked orders to everyone, keeping the barrel pressed against Francis's head, "All of you, sit on the floor with hands in the air, and don't move a muscle ... now!"

Everyone complied, except for Francis, "Hey ... no need for that.

My wallet is in my back pocket."

Naheed smacked the pistol against Francis's temple sending him tumbling to the floor. Karla moved to help him.

Naheed pointed the Glock at her, "I said not to move."

She moved the barrel to De Niro's head, "Stand up and keep your hands high."

De Niro stood with his hands raised, "Take what you want and leave."

Naheed smiled, "But, it's you I want, Mr. De Niro, the rest of you too."

She backed up and retrieved the bomb vest from the bottom of the cart then handed it to De Niro, "Put it on."

De Niro tried to take it from her, but she held it a moment, "Careful with it."

Tension grew as everyone realized what it was.

De Niro slipped his arms into the vest.

Naheed put the pistol to his head again, "Now raise your hands and keep them there."

De Niro hesitated slightly as he raised his hands, staring at the woman before him.

Those eyes … I know those eyes.

Naheed used her free hand to fasten the latches, which also acted as connectors completing an electrical connection. At once, a green LED light illuminated from the bottom of the vest. Lastly, she snapped the metal ring attached to the collar around De Niro's throat.

"The vest is made of heavy canvas and the collar is made of titanium, virtually indestructible. And take note of that light, Mr. De Niro … and the rest of you. If you attempt to take off the vest or tamper with the latches in any way, that light will turn from green to red. You will barely have enough time to kneel and pray, before it explodes killing you and everyone around you. Do you understand?"

De Niro nodded.

"Yes, well, now we all must take our leave. First, let me show you another way that the vest can be detonated." Naheed reached into her pocket and produced a small cell phone. "No need to make a call. I can simply tap the side button and the light will turn red. Do you all understand?"

Naheed didn't wait for replies. She waved everyone to their feet, "You may put your arms down." She took the bag out from under the cart. Everyone noticed a man enter the suite.

"My comrade, Khan, will search each of you as you exit. You are to place your cell phones, any weapons you may have, and anything else in your pockets into this bag."

One by one, each of them handed over their cell phones, wallets, pens, and change, followed by Mugsy who was the only person to also place a SIG Sauer 9mm Navy SEALs-issued pistol into the bag.

Naheed nodded to him, "Thank you. Now, listen and obey all of my orders. We will leave this room and head to the staircase at the end of the corridor. There, we will descend and wait just inside the back door until my friend pulls our vehicle around. We will quickly enter the truck. I will sit in the front passenger seat, and Mr. De Niro will sit directly behind the driver's seat. The rest of you may sit where you want."

She noticed Kevin Matthews looking in the direction of the doors behind her.

She approached him and placed the pistol to his head, "Is anyone else here?"

Matthews stared unblinkingly at her.

She pressed the barrel against his temple, "I asked you a question."

"No."

"No what …?"

He kept his stare, "No, no one else is here."

Naheed grinned unbelievingly. She began checking each room, starting with the dining room then bathroom then bedrooms, and finally ending up in front of the bedroom door Tonio had entered. She stepped in, turned on the light, and checked the closet and around each side of the bed before exiting the room. No one gave away their concern as she reemerged.

Naheed took off the white waiter's jacket she was wearing and handed it to De Niro, "Put it on."

De Niro complied and saw that the jacket was bulky enough to completely conceal the vest. She pulled handcuffs from the bag and slapped them on him. The sleeves of the jacket were long enough to obscure them.

Naheed motioned with the pistol, "Now, everyone follows Khan. You may walk in pairs or alone. The key is too look natural and not attract attention. If we pass anyone, you are to react casually. Once the truck pulls up, remember, Mr. De Niro, you are to sit behind the driver's seat and I will sit in the front passenger seat."

Everyone returned stern stares.

"Keep in mind. Khan and I are prepared to die. The question is, are you? If you aren't then I suggest you follow my instructions to the letter." She motioned with the pistol again, "Let's get going."

Naheed allowed everyone to leave then scanned the room once more. She noticed that the lights on the laptop were on, but the large monitor screen behind it was black. She considered taking it, but decided not to. Keeping the pistol in one hand and toting the bag was cumbersome enough while keeping watch on five people. She didn't expect these people to be foolish, but then again, people sometimes act irrationally in extraordinary situations. She didn't need the extra weight of the laptop to weigh her down.

Naheed walked into the dining room and popped a few tator tots into her mouth. Americans are so wasteful.

She walked to the door, placed the "Do Not Disturb" sign on the outer knob, and closed the door behind her.

Inside one of the bedrooms, the pillows began to move. Concealed under them, Tonio rolled over and stood up. "The one time I needed a piece, and I'm not carrying one!"

He walked to the door and scanned the corridor in both directions before hurrying out.

As he passed the laptop, he heard a voice, "Hey, you!"

Tonio turned, his hands balled into fists, "Who's that?"

Scipio's face reappeared on the monitor, "Who are you?"

Tonio shot an anxious look at the door, "I'd love to stay and chat, but—"

"If you're gonna go after them, you may get them killed, yourself with them."

Tonio furled his brows and leaned in close to the laptop, "I can handle myself. Who exactly are you, anyway?"

"My name is Scipio. What's yours?"

"Tonio."

"Tonio, listen to me, there should be a laptop bag somewhere near."

Tonio spotted the bag on the floor next to the chair, "I see it."

"Take it with you, but first, look inside. You should find earphones. Plug them into the laptop then unplug the laptop from the monitor and put the power supply in the bag."

Tonio moved quickly. After unplugging the monitor and stowing the power supply, he plugged in the earphones and placed them in his ears, "What now?"

"Now, carry the laptop open so you can continue to talk to me. Don't worry about staying connected. The laptop utilizes satellite technology. Head out of the room and down the corridor, in the direction of the back stairs."

"How do you know where they went?"

"'Cause I heard the British chick talking. Now, go, before they get too far."

Carrying the laptop open, Tonio headed out of the room and quickly down the corridor. He checked inside the stairwell before heading down the stairs. He stopped a half floor from the bottom, when he heard people below.

Tonio looked back at Scipio on the monitor, and whispered, "Hey, they're at the back door. I won't be able to follow them, if they get in a vehicle. I valeted my SUV."

"I don't need you to follow them. I need you get the license plate number and make and model of the car. Our people are already trying to set up satellite and camera surveillance, but they might not get it together in time."

Tonio heard the British woman's voice, followed by the sounds of them heading out of the back door. He descended the last flight of stairs and cracked the back door open, just enough to watch all of them get into a dark blue Chevy Suburban. He took his phone out and snapped a few photos of it.

As soon as the truck pulled away, he stepped out of the door and took pictures of the plate.

Tonio looked back at the monitor, "I took some pictures with my phone."

"Excellent," said Scipio, "text them to me. I just shot my number, to your cellphone."

Tonio felt his cell phone vibrate. He was about to ask how this crazy white guy got his number, but decided not to. He texted the photos.

"Now what?"

"I'll be landing within the hour. Can you pick me up at Coleman Young Airport?"

"I can get there in twenty."

"Good. I'll see you there."

Tonio closed the laptop, placed it into the bag, and walked back into the hotel.

CHAPTER 10

Terrell Briggs decided to camp near the stairwell, in case the guard got called away. The guard was posted there after his last breakout. Keeping hidden in the shadows, near a pile of cinderblocks, he stole another glance at the large guard, and sighed in frustration. He recognized the guard as one of the handlers.

Those handlers are all just waiting to kill someone. They don't care who or how ... infidel or one of us ... bomb or bullet ... and Allah gots nothin' to do with it!

As if hearing his thoughts, the guard spotted him. The heavyset thug pointed an AK-47 at Terrell, "What you doin' hidin'? Get your ass out here now!"

Terrell stepped into the light in the tight corridor just as clanging echoed down the stairwell, from the basement door opening to the street above. Losing interest in Terrell, the burly guard lowered his rifle and headed up the stairs.

Terrell quickly hustled into a dark corner further down the corridor and watched as the large thug, Khan, led five people – a black man and woman, followed by three white men, past him. Terrell noticed the last white man was wearing a white jacket like a waiter would wear.

That dude wearing thousand-dollar Christian Louboutin loafers don't look like no waiter!

Terrell was about to step out of the darkness to follow them when he heard Naheed's voice coming from the stairwell. She was talking to the burly guard, "Make sure the basement door is closed and locked securely and don't leave your post. Understood?"

"Yes ma'am," replied the guard, as he hurried up the stairs.

Terrell saw the tech guy--he couldn't recall his name--hurry past without noticing him. Naheed handed him the bag she was carrying, "Put this in the computer room."

With only darkness concealing him, Terrell held his breath and didn't blink, as the tech guy carrying the bag and Naheed passed within a couple feet. The two headed in different directions at the next corridor.

Terrell followed Naheed as she headed in the same direction as Khan and the others. He tailed her to what he thought was an un-utilized area and stopped just short of the doorway they all entered. The area outside the room was cluttered with broken, old furniture, with bed sheets thrown over them, all covered in an inch of dust.

He took a quick peek inside and discovered it was the boiler room for the apartment house over them. From their corroded condition, Terrell could tell the boilers had been inoperable for a while.

Naheed and Khan were standing with their backs to him just inside the doorway. Terrell could just see the five sitting on the floor in a star configuration, with their backs to one another. Khan was wrapping gaff tape around them, binding all of them together.

Terrell looked for cover. He ducked down behind an overturned table near the door, covering himself with one of the musty sheets and did his best to listen. Naheed was doing all of the talking.

"This is your new home. How long you will be here will depend, as much on your conduct, as our progress. If all goes well, you will never see us again, and hopefully, someone will find you here.

"But, if you cause any trouble by trying to escape … you need to be aware of a few things. First, this door is the only way in or out of this room. It's made of metal, and we've installed an unpickable lock. And, as you can see, the walls are made of solid cement.

"Second, we've installed cameras to monitor every inch of this room. If you even attempt to break free from one another, you will suffer the consequences.

"And third …," Naheed took the phone trigger from her pocket and held it out for all to see, "the bomb can be detonated with this, from anywhere."

She paused to let that sink in.

"Do you have any questions?"

Terrell heard someone ask, "Why not detonate the bomb now? Why keep us alive?"

"I know who you are, Mr. De Niro."

Terrell's eyes opened wide. Cris De Niro … the billionaire???

"Well, then you have me at a disadvantage."

"What matters is that I know who you are and all about that company you run. Something tells me, before too long your staff will notice you and these others are missing. So, I would prefer to keep you alive as an insurance policy, at least until my business here is done."

"And what business is that? I'm guessing nothing to do with a food franchise."

Naheed blinked then grinned.

"I thought you recognized me. As for my business, that is none of your business."

De Niro returned her grin, "And, after you complete your business, what then …? How do we know you won't detonate this thing?"

"Short answer, you don't. But, leaving you alive could serve another purpose."

"Another purpose …?"

"Public relations. Could you picture the headlines of the world press? The famous Cris De Niro and his legendary Watchman Agency disgraced."

"Disgraced … how?"

"As the saying goes, 'for me to know,' Mr. De Niro. Just make yourselves comfortable and remember … we're watching you."

Terrell held his breath again and froze, as he heard the heavy metal door being pulled shut and locked. He didn't move until Naheed and Khan's footsteps could no longer be heard, then he stood up and dusted himself off, before trying the door. The door didn't even rattle.

He banged on the door and spoke to himself, "Damn, Cris De Niro's in there!"

Terrell peered out of the outer room into darkness. He saw no one.

No guard. Guess they figure they don't need one with that door.

He looked back at the boiler room, "I'll be back, Mr. D. Count on it."

Then he disappeared into the darkness.

CHAPTER 11

MAIN TERMINAL
COLEMAN A. YOUNG INTERNATIONAL AIRPORT
DETROIT, MICHIGAN
7:30 PM (LOCAL), SUNDAY, JULY 03, 2016

Tonio sat in his black Cadillac Escalade SUV, parked at the curb, just outside the small airport's main terminal building. He watched as a small man, dressed from head to toe in black, exited the terminal. The man made his way over, opened the passenger door and offered his hand, "Tonio, right? I'm Scipio. Can I toss my bag in the back?"

Tonio popped the rear hatch. Scipio placed a large black duffel bag inside, shut the hatch, then jumped into the passenger seat.

Before Tonio could ask, Scipio tapped the screen of his cellphone then set it down in the cup holder between them, "From the plate number and photos you sent, we think we've located the vehicle."

A computerized female voice spoke from the phone, "Head east, then turn right toward Conner Street."

"Hold on," replied Tonio. "The plate can tell you the owner, but not the vehicle's current location, and there are probably hundreds of Suburbans in Detroit. We can't spend all day chasing them down."

Scipio fastened his seat belt, "That's true, but my agency can tap into--among other things--municipal and other governmental, as well as private security camera feeds. That allowed us to track the Suburban in question on part of its journey."

Tonio raised a brow, "That's Hollywood movie shit. You said part of its journey, then what?"

"Once we determined the direction it was traveling, we tied into satellite imagery. We have the ability to do that too."

Tonio kept his brow raised and shot Scipio a long stare, "You can do that, too? Who the hell are you people, CIA?"

Scipio broke a soft grin, "Nah. We're a private firm."

"That's right, owned by Mr. De Niro. I thought you people hunt for terrorists overseas."

"Unfortunately, we have terrorists here, too."

"Wait a minute. You saying they were taken by terrorists? But I heard that woman's voice. She sounded like she was from England."

Scipio picked up his phone and tapped the screen a few times, then turned it so Tonio could see, "If the woman's who we think she is, she was born and raised in England, and radicalized there in her early twenties. Since then, she's become something of a terrorist legend. The press gave her a nickname … White Widow."

Tonio remained staring. Scipio could see Tonio was street-savvy, but was having a hard time accepting what he was being told.

"But why would a British terrorist want to kidnap your people and my friend? And does this have something to do with my son's death? We went to the mosque my son used to attend. Are you saying there are terrorists in that mosque?"

"I'm saying there seems to be a connection between your son's death and the abduction of our friends, and that mosque is where we're heading. The Suburban is parked in the parking lot."

Tonio punched the steering wheel, "No wonder they didn't let me in. That explains their heavy hardware too."

"You mean they have armed guards?"

"Oh yeah … towel-headed niggas always standing outside wearing their Muslim dresses, concealing AKs."

Another thought crossed Tonio's mind. He lifted his jacket exposing the black handle protruding from his pants, of his Beretta Px4 Storm Type F Full Size .40 S&W pistol. He hit a button and opened the glove box. Scipio saw an identical handgun inside.

"You packing? Or else, feel free," said Tonio.

Scipio's grin returned, "Thanks, but I brought my toys. They're in my bag."

"So what we gonna do now, Mister Scipio? We gonna raid that place? Why don't you let me call a few dogs I used to run with? Trust me, we gonna need the help."

"It's just Scipio. Let's just the two of us check it out, for now. I think between you, me, and your friend tucked into your trousers, we can take care of business. Don't you?"

A wide smile grew on Tonio's face, "I like your style Brutha Scipio. Let's go take care of some b'ness."

Tonio screeched the tires leaving the curb.

CHAPTER 12

UNDERGROUND COMPOUND
BASEMENTS ALONG CHENE STREET
DETROIT, MICHIGAN
9:00 PM (LOCAL), SUNDAY, JULY 03, 2016

Syed, Naheed, Nabil, and Khan sat around a well-worn wooden table. On it were white take-out cartons filled with food from a Pakistani restaurant across town. They already finished off most of the tabbouleh, hummus, grape leaves, feta, labne, roasted beets, and lamb shawarma wraps, and were sipping their mango lassis. All but Syed Malik, who sat with his back to them, his eyes fixated on the TV. The channel was tuned to the local news.

Naheed noticed, "I told you Syed, nothing happened at the hotel to attract suspicion. You won't see anything on the news. The calls coming into their cellphones are going to their voice mail. I would wager the soonest any of their people will become concerned enough to contact Detroit police, will be sometime later tonight. At which time, Detroit's not-so-helpful constables will tell the concerned parties they must wait at least twenty-four hours before they can take a missing person's report. By then, all would've taken place, and we shall be gone."

Malik turned, raising his voice, "And what if the people working for that Cris De Niro decide to look for him sooner?"

Naheed glanced at the other men. They took the hint and left the room.

Naheed's tone became stern, "Syed, we are too close to success for you to inject doubt in the others."

He matched her tone, "You didn't answer my question."

"So what if they look. What can they find? We left nothing to trace us here."

Malik stood up, "Don't underestimate those people, Naheed. They were the ones who stopped the nuke from destroying Las Vegas."

Naheed got to her feet and walked in front of him, "I never underestimate my adversaries, Syed. That is how I've survived this long. I never underestimate, nor do I proceed without a contingency, which is why they are still alive."

Malik's anger turned to lust as he grabbed Naheed's face and kissed her. She did not resist, knowing so well the pacifying effect it would have. When their lips parted, Malik took her by the hand and led her to the room where he slept.

As soon as they heard a door close, Nabil and Khan walked back in and began finishing their meals. Khan nodded toward the door as he took a bite of shawarma, "I wouldn't mind having a go with that one. Believer or non-believer, white women are all sluts."

Nabil found his lassi and finished it, "I've been with Ms. Samantha for over 10 years. In that time, she's been married twice, and has had twice that many admirers … with whom she's gone behind closed doors." He looked up at the brawny Khan, "None of them are still alive."

Khan stopped chewing. Nabil smiled, "Another reason I guess she's called the White Widow."

CHAPTER 13

PROPERTY OWNED BY THE NORFOLK SOUTHERN RAILROAD
(ACROSS THE STREET FROM THE FAISAL ISLAM MOSQUE)
DETROIT, MICHIGAN
10:00 PM (LOCAL), SUNDAY, JULY 03, 2016

Scipio had Tonio park his SUV several blocks away from the Faisal Islam Mosque. From there, he led them to an overgrown area that ran along the train tracks, across the street from the mosque. Scipio found a spot that gave them a clear view of the front and back of the one-story building.

After peering through, Scipio handed the sleek Swarovski SLC HD 15x56 night vision binoculars to a curious Tonio.

Tonio whistled, "Damn, if I can't read the words on the car tires around that mosque!"

"Check out the back lot. Look familiar?"

Tonio scanned to the right, "That's the Suburban."

"Now look on the front side of the building."

Tonio scanned left. It took a moment before he saw the familiar black men wearing dishdashas.

"I see two guards."

Scipio took the binoculars, "I saw four more. Something tells me they've been put on alert."

"But they can't know we're coming."

Scipio dropped the binoculars in the duffel bag and retrieved a balaclava, lock pick set, and a Tavor X-95 bullpup assault rifle.

Tonio pointed at the rifle, "You got another one of those?"

Scipio pulled the black mask over his head, "Know how to use one?"

Tonio took the compressed weapon from him, tucked it into his shoulder and hit the clip release with his index finger. He checked it, reinserted it, then flipped up the front and rear sites and took aim before handing it back to Scipio.

Tonio winked, "It's like a Polaroid … point and shoot."

That made Scipio smile, "I'll tell you what you can do. Go around the front. Stay across the street but make your presence known. Try to draw their attention, but don't get yourself killed and try not to kill them."

"I can do that. And what will you be doing?"

"I need to get inside to look for our friends."

"And if you find them, then what? Point and shoot?"

Scipio reached into the bag and pulled out two Invisio® M30 remote communication devices. He slipped the device onto his index finger and had Tonio do the same with his. "Put this transmitter in your pocket, then run the wire from the remote to the transmitter through your sleeve and under your shirt."

Tonio did as he was told, "Now what?"

"Put this bud in your ear. Now I can talk directly to you without anyone hearing, even if they were standing right in front of you. When you want to talk to me, just press the button on the remote and talk normally."

"Okay, now that we can communicate, answer the question, if they're inside, what then?"

"If I find them, I'll let you know what to do. It might require firing that thing. You okay with that?"

"If they be in there, that means they probably had a hand in my son's death. I gots no problem puttin' a cap in all their asses."

Scipio winked, "Just make sure you don't put a cap in my ass, when I come out."

Tonio pulled his pistol, chambered a round and placed it back in his belt, "Let's do this thing."

Scipio patted his shoulder and led the way.

CHAPTER 14

Much of the talking had ebbed, between Cris, Mugsy, Johnny-F, Karla, and her brother Kevin. De Niro was now spending part of his time praying and the rest thinking about his sons, Richard, and Louis. The thought of them losing their dad after losing their mom weighed heavy on Cris. Yet, at the same time, he couldn't help feeling a special sense of peace in dying and seeing his wife Lisa again.

As a Christian, Cris believed he would see Lisa again in God's Kingdom if he was found worthy, and there, they would serve the God Almighty forever, in love and peace. His beliefs grew ever stronger, after being challenged by Lisa's murder in the North Tower of The World Trade Center on 9/11.

There was a point when he contemplated suicide, yet his faith and trust in God saved him. More than that, it focused him. He became committed to using all his wealth and resources to prevent other terrorist acts.

Sitting with a suicide vest locked to him, De Niro wondered if dying there was his fate. If he was alone he could accept it, but not if the others were harmed. So, he prayed more.

Karla and Kevin remained quiet, with their heads down, while Mugsy scraped a shard of metal against the floor. He found it after discovering quite painfully that he was sitting on it.

Mugsy stopped scraping the shard and held it up for Francis to inspect, "Whaddaya think so far?"

Francis had told the others he was convinced the cameras over their heads were not equipped with microphones, so it was safe to speak out loud to one another.

Mugsy waited for a reply.

"John?"

"Forget it, he's sleeping," replied De Niro.

"Sleeping ... seriously, now?"

De Niro knew his old friend well, "Trust me, when he gets stressed out, John can sleep in a lion's cage. Switch it to your other hand, so I can take a look."

Mugsy passed the metal fragment from his right hand to his left, and did his best to hold it up.

De Niro strained his neck to take a glimpse, "Looks good."

"Should I give it a try?"

"Try what?" asked Karla.

"I think I can cut through the tape," replied Mugsy.

Karla replied softly, but sternly, "They're watching us!"

"We need to try," Mugsy insisted.

"But if they see ... Cris!" replied Karla.

Kevin reached for and took hold of his sister's hand. She turned to him and their eyes met, "Sis ... we can't just do nothing."

"No—" Karla was interrupted by another voice.

"Give it a try," the voice was De Niro's.

"Karla, from the angle of those cameras I don't think they'll be able to see what Mugsy's doing," replied Francis.

"Now you wake up?" replied Mugsy, with strain in his voice as he began scratching the shard against the gaff tape.

"I heard a damsel in distress. Besides, my nose got itchy."

"If Mugsy can cut through the tape, everyone remember to remain still," warned De Niro.

"What good will it do?" asked Karla.

"Karla, if I know Scipio, he'll find us. When he does, it'll be better if we're at least free of the tape. How's it coming Mugs?"

Mugsy shook sweat from his brows and sighed audibly, "This isn't gonna be easy. That asshole must have used an entire roll of tape. It's gonna take some time."

"You'll have as much as they give us," replied De Niro. "Keep at it."

"Karla, do me a favor?" asked Francis.

Karla turned to find Francis straining his neck to extend his face toward hers.

"What are you doing??"

"My nose is itchy."

"So, what do you want me to do about it?"

"Rub your nose against mine?"

"Not in your wildest dreams!"

"Please … Karla I'm dying here!"

"I'm wearing a kilo of explosive, but Johnny-F is dying because his nose is itchy."

Everyone heard the levity in De Niro's voice. Kevin was the first to laugh. De Niro was next, followed by Mugsy and Karla. Francis was the only one not laughing. He stared hard into Karla's eyes and twitching his nose, "Karla, PLEASE!"

The room became silent for a moment, before being broken by

the sounds of Francis's oohs and ahhs.

"Sounds like they're having a good ole' time over there," remarked Mugsy.

"Hey, what are you doing with my sister?" Kevin was unable to sound serious.

"If any of you EVER breathe a word of this to anyone!" Karla said sternly.

De Niro looked up at one of the cameras, "At least we're giving our friends a show."

* * * * *

Nabil peered closely at the monitor, before sitting back and smiling. Khan lounged behind him nodding toward the screen.

Nabil turned to him, "It looks like they are fighting amongst themselves. We should've installed microphones." Nabil chuckled and added, "Americans are such cowards."

* * * * *

Quietly, Terrell made his way back to the door of the boiler room, carrying a small pad and two pencils. He knelt and jotted something on the pad, then tore the top sheet and slid it under the door. Next, he tried pushing the pencil under the door.

"Damn!"

The pencil wouldn't fit.

* * * * *

Her neck sore from turning to talk to the others, Karla faced forward, having nothing to look at except the door. She stared at it, wondering if Scipio really would find them, when she saw the note emerge.

Thinking fast, Karla glanced up at the cameras then shrugged her shoulders and tossed her weight, conspicuously, from one leg to the other, "My feet are killing me!"

Her brother and Johnny-F watched in confusion as Karla slipped her foot out of her heel and stretched her leg to reach the note with her toe. It took some flexing to keep it concealed while sliding it to her hand.

"Now that was impressive," said Francis.

She turned to him, "I owe a debt of gratitude to my ballet mistress. Do you think they saw?"

Francis looked up at each camera, "I can't be sure, but I doubt it. Those cameras have terrible resolution and I can't believe someone is staring at us every second. Besides, I could hardly see that piece of paper and I'm sitting right next to you."

"What piece of paper?" asked Mugsy.

"A small slip of paper was slid under the door," replied Karla.

"That could be Scipio. Is there something written on it?" asked De Niro.

She looked down and reoriented it. It was a message written in pencil:

I want to help you get out of the room.

Karla read it out loud then added, "Who could it be?"

"I don't know, but we need to find a way to send a message back," replied De Niro. "Everyone, look around you for something to write with."

* * * * *

Terrell tried to force the pencil under the thick metal door, but only the pencil tip would fit under it. Frustrated, he pushed on the eraser end with all his strength and heard a crack. Pulling the pencil out, he gritted his teeth when he saw the graphite tip had broken off.

"Damn … damn!"

Terrell closed his eyes to calm himself. A thought came to him. He tore two sheets from the pad and gently pushed them underneath the door where he smashed the pencil. He thought he felt the broken piece of graphite being pushed by the paper, but he couldn't be sure.

* * * * *

Everyone scanned the debris scattered around them. They were surrounded by chunks of cement and trash of all sorts – plastic children's toys, empty paint cans, various rusty nuts, bolts, screws, and nails of all shapes and sizes.

Everything except something to write with!

Her neck sore, Karla looked straight again. She couldn't believe her eyes when something small and black rolled out from under the door. Repeating her movements, she stretched to reach whatever it was with her toe. It took even more dexterity to roll the small item to her hand than it did the slip of paper.

"That is just … so sexy," said Francis. "I hope whoever it is keeps slipping things under that door!"

"Knock it off, John," replied Karla. "I'm a married woman."

"But we rubbed noses. That's gotta count for something."

"John …," De Niro took over. "Karla, did you find something?"

"Whoever's out there just pushed the point of a pencil under the door. I have it in my hand."

"Good. Think you can write what I tell you?"

She placed the slip of paper on the floor directly under her hand then pinched the pencil point between her index finger and thumb, "I think so."

As he recited the message, De Niro stopped a few times to think carefully about what to say, "That's about it. Read it back, Karla."

"Cameras on us. Knock three times before sending replies. Only have tip to write with. Who are you? Door locked on outside too? Can you go for help? If not, can you make a call?"

"That's about right," replied De Niro. "can you slip it under the door?"

Karla placed the note under her toe, and in reverse fashion, pushed it all the way to the door.

"I need to scoot just a few inches closer."

"Alright," said Mugsy," Everyone scoot a few inches toward the door on three, and don't overdo it. Ready … one … two … three."

The five of them moved about three inches, in unison.

Karla repeatedly scrunched her big toe and straightened it, moving the note inch by inch, careful to keep its long edge perpendicular with the door until it disappeared under it.

"Karla, did I ever tell you I'm a foot man?"

"Shut up, John."

* * * * *

Terrell sat on the floor next to the metal door, leaning his chin on his hand. Minutes felt like hours as he waited with no idea if his note had even been found.

A beam of light entered the room from the dark corridor.

"Shit, guards!"

Terrell pulled the sheet over him and froze. The familiar beam from a flashlight passed over him twice before everything went dark again. He waited a few additional minutes before coming out.

He scanned the corridor. It was empty. Then he turned back to the door and smiled when he saw the slip of paper jutting out from under it.

He read the reply:

Cameras on us. Knock 3 times before sending replies. Only have tip to write with. What's your name? Door locked on outside too? Can you go for help? If not, can you make a call?

Quickly, he scratched the pencil against the floor to make another point then started writing on another slip:

I'm Terrell. Door is locked out here too. Can't go for help or make a call and can't wait around here much longer. I'll be missed. Want to help. What can I do?

Terrell knocked three times on the door then pushed the note under.

* * * * *

When they heard the three knocks, as a diversion, they all stretched their legs and tapped their feet against the floor, while Karla retrieved the note the same we she had before.

She read the note out loud to them.

"Could that be the same Terrell we were going to look for?" asked Francis.

"I think it is," replied De Niro.

"What now?" said Mugsy. "Apparently, we're locked in on both sides, and he can't go for help."

De Niro thought a moment then told Karla what to write in reply, "Anyone have anything else to add?"

"Karla, tell whoever it is to tell Scipio to bring my phone when he comes for us," replied Francis.

"Your phone?"

"Yeah, I built a new toy into my cell phone, a prototype 100-kilowatt direct diode laser. One of the companies that Cris and I invested in came up with a metal-cutting direct diode laser, with a conversion efficiency of 80%. The company is gonna make a mint competing against CO_2 and fiber lasers—"

"John, John, John," Karla cut him off, "So, you built a laser into your phone. So what?"

"Oh, so, from the look of it, the collar of the suicide vest Cris is wearing is made of titanium."

"And …?"

"And the laser can cut through it without burning a hole in Cris's neck. At least, I think it can. It should. I mean, I never tested it on titanium, but—"

"Karla, add the request to the note," replied De Niro.

Karla added Francis's request and once again pushed the note under the door.

* * * * *

Terrell wiped sweat from his forehead as he waited for the reply. He knew he couldn't be gone much longer without someone noticing he was missing. Relieved when he saw it appear, he grabbed and read it:

Man named Scipio is coming. He wears black. Guide him to us. Tell him about cameras and suicide vest I can't take off. Destroy notes. Knock 2x if you understand. p.s. Your Grandmom loves you. p.p.s. Tell Scipio to bring Johnny-F's cell phone.

Tears filled Terrell's eyes at the mention of his grandmother. He tore the notes up and scattered them in each of the dark corners of the room, then hid the pencil and pad under the sheet. Returning to the door, he wiped tears from his eyes, knocked twice, then hurried out.

CHAPTER 15

Leading the way through the littered underbrush, Scipio stopped and crouched under an old, Dutch Elm tree near the chain link perimeter fence. Tonio did the same.

Tonio scanned the street running between them and the mosque.

"Man, they couldn't have placed that mosque in a more barren spot. Half a football field of dirt, from the curb to the side of the building, and we can't even get to the dirt without walking across a brightly-lit street."

Scipio unzipped the duffel bag and removed a small cardboard carton. The carton was painted black on the outside and was open one end. Tonio saw just one LED light inside the carton.

"What the hell is that?"

Scipio pointed to a rectangular metal junction box, two feet from the nearest street light.

"Hop the fence and place this on top of that junction box Then throw this switch, with the open side facing us, and you'll see."

Tonio took the carton with a look of doubt on his face, and crept to the area directly under the old tree where its branches overhung the fence. Deciding he couldn't scale the six-foot fence with the carton in his hand, as gently as he could, he held it up and dropped it over the other side. It landed softly. Tonio looked back at Scipio, but he couldn't find him. That boy's like a ninja.

Tonio scaled the fence with some difficulty and retrieved the carton, then checked across the street to see if he attracted attention. None of the figures in the front or back of the mosque seemed to notice.

Tonio considered sneaking over to the junction box when a thought came to him.

Shaft wouldn't creep!

He stood up, glanced back toward the tree looking for Scipio, then walked with a spring in his step the fifteen feet to the junction box. He placed the carton on top of it, switched the light on inside, and walked away slowly.

Tonio tapped the switch on his index finger, "Where the hell are you?"

Instantly, he heard Scipio's voice in his ear, "I'm watching. Had a problem hopping that fence, did you?"

"Shit … if I knew we'd be hopping fences I would've worn sneakers. I don't see nothin' happening. Now what?"

"Wait for it."

"Wait for what?"

"Wait for it …."

Tonio shrugged then stopped in his tracks as, one by one, he saw the street lights go dark, up and down the street.

"What the hell …?"

"That box controls all the street lights in the area," Scipio's voice didn't come from his earbud, but from directly behind him.

Tonio jumped, "Don't you know better than to sneak up on a brother, in Detroit?!" He couldn't see Scipio's mouth from the balaclava, but he could see he was grinning from the glimmer in his eyes.

The street and sidewalks between them and the mosque were now covered in darkness.

Scipio flipped night vision goggles down over his eyes and handed Tonio a pair, "The switch to turn them on is on the side. I'll wait until you're in position directly across the street from the front of the building. As soon as you get there, make your presence known."

Tonio placed the goggles on his head and adjusted the fit, then turned them on, "Nice! Not a problem, my brother. I'll make my presence known, for sure, with these things."

"Remember ... don't shoot anyone, unless I tell you to."

Tonio flashed a grin and started across the street.

CHAPTER 16

IMAM MOHAMED YASIR ELSAYED'S OFFICE
FAISAL ISLAM MOSQUE
DETROIT, MICHIGAN
11:00 PM (LOCAL), SUNDAY, JULY 03, 2016

Imam Elsayed reclined in his chair, sitting behind his desk. The sixty-year-old man rubbed his white beard as he listened to Khan's raspy voice from the speaker on his cell phone.

"I told her it was a mistake to bring them here."

"Where are Syed and the woman now?"

"He has taken the slut to bed. She does not even care that we can hear her lustful groans. Imam, please let me kill the infidels now."

The Imam didn't reply right away. He didn't like the idea that the British woman, known as the White Widow, was even contracted by Syed. He was deeply disappointed in him. Yet, he knew the importance of completing this multi-target attack, and he also knew of the woman's track record of successful operations. Still, Imam Elsayed did not like a woman being in command and control of anything, especially one of infidel bloodline.

"No. The woman and Syed are in command. Despite her decision to bring them there, her reasons for keeping them alive are valid. Follow their orders."

"Yes Imam. I still believe it was a mistake to bring them here."

The Imam found the serious tone of Khan's voice disturbing. He knew Khan was a violent, devout man who feared nothing and no one outside the true faith. He also knew the man respected his superiors. Both Syed and the British woman were his superiors. The Imam was alarmed that he was defiantly and repeatedly calling their decisions and actions into question. He replied with irritation in his voice, "Would you prefer that she blew them up at their hotel?"

"No Imam, I did not think they posed enough of a threat to take any action, in the first place."

"You did not think they posed a threat? They spoke to the grandmother of Hooman. She could have told them about the mosque."

"But Imam, we warned you about that, and you have taken the proper steps. I personally chose the guards outside the mosque. They are our best fighters. No one will get past them."

"The White Widow believes that those people pose a real threat to us."

"Imam, I ask again, let me slit their throats and the threat goes away."

"Enough!" cried Imam Elsayed. "You are to obey the White Widow and Syed. Is that understood?"

"Yes, Imam."

The Imam disconnected the call as he heard a knock on the door. "Enter."

One of the guards Khan sent opened the door and took a step inside, "Imam ... that man is back."

"What man?"

"The father of Tariq Ali."

Imam Elsayed rose to his feet, "Where is he?"

"He's standing across the street from our front door."

"Across the street … what is he doing?"

"He's … looking at us … with night vision goggles."

"Night vision goggles … what are you talking about?"

"Imam, all the street lights went dark and then there he was, staring at us from across the street. We—"

"Wait, you say the street lights all went dark and then he appeared?"

"Yes Imam. As soon as we saw him, we approached and recognized him."

"Then why is he still out there? Did you not order him away?"

"We did, Imam, but he is armed."

"So are you!"

"Yes Imam, but Khan told us earlier that we must not have altercations tonight. That is why we also did not call the police. Khan said we must not attract police presence."

Imam Elsayed stroked his beard again, with strain apparent on his face.

"Show me this man."

The guard led the Imam to the front entrance, but the guard at the entrance prevented him from exiting the building. "Imam, the man is armed. We cannot allow you outside."

The Imam stared out the glass door. He could see the green reflection from Tonio's night vision optics.

"I will go to him."

"Imam—"

The Imam held up his hand, "He did not come here to shoot me."

"How do you know?"

"Because he would have already shot you."

"Then why did he come, and why is he armed and wearing night vision?"

"That is what I will ask him."

The Imam waved his hands in front of him for the guard to open the door. The guard did so, while the other followed after him, waving three other guards over to join them. The five crossed the street heading for Tonio.

* * * * *

Tonio watched as a white-bearded cleric stepped out of the mosque's main entrance and headed for him. Behind the cleric, four armed guards followed.

Tonio tapped the button on his index finger, "Looks like the head honcho is heading my way. It's a good time for you to do your thing."

Scipio's reply came a second later, "Roger that."

* * * * *

Scipio sprinted across the bleak, grassy field leading from the sidewalk to the mosque, keeping his night-vision optics focused on Tonio, and the attention he was gathering. His original plan was to scale the side of the one-story building, and either break in via one of the windows or through the roof. When he reached the side of the mosque, he realized that wouldn't be necessary. Tonio not only had attracted the attention of every guard at the front of the building, the Imam himself had exited the building. No one was left guarding the main entrance.

Scipio simply snuck around the front and entered the mosque through the front doors. He hurried through the front lobby and into the main corridor.

I have no idea if there are more guards lurking about in here. I doubt it at this hour. I bet all their guards are outside, in front and behind the building.

Moving quickly, he made his way back to the Imam's office. The door was ajar.

That's convenient.

Scipio hurried around the front of the desk and glanced out the window. He could see the Imam and four guards crowded around Tonio. Scipio tapped the button on his index finger, "I'm inside the Imam's office. Buy me as much time as you can."

Scipio wasn't expecting a reply as he began rifling through the Imam's papers.

* * * * *

Tonio heard Scipio's message but couldn't reply. The Imam and the guards were standing in front of him.

"I am Imam Elsayed. You are the father of Tariq Ali?"

Tonio raised the night vision optics from his eye, "No, but I was Teddy Brown's dad."

The guards drew their rifles from under their cloaks and moved toward Tonio, but the Imam waved them back.

Tonio showed them his hand on the handle of his pistol tucked into his belt.

"Why are you here?"

"I want answers."

"But you have not asked any questions."

"I have, too ... I've come here before and asked your goons, but they wouldn't talk. And they wouldn't let me come in and speak to you, either."

"You must forgive us. There are many in this city that wish to do us harm because we are Muslim."

"Maybe, if you didn't greet strangers with armed thugs we might like you more."

The Imam had to halt the guards again by raising his hand.

Tonio held the photo of his decapitated son out, "Who did this to my son?"

The guards held their ground, but now their rifles were pointed at Tonio.

Imam Elsayed examined the photo with tired eyes then looked up, "You should leave. There are no answers for you here."

The Imam turned to walk away when he felt the cold steel barrel of Tonio's pistol being pressed against the back of his head.

Immediately, the guards rushed around with rifles raised and trained on him.

Tonio spat into the Imam's ear holding him close, "Call your dogs off now, or the next face you see will be Allah's."

The Imam grinned, "His face, beautiful and radiant, would be a most welcome sight."

Tonio moved the pistol from the back of the Imam's head to the small of his back, "On second thought, a hole down here won't kill you … just hurt like hell before it paralyzes you."

The Imam's grin disappeared, "Put your weapons down!"

Tonio pointed with the pistol, "Put 'em on the ground and take five steps back, with your hands behind your heads, now!"

The guards looked to the Imam, who nodded. One by one, they placed their rifles on the ground and their hands behinds their heads and stepped back.

The Imam tried to turn, but Tonio wouldn't let him, "What do you hope to accomplish by doing this?"

"I told you, I want answers, starting with who murdered my son." Keeping one arm around the Imam's throat, Tonio fanned the pistol in the direction of the guards, "Are they responsible?"

He raised his voice to speak directly to the guards, "Did you murder my son? Speak up!"

* * * * *

Scipio sifted through the paperwork on the Imam's desk then rifled through the desk drawers, but he could find no mention of Cris and the others, or of the woman who took them hostage. He continued to glance out the window and saw Tonio was now holding a pistol to the Imam's head and pointing at the guards.

Dude is crazy. At least he had them drop their rifles. He better hope they're not carrying any other weapons.

Another thought crossed Scipio's mind.

Everyone uses a computer of some sort. I don't see a desktop or laptop. If he's not using a computer …, Scipio tapped the button on his index finger, "Tonio, tell the Imam to give you his cellphone."

* * * * *

Tonio heard Scipio's order and placed the pistol against the Imam's head again, "Hand me your cellphone."

The Imam reached into his pocket.

Tonio whispered into his ear, "Drop it and I'll drop you."

The Imam pulled his cellphone from his pocket but hesitated handing it back. Tonio detected beads of sweat on his forehead. Man don't sweat from a gun pressed against his head, but from giving up his cell phone?

Tonio tapped the barrel against the side of the Imam's head, "I said hand it back to me."

The Imam did so with tension in his movement.

Tonio now held the pistol in one hand and the Imam's cell phone in his other. When he attempted to ask Scipio what to do next, the problem became evident.

Taking his arm from around the Imam's throat, Tonio tried stuffing the cellphone into his pocket.

Sensing he was no longer being held, Imam Elsayed signaled the guards with his eyes. Rapidly, he dropped to his knees.

Caught by surprise, Tonio looked down at the Imam, before noticing the guards diving for their rifles. He raised his pistol, but the Imam reached up and grabbed at it. The two men struggled for control of the weapon.

Tonio watched helplessly as the guards picked up their rifles and took aim at him. Finally wrestling his pistol from the Imam, he knew it was too late.

Tonio raised his hands over his head but knew that wouldn't stop them from filling him full of lead.

He stood there with a look of defiance on his face, when the sound of automatic weapon fire cracked through the air, once, twice, three times, then four, in quick succession.

With each shot, a guard's body crashed to the ground.

Mindlessly, Tonio checked his torso for bullet holes. Then he saw who had fired. Scipio came jogging from the mosque, holding his rifle.

Tonio looked down at the Imam cowering at his feet, "Get up."

Covering his head with his hands, the Imam didn't move.

"Leave him," cried Scipio as he ran past. "We gotta get out here now!"

Tonio returned the night vision optic over his right eye, and could see the guards from the back of the mosque heading his way.

He looked back down at the Imam, and placed the gun to the top his head, "If you didn't murder my son, you know who did. Tell me now!"

The Imam remained still and quiet.

Tonio squeezed a round off just to the right of the crouching man. The Imam twitched from fear.

Tonio looked up. The guards were slowed by the darkness and uncertainty, but they were getting closer. Their shouts could now be heard, clearly.

Tonio pressed the hot barrel against the Imam's neck, "Tell me a name or the next one goes down your spine!"

The Imam muttered something in a nervous voice.

"Who ...?"

"Hooman Halim ... Hooman Halim put your son to death!"

The name stunned Tonio into silence.

The Imam repeated, "Hooman Halim ... was your son's friend, Terrell Briggs."

"Terrell ...?" Tonio stood dazed trying to grasp what he was just told.

"Tonio ... what are you doing?!" Scipio shouted from the street. "Leave him and let's go!"

Tonio looked out to the guards. They spotted him and were running at full speed with weapons drawn.

"I told you his name," said the Imam, "now you have your answers."

Tonio squeezed the trigger rapidly twice stopping the rushing guards in their tracks. They dove for cover as blood spurted from the Imam's head.

Tonio kicked the Imam's body over and placed the gruesome photo of Teddy on his back, "That's for pretending to be a holy man when you're no better than a thug."

Tonio took off after Scipio.

The guards relented when they came upon the Imam's body.

Scipio waited for Tonio to catch up. He watched the whole scene through the night vision optics.

Both men stopped when they reached the old tree. Scipio pulled the optics and balaclava from his head. The men's eyes met. Not a word was spoken.

Scipio placed the night vision back on, patted Tonio on his shoulder and took off running. Tonio followed him.

CHAPTER 17

UNDERGROUND COMPOUND
BASEMENTS ALONG CHENE STREET
DETROIT, MICHIGAN
12:30 AM (LOCAL), MONDAY, JULY 04, 2016

Khan answered his cell phone after the second ring, simply saying his name, with his eyes still closed. He had just fallen asleep on
his bunk.

"Khan …."

The voice on the other end of the line was one the men he sent
to the mosque to guard it. He listened, then his eyes snapped open,
"What …?"

Khan threw his legs over the edge of the cot and slipped his
socked feet in his boots, "Stay on the line."

He hurried to Malik's sleeping quarters and banged on the door.
He was about to bang again when he heard Malik's voice, "Who is
it?"

"It's Khan. Something's happened at the mosque."

Khan waited impatiently as almost a full minute went by before
the door opened. He was surprised to see Naheed open the door.
She was wearing the pants and shirt she wore when she entered his
room, though the shirt was untucked and she was barefoot.

"What happened?"

"Two men attacked the mosque. The Imam and four guards are dead." He held his cell phone up, "One of the guards is on the line. He wants instructions."

Naheed grabbed the phone and headed into the meal room, as she spoke. Khan and Malik followed her.

"You're certain they're all dead? When did this happen? Did you get a look at who they were? They were wearing what? You think they were wearing night vision goggles. What about the other? You couldn't follow them? Have the police responded? Do you think anyone else saw ... all the lights in the area are out? What else? A photo of what ...?"

Naheed looked over at Malik and Khan with concern.

"Okay, I want you to place the bodies in the trunk of the Imam's car. Lock up the mosque then have two of the men drive the car, and look for a commercial park, one where all the businesses will be closed for the Fourth of July.

"Tell them to park the car in a remote spot of the parking lot, and remind them to wear gloves. Follow them in the SUV, and as soon as they're done, all of you head here. Make sure not to park within ten blocks, understood? Now, hurry."

Naheed tossed Khan's phone back to him, "Two men attacked and killed the Imam and four of the guards."

"The Imam is dead?!" Malik's voice cracked from emotion. "But how ...? Khan, you sent so many guards!"

"I sent eight of my best men ... men I recruited and trained in Syria."

Malik sneered at Khan, "Your best men weren't good enough, were they?"

"Enough!" Naheed put her face in Malik's.

He wiped a tear from his eye, "Do they know who did this?"

"They said they saw a black man wearing night vision goggles. He was the one that murdered the Imam. And afterwards, he left the photo you took of Tariq Ali's corpse on the Imam's body."

"He what …?" Malik's face contorted into a confused stare.

Naheed paced, holding her chin in her hand, "It must be Tariq's father … that drug dealer."

"Wait," Malik stepped in front of her, "is our plan for today in jeopardy?"

"I don't know. The guard who reported wasn't sure if the mosque itself was broken into. He said the shooting took place outside the main entrance."

"But why would the Imam leave the safety of the mosque to confront that man?"

"I don't know," replied Naheed. "The guard said the lights had gone out in the entire area and that both men were wearing night vision goggles. That can't be a coincidence."

"Who is the other man?"

"Indeed …," Naheed sat at the table, "who is the other man? Something tells me our guests know who he is. First, we need to be sure that our operation hasn't been compromised. You both know the Imam better than I. Would he have kept any information that could be traced back to us in his office … perhaps on his laptop?"

Malik shook his head, "The Imam did not use a laptop, at the mosque, nor would he ever keep paperwork on any of our activities."

Naheed look over at Khan, "Khan …?"

The broad-shouldered man blinked in thought, "Imam used his cell phone for everything. He always had it with him."

"His cell phone …?" Naheed thought for a moment, "Khan, call your men. Tell them to search the Imam's body for his cell phone!"

They waited as Khan made the call, "They searched the Imam's body. His cell phone is not with him."

Naheed thought a moment then looked up at Khan, "Go wake up Nabil. Tell him what happened then give him the Imam's cell-phone number and tell him I want him to trace the Imam's phone. Tell him quickly!"

Naheed got up and headed back into Malik's room. He called after her, "Where are you going?"

"To put my shoes on, it's time we have a talk with our guests."

CHAPTER 18

Drenched in sweat, Mugsy continued the sawing motion with the sharpened piece of metal in his hand. At regular intervals, he stopped sawing to apply pressure to the cut with his arm.

Finally, he heard the tape rip. He used all his remaining strength to break free. The tape began to stretch and rip further and further.

"John, the tape is splitting between us. Help me apply pressure. On three ... one ... two—"

They froze at the sound of the lock being turned in the door. The door was pulled open. Malik entered first, followed by Naheed. Khan stood behind them with an AK-47 pointed at the floor.

Kevin Matthews looked over his shoulder, "If it isn't the pita restaurateurs."

"I knew it was too good to be true ... a good fast-food pita joint ...," added Francis.

"Silence!" shouted Malik.

Naheed walked around them until she was standing in front of De Niro. Khan followed.

De Niro looked up at her.

Naheed whacked De Niro across the face with her pistol.

Mugsy and Kevin Matthews struggled on each side of De Niro, until Khan pointed his rifle at them.

Naheed crouched so she was face-to-face with De Niro. She placed the barrel of her pistol against his head, "I ask the questions. You answer the questions. How much do you and your people know about our intentions?"

De Niro kept his eyes focused on hers but didn't reply.

She slapped the pistol across his face again. This time blood dripped from the side of his mouth.

De Niro straightened up. His eyes found hers again.

Naheed flashed a soft smile, "So, you're the macho type." With a sultry gaze, she leaned in and licked the blood from his lip.

She brought her lips to his, rolling her tongue in her mouth, "Mmm, I love blood. Spilling the blood of infidels … seeing the life force drain from their bodies."

She let her lips brush against his, "Tell ya what … let's play a game. Each time you don't answer a question, I'll put a bullet into the thigh of one of your friends here. Then we can see who lives longest before bleeding to death."

"We don't know anything about your intentions."

Naheed smiled, "Ah, so the game begins. One more rule. If you lie, someone will die." She started pointing the pistol at each of them, "So, who shall it be?"

"I'm not lying!"

She continued to point the pistol at the upper legs of each one of them, "Then why did you go to Hooman Halim's grandmother's house?"

"You asked if we know about your intentions. We don't. We were simply trying to look into the death of a friend of his."

"And what could that old woman tell you about Tariq Ali's death?"

"Just that her grandson attended the Faisal Islam Mosque with Teddy Brown."

"I told you they knew nothing!" hollered Malik.

Naheed ignored him and leaned in close to De Niro again, "You saw the photo of Tariq, yes?"

De Niro blinked before replying, "We saw it."

"And what did you deduce from it?"

"That whoever did that to that young man was an animal."

"What else?"

"What do you mean?"

Naheed stood up straight, "Come now, Mr. De Niro, you own a counter-terrorism firm. Some of your staff is sitting next to you. They saw the photo too, and none of you deduced anything from the method of violence inflicted on that young man?"

De Niro hesitated before replying.

She leaned down again, "We are still playing the game, Mr. De Niro. You are not answering."

"We deduced that it might have been an execution."

"Perpetrated by whom?"

"By someone associated with the mosque."

"Now we're getting somewhere." She looked up, "See Syed, they do know something."

Her eyes met De Niro's again, "So you sent a man to the mosque to assassinate the Imam, but why? Just to allow the boy's father revenge, or was there another reason?"

De Niro spit some blood from his mouth, "I don't know what you're talking about."

"You don't know what I'm talking about? That's a lie!" Naheed walked over to Kevin Matthews and placed the pistol against his head.

"No!! Please don't!" Karla cried out.

"I'm telling you, we didn't send anyone to the mosque!" replied De Niro. "You grabbed all of us, remember?"

"The father of Tariq Ali was with you at that woman's house, and then he was seen shooting the Imam with one of your men!"

"How do you know it was one of our men?"

"Because they were wearing night vision goggles."

Naheed saw the look on De Niro's face change. She pulled the pistol from Matthews' head, "Not something a Detroit drug dealer would wear, but it's something a counter-terrorism operative would. Wouldn't you agree?"

She aimed the gun at Matthews' thigh, "You are not replying."

"Perhaps … but we didn't send anyone."

"But you know who it might be?"

"I don't. No one else from my firm was supposed to be here in Detroit."

"You're a liar."

"I'm not lying."

Naheed placed the gun against Matthew's head again and leaned toward Karla, "I think he is lying, but I can't tell for sure, so I'll ask you. Same rules apply. If you lie, your brother dies. Do you know who accompanied Tariq Ali's father to the mosque?"

Karla didn't look at Naheed. Her eyes and those of her brother's were locked.

"I do not. None of us do."

"Ya know, you can buy night vision goggles online," Francis twisted his head around so he could see Naheed. "I'm just sayin."

"Besides, we're a counter-terrorism firm, not an assassination squad," added Mugsy.

Naheed looked from Francis to Mugsy and back to Karla before taking the gun from Kevin Matthews' head and tucking it back in her belt. She walked to the door and spoke without turning back at them, "If you have lied, and someone even attempts to rescue you, they will die, and so will you."

Naheed walked out of the room followed by Malik. Khan waited for them to exit before walking over to De Niro with his rifle still pointed at the floor.

"The Imam was a holy man. Whoever took his life will die by my hand."

Khan locked the thick metal door behind him.

"For a minute, I thought that maniac was gonna do something to Cris," said Francis.

Mugsy jerked his body. The gaff tape split with a loud pop. He held the metal shank up, "If he would've tried, he would've died by my hand."

* * * * *

Hurrying through the underground corridors, Syed Malik caught up to Naheed, as she spoke on her cellphone. He waited for her to finish the call.

"We learned nothing from them. We should put them to death now."

Naheed didn't reply, prompting Malik to grab her by the arm.

"Give me the trigger to his jacket and I will do it."

Naheed watched as Khan caught up and stood behind Malik. She knew he stood behind his desire to kill the infidels.

"Killing them now serves no purpose. We know they have a man out there, and whether they sent him or not, he's looking for us with the boy's father."

A grin grew on Naheed's face, "I think we should gather them all together and detonate the bomb."

Malik looked back at Khan. He showed no emotion.

"Nabil was able to track the Imam's phone?"

Naheed's grin turned into a smile, "They are less than a mile from the mosque, probably sitting in a parked vehicle, at the GM Detroit Assembly Center.

"Khan, have your men rendezvous here and take the sniper rifle. Use your men's vehicle and remain in contact with Nabil. He will guide you to the exact location.

"When you're close enough, park outside of the Assembly Center's property. Approach on foot then find someplace that gives you a clear line of sight. Be sure to station your men as close to the location as possible without the being seen. Once everyone is in position, call me before acting. Is that understood?"

Khan nodded.

"And Khan, I heard what you said in there. Do not fire unless and until I give you the order. Understood?"

Khan gave Naheed a long stare, recalling what the Imam had told him. He closed his eyes and nodded, "By your command."

CHAPTER 19

GM DETROIT-HAMTRAMCK ASSEMBLY CENTER
ACROSS THE STREET FROM THE FAISAL ISLAM MOSQUE
DETROIT, MICHIGAN
3:00 AM (LOCAL), MONDAY, JULY 04, 2016

As they waited in Tonio's SUV for a call back from The Watchman Agency, Scipio looked over at Tonio. He was sleeping, with the driver's seat reclined.

Scipio gazed out the window. He thought it ironic to be sitting in an Escalade parked in the GM Assembly Center parking lot, which fed out onto Cadillac Assembly Plant Road.

Sort of like this SUV came home.

Scipio's cellphone vibrated. He looked at the caller ID before answering, "That took long enough. Tell me you got something."

The voice on the other end of the line was Michelle Wang's, Vice President of Intelligence Services for The Watchman Agency.

"Apologies, but Johnny-F's techno-weenies told me they had problems decrypting the Imam's phone. I'm sure all this would've gone faster if John was here. Apparently, the Imam was using Tor Network – VPN, and deleted all his files with iShredder®, both favorites of ISIS."

"So, you don't have anything?"

"I was just told, we might. Instead of using the Imam's data to find where they might be holding our people, the tech team focused on the phone's location history."

"You're telling me the Imam was savvy enough to utilize VPN and advanced file deletion, but didn't turn his location history off?"

"Apparently not. Google stores the history, and we were able to retrieve it. The problem is … the Imam was a very active traveler. Not only did he frequently travel overseas, he also traveled extensively within the U.S., and all over Detroit."

"Send me access to the phone's location history."

"On its way."

"Thanks, Michelle."

"Anything else you need—"

"I'll be sure to ask."

"Get them back, Scip … and be careful."

"Will do."

Scipio could hear the concern in Michelle's voice, especially for her fiancé, Mugsy.

Scipio clicked on the link that appeared on his Big-Brutha phone. It opened a Google map, with a multitude of small red dots denoting all the places the phone had been.

Scipio tapped Tonio's arm.

Tonio blinked the sleep out of his eyes, "They found 'em?"

"No, but we might." He showed Tonio the screen, "Those little red dots are all the places the Imam has been."

"That's a hell of a lot of red dots."

"Yeah, but all we have to do is focus on Detroit …," Scipio clicked on the screen. The map changed from a view of the whole Earth to a view of the city.

Tonio raised his brow, "That's still a whole lot of red dots, brother."

Scipio scratched his head, "Well, let's start with the past thirty days. Just click on each one and see where—"

The chime of a cellphone ringing cut Scipio off. Tonio looked at his phone then shook his head.

Scipio put his phone down and picked up the Imam's. It chimed again. Scipio looked at the caller ID.

The screen read, Private.

"Who'd be calling the Imam at this ungodly hour?"

Tonio shrugged, "One way to find out …."

Scipio answered the call on speaker. There was silence for the first few seconds, then a British-laced female voice broke in.

"I assume I am speaking with one of Mr. De Niro's men, the father of Tariq Ali, or perhaps both."

"You're speaking to the person answering the Imam's phone. The Imam is permanently indisposed. Perhaps, I can help."

"You think this is a joke … look at your friend."

The red dot of a laser sight appeared on the side of Tonio's head.

Tonio saw the curious way Scipio was looking at him, "What …?"

"Here are your options. You will both exit the vehicle now leaving all your weapons, phones, and belongings inside, or you will watch your friend's head explode a moment before your own. Which shall it be?"

Tonio turned and caught sight of the red dot dancing on his forehead, "Shit!"

"Tell your men not to shoot. We're getting out."

Scipio disconnected the call. A moment later the red dot disappeared from Tonio's head.

"Tonio, listen to me—"

"How the hell did they find us?!"

"The same way we saw where the Imam took his phone—"

"They saw where we took it. Shit, brother, I thought you were some kind of expert at this shit!"

"Shut up and listen to me. We don't have time. They probably have a few armed men out there, in addition to the sniper. There's a good chance they're gonna take us to where they're holding the others. Whether they do or don't, be ready when I make my play."

"Your play …?"

There was a banging on the doors of the SUV. Four men armed with AK assault rifles stood outside on each side of the vehicle.

Scipio and Tonio tossed their weapons and phones on the back seats, then stepped out and placed their hands on the backs of their heads. Two of the men took hold of them, while the other two kept rifles trained on them.

Khan approached from across the lot. He stepped in front of Tonio first, slamming the butt of the sniper rifle into his mid-section. Tonio would have collapsed to the ground, if it weren't for the man holding him.

Khan slipped a hood over Tonio's head, then stepped in front of Scipio, "I know it was that son of a dog who murdered the Imam. He will die by my hand."

Khan stripped Scipio's utility jacket off, leaving him wearing a black turtleneck underneath, then slipped a hood over his head.

"You will die with your friends."

Khan motioned to two of his men. Instantly, the men slammed the butt of their rifles into the backs of Scipio's and Tonio's heads. Both fell face first to the pavement. Khan shouldered his sniper rifle and began walking in the direction of their truck. He waved his arms without looking back, "Bring them."

CHAPTER 20

UNDERGROUND COMPOUND
BASEMENTS ALONG CHENE STREET
DETROIT, MICHIGAN
4:00 AM (LOCAL), MONDAY, JULY 04, 2016

Terrell lay on his sleeping bag staring up into darkness surrounded by thirty-eight fellow bombmakers, drivers, handlers, and bombers. Most were asleep, except for a few like him, too afraid to slumber. The White Widow professed sleeping, eating, training, and worshiping together to bond them. Yet, after witnessing Tariq's beheading, most isolated in terror.

Though the room was air-conditioned, Terrell was covered in sweat. His heart raced, as thoughts raced through his mind of the man dressed in black coming to rescue Cris De Niro, the others, and him too, he hoped.

I gotta do something to help those people and myself!

Terrell recalled seeing Naheed hand the "tech guy" a bag when she came back with Mr. De Niro and the others.

The note said to tell Scipio to bring Johnny-F's cell phone.

I bet their phones are in that bag. Grabbing it could put me right with that guy Scipio and bring me one step closer to getting out of here!

What's the worst thing that can happen? I get my ass caught and that big mo-fo Khan does to me what they made me do to Teddy.

Tears welled in his eyes.

He muttered under his breath, "At least this shit'll be over and done, one way or the other."

Terrell rose from the mattress as quietly as he could and looked around. He saw some with their eyes open, but none taking any notice of him.

Softly, he stepped into the dark corridor, checking both ways before heading for the "Tech Room." The room was filled, from floor to ceiling, with high-tech equipment operated by a man Terrell and the others referred to as the "Tech Guy." Terrell never learned the Tech Guy's name, but the name was befitting. The Tech Guy was always in that room fiddling with the equipment.

Turning a corner, he heard footsteps approaching. Terrell retreated as Khan and his men led two men down the corridor. Terrell recognized Teddy's dad Shah, and the other was a small man dressed in black.

Shit, that must be Scipio. He's caught! Now what?!

Terrell looked on from a distance as the men were brought to the meal room. The door was closed and guards were stationed outside.

I can't break them out, but I gotta do something!

Behind him, someone emerged from the tech room.

Shit … nowhere to hide!

Without taking notice of him, the tech guy walked past and entered the meal room.

Terrell exhaled audibly.

I might as well stick to my original plan and see if I can find that phone. Hopefully, they don't kill 'em.

He walked with purpose to the door of the computer room, then paused to glance down the corridor at the guards outside the meal room.

They're looking my way, but not paying attention.

Terrell entered the cluttered room. Along the walls were tables topped with all sorts of gadgets, parts, and tools. In the center of the room a U-shaped desk was covered with computer monitors and keyboards.

In the far corner, Terrell spotted the bag. Sneaking one more look down the corridor, he grabbed the bag, placed it atop one of the tables, and opened it.

"Shit …," he whispered.

Reaching in, he took a pistol from the bag and tucked it into his belt then quickly examined the rest of the contents.

One of these phones must be the one.

Terrell zipped the bag and headed to the door. He noticed the guards in front of the door weren't looking his way any longer. Instead, they were talking to each other with their backs to him.

He slipped out the door and turned the corner as quickly as he could.

Now what? I can't shoot my way in. Better to wait and think. I've gotta get this bag into that Scipio's hands.

Terrell squatted and continued to peak around the corner.

Just gotta wait and see. If they come out alive or dead.

CHAPTER 21

UNDERGROUND COMPOUND
BASEMENTS ALONG CHENE STREET
DETROIT, MICHIGAN
4:15 AM (LOCAL), MONDAY, JULY 04, 2016

Khan forced Tonio and Scipio to their knees.

"Hands behind your heads and lock your fingers."

Naheed and Malik entered from his room. Standing behind Khan were two of his men. Nabil was at the table sipping tea.

Naheed walked over to Tonio and Scipio and pulled the cowls off their heads. They looked around trying to focus, pain still evident on their faces.

Naheed stood in front of Scipio with her head tilted, "I must say, I'm quite disappointed. After reading all about the heroic exploits of the famed Watchman Agency, I would've never thought it this easy to have so many of you locked away or on your knees."

Scipio looked at her, but didn't reply.

"We need to know if you've told anyone else. Are there more of Mr. De Niro's men out there looking for us?"

Scipio grinned, "I'm sure the ones not locked away or on their knees are out there looking for you."

Naheed returned his grin with a strained one of her own. She nodded to Nabil, "Go up and look, but be careful."

Nabil got up and jogged out of the room.

Naheed looked down at Tonio, "As for you, you murdered the Imam for no reason. The Imam didn't kill your son."

Tonio stared at the floor, "Then who did?"

Naheed glanced at Khan.

Tonio looked back at him, "Him?"

Naheed ignored his question, "The Imam was a man of peace."

Tonio turned back to her and glared, "He's no different than a gang leader. He recruited my son into your bullshit religion and—"

Khan stepped behind Tonio placing the blade of a large knife to his throat, "He does not deserve to live another moment. You want to know who killed your son. His friend, the one called Terrell cut his head off."

Spit shot from Tonio's shouting, "NOOO!!! I don't believe you!!"

Khan shrugged, "Believe what you want. We all watched and laughed as he did it!"

In a single motion, Scipio grabbed Khan's leg with one hand, while punching him squarely in the groin with the other. The husky man doubled over in pain with the knife still in his hand.

Khan's men charged at Scipio.

Grabbing Khan's knife-wielding hand, Scipio spun Khan around so he was now facing the charging men with the long blade held to his own throat. The men stopped in their tracks.

Scipio heard the familiar sound of a semi-auto pistol's slide being racked an instant before feeling something hard-tap against the back of his head.

"That just won't do," said Naheed.

Scipio looked behind him to see Malik holding a pistol to Tonio's head, as Naheed was holding one to his. He retracted the knife from Khan's throat and handed it to Naheed.

"Khan, you will exact vengeance for the Imam, but do so inside the boiler room. I don't want our fighters to see any more bloodshed before they martyr themselves."

Naheed removed the barrel from Scipio's head and tucked the pistol in her waist, "Besides, it will make for a good show for our guests."

From behind, Khan grabbed Scipio around the neck. This time, Scipio elbowed him in the groin before backhanding him to his face and turning to face him.

That blow would have decked most guys.

Doubled over, Khan let out a roar. His eyes, filled with fury and locked with Scipio's. Like a bull in a ring, he charged at Scipio, and like a matador, Scipio side-stepped the rushing bull, sending Khan crashing into the meal table.

Naheed pulled her pistol and placed it against Scipio's neck, "Enough!"

Ignoring her, Khan spun around and charged at Scipio again. This time Scipio side-stepped and delivered an elbow to the back of Khan's neck, sending him crashing to the floor.

Naheed fired a round into the ceiling, "I said enough!!"

Scipio and Khan froze, their eyes locked on one another's.

With the barrel of her gun against Scipio's head, Naheed nodded to Malik, "Bind their wrists."

Malik tucked his pistol away then took long black wire ties from his pocket. He bound their wrists tightly behind their backs.

Naheed tossed a key to Khan, "You, your men, and Syed, take them to the boiler room." Naheed held Khan's knife by the blade, with the handle out, "Make it painful on behalf of the Imam."

Khan took his knife back then grabbed Scipio by the neckline of his shirt and shoved him in the direction of the door.

* * * * *

Terrell watched as the doors to the meal room opened. The first one to emerge was the small man dressed in black. Khan was behind him. After Khan gave the two guards at the doors orders they led the way, followed by Scipio, Khan, Tonio, and Malik.

Terrell concealed himself behind a column, as the procession approached and headed down the corridor, in the direction of the boiler room.

Terrell let them disappear before picking up the bag and following.

CHAPTER 22

UNDERGROUND COMPOUND
BASEMENTS ALONG CHENE STREET
DETROIT, MICHIGAN
5:00 AM (LOCAL), MONDAY, JULY 04, 2016

Terrell reached the junction of the corridor and the outer area of the boiler room then set the bag down to peek into the room. He saw Khan inserting a key into the heavy door lock. Behind him were Scipio and Tonio with a guard on each side of them. Terrell could see the guards were carrying AK-47 assault rifles, but Khan was empty-handed.

He probably has that big knife he forced me to hold ….

The memory ran down Terrell's spine as a shiver.

The clanking of the key turning inside the lock echoed, followed by the squeal of rusty hinges, as Khan pushed the heavy metal door of the boiler room open.

This is for you, Teddy!

Terrell drew the pistol he found in the bag from his belt and slowly racked the slide. He took three deep breaths, turned the corner and charged in, gun blazing.

One bullet pierced the arm of the guard standing to the left of Tonio, while another slammed into his forehead. A third hammered the shoulder of the guard standing to the left of Scipio. Two more bullets narrowly missed Khan, as the burly man dove into the boiler room. The rounds ricocheted off the metal door and flew into the room over the heads of the five taped together. Terrell couldn't continue to fire without the risk of hitting Scipio or Tonio.

* * * * *

When the shots rang out, Scipio, Tonio, and the two uninjured guards had all ducked to their knees. Tonio saw the guard behind him raise his rifle. Throwing all his weight at him, he barreled over the guard knocking them both to the ground.

Without turning, Scipio smashed the back of his head into the guard behind him, breaking the man's nose, then bull-rushed the injured guard in front of him, who was trying to lift his rifle with his uninjured arm.

* * * * *

Inside the boiler room, everyone watched as Khan pulled his knife and peeked out the door.

With the sharpened metal shard in his hand, Mugsy twisted his body hard, breaking free of the gaff tape. It caught Khan's attention.

Khan turned and waved his hand, "Come …."

* * * * *

Terrell raced over and pointed the gun at the head of the guard he winged in the shoulder. Lying on the ground, the guard placed his hands over his head and interlocked his fingers.

Vengeance filled Terrell's heart, until he saw the helplessness of the man lying on the floor. For a moment, he envisioned Teddy on his knees.

Scipio saw the guard that was wrestling with Tonio overpower him and regain his rifle. He shouted at Terrell as the guard took aim, "Look out!"

Terrell looked at Scipio with confusion.

The injured guard at Terrell's feet took advantage of the situation, grabbing Terrell's legs and knocking him to the floor, just as bullets fired by the guard near Tonio zipped overhead.

Regaining his footing, Tonio kicked the guard in his back, while simultaneously, Scipio got to his feet and kicked the other guard in the face.

* * * * *

Inside the boiler room, Mugsy circled around the others still trying to break free of the gaff tape until he squared off with Khan. Khan kept waving for him to attack, as he began lunging at Mugsy with his long blade.

Mugsy parried a few of Khan's thrusts and then rushed him. The two men grabbed each other's wrists, using all their strength to stab the other.

* * * * *

Scipio rushed over and delivered an NFL punter-style kick to the side of the head of the guard holding Terrell's legs. The guard went limp and Terrell quickly freed himself from the grip of the unconscious man.

Scipio lifted Terrell to his feet then waved in the direction of the boiler room to Tonio, "Get inside!"

"Wait," cried Terrell. He broke out of Scipio's grip and took off running into the corridor disappearing around the corner.

With the guard's hand's around his throat, Tonio gasped as he cried out, "Scipio … I could use a little … help!"

Scipio hustled over. He put his hands over the guard's and with skilled force, peeled the guard's fingers back, until he broke all of them, except for his thumbs.

The guard stood there screaming in pain. Catching his breath, Tonio punched the guard in the throat. The guard's screams were replaced by strained gurgling sounds, as he collapsed to his knees before falling to the floor.

Still enraged, Tonio began stomping on the guard's head over and over until Scipio pushed him away.

Scipio pointed at the boiler room, "I said get in there, now!"

Scipio had seen Terrell disappear around the corner, in the corridor. He looked in that direction again, and saw Terrell reemerge, carrying the bag he had seen before.

Scipio nodded toward the boiler room, "Let's go!"

* * * * *

Inside, Mugsy and Khan were locked in a death struggle, while the others freed themselves from the gaff tape. Mugsy and Khan remained locked holding each other's wrists, but Mugsy was losing the contest. Khan's blade inched closer and closer to the former SEAL Captain's neck.

De Niro freed himself and got to his feet. Seeing the tip of the terrorist's blade piercing his brother-in-law's neck, De Niro sprang at Khan grabbing his arm.

"Cris, get the hell away with the vest on!" cried Mugsy.

Struggling in unison, Mugsy and De Niro were barely able to bend the brawny man's arm back enough to remove the tip from the bloody wound.

Johnny-F was next to break free and join the tussle. He jumped on Khan's back and began choking him to no avail. The tip of Khan's blade remained only an inch from Mugsy's neck.

Leading Tonio and Terrell into the room, Scipio stepped behind Khan and with the precision of a martial arts master landed a kick to the back of the powerful man's right knee.

Khan collapsed taking Mugsy, De Niro and Johnny-F to the floor with him.

Before he could help them, Scipio saw the two guards now bleeding from their faces and grabbing their rifles.

He turned to De Niro, Mugsy, and Francis and pointed at Khan, "Quick, we gotta throw him out of the room!"

Johnny-F now being crushed by Khan who was lying on top of him looked over at Scipio, "Throw him … I can't even feel my legs!"

Mugsy and De Niro lifted themselves from Khan, allowing the powerful man to get to his feet.

Making eye contact with Mugsy, De Niro waved at him, "Come on big guy. Now that I'm free, let's see what you got."

Khan showed his teeth then began thrashing his knife at De Niro from side to side.

De Niro took a step back, "Come on big guy, one stab and we all go boom!"

Khan hesitated.

De Niro waved him on, "What's the matter, you afraid there's no virgins waiting for you in paradise?"

Khan snarled again and charged ahead, swinging his dagger wildly in front of him. De Niro took another step back as Khan advanced until he was standing in front of the open door.

Mugsy made his way behind them and delivered a drop kick to Khan's back that propelled the powerful man out of the room.

Scipio slammed the heavy metal door shut, just in time to shield them from a barrage of 7.62x39mm rounds.

De Niro patted Scipio on the back, "Good to see you, Scip."

"And not a moment too soon," added Mugsy.

Scipio raised his brow, "I can see that, what with our beloved leader egging the big guy on to blow us all to smithereens."

Kevin and Karla Matthews helped free each other from the gaff tape, and with their arms around each other's waists, joined the others.

Johnny-F wiped dirt from his arms as he walked over, "Excuse me for breaking up the love fest," he turned to Scipio, "but correct me if I'm wrong ... didn't you just lock us in again?"

"They were about to shoot us."

"So now, instead of shooting us, they'll just blow Cris up taking all of us with him."

"Not if we can get that jacket off of him."

"Did you bring my phone?"

"What phone?"

Mugsy used the shard to cut the plastic zip ties from Scipio's wrists. He headed over to Tonio next.

"My phone," Francis pointed at Terrell, "we told the kid to tell you to bring my phone."

"The kid and I never got the opportunity to talk."

Terrell held the bag up, "But hey, I got—"

As soon as Mugsy cut Tonio's wrists free Tonio charged at Terrell, tackling him to the floor, with his hands around the young man's throat.

"You killed my son! You killed Teddy!!"

De Niro put his arm around Tonio's neck, "Tonio, stop it!"

Tonio continued to choke Terrell, "He killed Teddy!"

De Niro applied more pressure to Tonio's throat, "I said, stop it!"

Gasping, Tonio finally let go and held his arms up, "Alright …."

De Niro released him.

Scipio helped Terrell up, "What message were you supposed to give me?

"I was supposed to guide you here, and tell you about the security cameras in this room …."

Scipio looked at Johnny-F who pointed at the cameras in the ceiling.

"I was also supposed to tell you Mr. De Niro is wearing a suicide vest and to bring Johnny-F's phone."

Scipio gave Francis a dubious glance, "Why your phone?"

"Because I have a prototype laser built into it that could cut through the titanium collar around Cris's neck. Really wish you would've gotten the message … and not have gotten caught … and not have locked us back in here."

Scipio looked at Terrell, "It's in the bag, isn't it."

Terrell nodded, "I think so. There's a bunch of phones, and this pistol was in it too."

Mugsy held his hand out, "That's mine."

Scipio took the bag from Terrell and handed it to Francis. Francis unzipped it and searched, "Voila!"

He tapped the screen, and after a moment, a narrow green beam shot up from the top of the phone, "Gentleman, behold, the first metal-cutting laser built into a cell phone."

Scipio patted Francis on his back, "It's beautiful. Now get to work on the collar."

One by one, Mugsy took aim at the cameras in the ceiling, shot them out, then tucked the pistol into his waist, "John, if you can … work fast. I'm not sure why whoever is watching us didn't already detonate Cris's vest."

"That's because the tech guy wasn't in the computer room," replied Terrell. "He would be the one to detonate the vest, but I saw him run out of the meal room heading for the street. I doubt he'll be gone for long though. He's never out of that room for long."

Terrell noticed Tonio sitting on the boiler slab holding his head in his hands. He walked over to him, "Mr. Brown, I'd like to explain what happened to Teddy."

Tonio didn't acknowledge.

Terrell took a seat next to him, "Mr. Brown, I think you know that Teddy was my best friend." His voice cracked, "I loved him like a brother."

The emotion in the young man's voice got to Tonio. He glanced at him with one eye, "Why'd that big dude tell me you killed him?"

"He killed him!!" Terrell wailed. "He forced that big knife into my hand and made me hold it! I tried to stop him, but the dude was too strong for me!"

Tears began flowing down Terrell's cheeks. "He put the knife to Teddy's throat with my hand on it and I tried to scream!! I tried to scream … I couldn't …." Terrell broke down in tears and wept.

Tonio blinked as a tear drizzled down his scarred cheek. He looked at De Niro. De Niro nodded back at him.

Gently, Tonio put his arm around Terrell and pulled the young man's head to his chest.

"It's okay, son. It's okay. It wasn't your fault."

Francis stepped behind De Niro and hesitated, "Cris, I never did this before. I mean, I never used the laser so close to a person's neck."

"I figured you haven't, John," replied De Niro. Just make sure you cut through the collar and not my brain stem."

"Right … don't move, okay. I don't have the best aim."

"Now you tell me."

Mugsy examined the door, "The lock isn't even accessible from this side of the door. I can't shoot it open."

"If John can get this thing off me, we won't have to shoot it open."

Scipio winked at De Niro, "Good idea, boss."

CHAPTER 23

UNDERGROUND COMPOUND
BASEMENTS ALONG CHENE STREET
DETROIT, MICHIGAN
6:00 AM (LOCAL), MONDAY, JULY 04, 2016

Khan sheathed his knife and jumped to his feet. Unusually nimble for a man of his size, he grabbed a rifle lying near one of the guard's bodies and began firing. The bullets ricocheted off the metal door as it was slammed shut.

Khan slung the rifle over his shoulder and turned to his remaining men, "Stay here. They locked themselves in again. No one is to enter or leave that room, understood?"

The two uninjured guards nodded then took positions near the door.

Khan examined the injured guard's shoulder, "You are losing blood. Can you walk, or must I carry you?"

"I can walk."

"Good, then follow me back to Syed. I must let the Widow know what's happened."

Khan took off into the corridor.

* * * * *

Nabil returned to the meal room. Naheed and Malik were seated at the table. Before them were plates of scrambled eggs, buttered English muffins with jam, and a pot of Yorkshire tea.

"I saw no one on the street in either direction. I even went up and down the block and checked the cross-streets. There wasn't a person or vehicle, not as much as a dog or bird anywhere in sight."

Nabil began spooning eggs, from a large bowl, onto a plate.

Naheed looked at her watch, "It's been an hour. Go check the monitor. Khan should have carried out the executions by now."

Nabil frowned, "Naheed, I'm starving. Khan couldn't wait to behead them. Let me eat first."

Naheed took a bite of her jam-covered English muffin and spoke with her mouth full, "Check now. He should've been back by now."

Nabil mumbled under his breath as he dumped the eggs back into the bowl and left the room.

Malik grabbed the remote and switched on the TV. The screen came alive tuned to local news. He turned the volume up as the male anchor was speaking, "… our Fourth of July weather is going to be very hot and muggy with temperatures approaching 90-degrees. The good news is, no rain expected this evening, so the area fireworks displays should 'go off' without a hitch. The largest display begins at nine o'clock. The Salute to America celebration will take place at the Henry Ford Museum and Greenfield Village …."

Naheed took another bite of her food, "You see, Syed, Allah is with us today. Nothing will stop us now."

* * * * *

Nabil entered the computer room and flopped into his chair in front of the bank of monitors. It only took him a moment to see something was wrong. The monitor with the split screen, showing the camera feeds from the boiler room, was black.

He checked the cables going into the computer and monitor, then typed commands into the security application to run a diagnostics program. After a minute, the results flashed on the screen:

Camera 1: malfunction, no feed or camera not powered.

Camera 2: malfunction, no feed or camera not powered.

Camera 3: malfunction, no feed or camera not powered.

He scratched his head, "What the hell …!"

He checked the camera feeds from the outside door, and then the feeds from the meal room, fighter's quarters, and various corridors. All of them were functional except for the three cameras inside the boiler room.

The realization came to him, "Shit!"

Nabil raced out of the room.

CHAPTER 24

Out of breath, Nabil threw the door to the meal room open and crouched. Naheed and Syed Malik looked at him.

Malik spoke with annoyance in his voice, "What's the matter with you?"

Nabil took a moment to collect his thoughts, "The cameras in the boiler room are not operating."

It was Naheed's turn to express annoyance, "What do you mean, not operating?"

Nabil stood straight with hands on his hips, "I mean, I ran a diagnostic that isolated the problem to the boiler room."

Naheed turned back to finish her tea, "So … a camera went dead in the boiler room, hardly something to get upset about."

Nabil approached the meal table, "All three cameras, at the same time?"

Naheed and Malik rose from their chairs as Khan burst into the room.

The annoyance in Naheed's voice turned to anger, "Khan, what happened?"

"Hooman attacked us with a pistol, killing one of my men and wounding another."

"What about the two …?"

"They escaped into the boiler room and locked themselves inside. I left two of my uninjured men to guard the door. The other has a bullet in his shoulder. He's on his way here."

Naheed ignored the news about the injured guard, "They locked themselves inside the boiler room, you say?"

"Yes, it was a prudent decision by the one dressed in black."

Naheed could see on Khan's face there was more, "Nabil just told us the cameras are no longer operational inside the boiler room."

Khan nodded, "The ones inside have broken free and Hooman is with them."

His temper flaring, Malik stepped closely and stood nose-to-nose with Khan, "What else?"

"Hooman was carrying a bag. It looked like the one that contained their belongings."

Malik exploded in anger, "You fool!"

Naheed grabbed Malik's arm, "Now is not the time to lose our cool!"

Malik bit his lip and stepped back.

Naheed began pacing, "Nabil, go check if the bag is still in the computer room."

Nabil nodded and ran off.

Khan walked past Malik to Naheed, "If Hooman took the bag, that's where he got the pistol.

Malik joined them, his anger turned to concern, "So, what else do they have that we must worry about?"

Naheed thought a moment, "If I remember correctly, one pistol, not fully loaded, and five cell phones?"

Malik's concern turned to panic, "They will call for help!"

Khan's injured man stumbled into the meal room covered in blood.

Naheed motioned with a nod, "Syed, tend to him."

Malik ignored her instruction, "Did you hear me?! We must leave here, now!"

Nabil returned, "The bag is gone!"

"I thought as much," replied Naheed. She reached around her belt and produced the small cell phone-detonator then turned again to Malik and nodded to the injured guard, "I said tend to him!"

Malik didn't move.

Naheed softened her tone, "Syed, their phones may not even work from the boiler room. Even if they're functional, by the time anyone comes to rescue them, we will be gone," she shook the phone-detonator, "and they will have to scrape Mr. De Niro's remains from the walls."

Malik's panic subsided. He nodded then led the injured guard out of the room.

Naheed waited for them to leave before continuing, "Khan, return to the boiler room and contact me when you get there. Position yourself and your men away from the door. We can't be sure where Mr. De Niro will be now that they are free to move around. If he stands on top of the door, the blast could open it. And the people inside could survive the blast if they take shelter behind the boilers, so be ready with your men to storm inside as soon as you hear the explosion."

Khan nodded and turned for the door.

"Khan … this time, no vengeance, no blades, just shoot them all dead, understood?"

Khan nodded and left the room.

CHAPTER 25

UNDERGROUND COMPOUND
BASEMENTS ALONG CHENE STREET
DETROIT, MICHIGAN
6:30 AM (LOCAL), MONDAY, JULY 04, 2016

Sweat dripped from Johnny-F's chin as he held his cellphone as steadily as he could at the back of Cris De Niro's neck. An intensely green laser beam emitted one inch from the top of the cellphone. It was aimed directly at the titanium collar of the suicide vest De Niro was wearing. Acrid smoke rose from the melting alloy.

De Niro was also dripping sweat as he tried to remain as still as possible, standing with his hands against the wall and his back to the room.

"How's it going, John?"

"It's going," replied Francis as he wiped the sweat from his chin onto his shoulder. "Just a little ... bit ... more ...."

The high-pitched din of brittle metal snapping could be heard by everyone.

Francis turned off the laser and stepped back, "Voila, now what?"

Mugsy took his place behind De Niro with the sharpened metal shiv in his hand, "Now I cut the vest off from the back, keeping the connections intact, in front."

"Are we sure it won't detonate from cutting it?" asked Karla.

Mugsy pulled the fabric taut and stabbed through the top near the collar, "No, but we can be sure that as soon as that thug gets back to the woman, she'll detonate the vest."

"I hear you, you know," De Niro kidded.

Mugsy slashed down hard, again and again, until he cut through the bottom.

Scipio turned De Niro to face him, "Hold your arms out."

De Niro extended his arms.

Scipio pointed behind the boilers, "Quickly, everyone get behind them and stay low."

Scipio waited for everyone else to comply before slipping the vest from De Niro's torso and sliding it off his arms. With care, he placed the vest snuggly against the door, directly under the knob, then grabbed De Niro and together they dove between the two corroded boilers.

* * * * *

Khan turned the corner and pointed to his men, "Stand away from the door and be ready. The Widow is going to detonate the vest. Then we will enter and kill whoever is still alive."

The two men stepped back from the door with their rifles raised.

Khan tapped his phone and placed it on speaker, "Naheed, I am here. My men and I are in position."

Naheed's voice crackled from the small speaker, "Okay. Get ready ... three ... two ... one ...."

Even with the countdown, Khan and his men weren't prepared for the force of the explosion. The thick metal door blew open. Heat from inside the room billowed out and scorched them as they were knocked from their feet. Thick white smoke poured from the boiler room filling the outer area.

Naheed's voice could still be heard, "Khan, are you there?"

Khan took the phone off speaker and put it to his ear, "I'm here. We are going in."

CHAPTER 26

Khan ordered both his men into the boiler room ahead of him. They walked into a darkness permeated by a thick, choking cloud laced with burning ash. Khan had to get close to them to motion with his hand to split up.

Khan remained near the door as each man took his time advancing toward the dilapidated boilers. They couldn't see their own footsteps, but could feel the mounds of debris onto which they were stepping. They paused when they reached the slab to listen for signs of life. They heard nothing.

Khan's voice cut through the bitter fog, "Do you see anything?"

"No," their replies came almost in unison.

"Check behind the boilers."

Both men started around the outer sides of each boiler, carefully placing one foot in front of the other, with their assault rifles pointed in front of them.

The man on the side of the boiler nearest the door reached the back first. At twenty-five, he was the older of the two. Bald headed, but bearded with his back covered in hair, the others nicknamed him, "Grizzly." Taking a deep breath then turning the corner, Grizzly felt a cold, sharp metal fragment slam just under his ear. It was the last thing he felt.

Scipio caught the man in his arms with a look of shock on his face as he collapsed. He lowered him to the ground before pulling the shiv from his neck. Quietly, Scipio wiped the blood off the shiv onto the now-dead man's shirt, before placing it in his pocket and taking his rifle.

The second man, Aamil, at only nineteen years of age, stood six inches taller than Grizzly, and was subordinate to the older man. He reached the end of the boiler near the far wall and stopped in his tracks. His eyes were tearing from the soot. Unable to suppress it, he coughed uncontrollably, which made his heart race in fear that he had given his position away.

Unsure of what to do, he called out, "Grizz … are you there?"

Aamil heard scuffling followed by a gurgling sound, and then nothing. He looked behind him. The soot was even thicker, so he decided to press forward.

Slowly, he peered around the back of the boiler, until he realized he was staring straight down the barrel of a pistol.

Mugsy only fired once, point blank, between Aamil's eyes.

* * * * *

Khan heard the gunshot. Holding the rifle at his waist, he began spraying bullets wildly into the smoky room. Some rounds chopped into the walls, adding cement dust and fragments into the dense air, while others pierced through the rusted shell of the boiler.

* * * * *

Kevin Matthews cried out in pain, as one of the bullets sliced through the back of the boiler he was using for cover, and penetrated the back of his thigh.

Karla screamed out to her brother, "Kevin!"

He bit his lip in agony. After a moment, he hollered, "I'm hit!"

"Quiet," whispered De Niro, surprising Matthews from the gloom, "we don't want them knowing you're wounded."

De Niro inspected the wound. Dark blood poured from it.

"Don't move. I'll be right back."

Matthews flashed a pained grin, "I'm not going anywhere."

De Niro glanced around the side of the boiler, before making his way over to Karla. He saw the tension on her face.

"How's Kevin? Is it bad?"

De Niro took hold of the bottom hem of Karla's dress, "May I …?"

He waited for Karla to nod before stabbing the fabric with his pen and tearing it. He continued the tear all the way around the bottom of the dress, until he was holding a four-inch band of material.

De Niro kept his voice down, "He caught a round in the back of his thigh."

Karla started standing up, but De Niro stopped her, "You stay here, until you hear 'all clear,' understood?"

De Niro saw tears welling in the stately woman's eyes as she nodded. He made his way back to Kevin. Tonio and Terrell were crowded in front of him.

"This may hurt. Steady yourself," De Niro folded the material into a four-by-four patch then pressed it to the bullet wound.

Matthews cringed in pain as De Niro took his hand and placed it over the patch, "You have to hold it there as tightly against the wound as you can, understood? We have to try to get your blood to coagulate."

Matthews nodded. A tear trickled from his eye as he pressed down.

De Niro depressed a small access panel on the side of his Big Brutha phone releasing two small earbuds. He placed them in his ears then tapped on Johnny-F's push-to-talk app and began speaking softly.

"Mugsy, its Cris. Kevin caught a round in his leg. I've applied a make-shift bandage. I don't hear anymore shooting. Do you think the coast is clear?"

* * * * *

Taking a position just outside the door, Khan pulled the empty clip out of his AK-47 and reloaded from a pouch attached to his belt. Without aiming, he twisted the rifle around the entrance and fired blindly.

* * * * *

Shaking cement debris from his head, Mugsy replied, "The coast is definitely not clear. Scipio, how do you want to proceed?"

Scipio's voice cut in, "I got my guy's AK. Did you get yours?"

"Affirmative."

"Then toss Cris the pistol. On three, we all step out guns blazing and charge the door."

"Scip, we have limited ammo and we have no clear targets."

De Niro looked down at Kevin Matthews. His complexion was turning pallid, "Mugs, we have to get Kevin out of here. Toss me your pistol and let's do this."

"Aye, boss." Mugsy spotted De Niro through the lifting smoke. He tossed him his pistol then spoke again, "Okay, on three … one … two …."

* * * * *

Khan twisted his arms around the corner of the entrance and fired. Bullets ricocheted off the cement walls and floor. The ramshackle boiler casings were speckled with bullet holes.

* * * * *

"Three!"

Together, Scipio, De Niro, and Mugsy stepped out from behind the boilers with weapons blazing and did their best to charge the door. Their rounds bounced off the thick metal door and careened out of the room.

The three reached the door and ceased firing. Mugsy pointed at Scipio then to his own eyes, signaling for Scipio to take the first look outside the door.

Scipio used his fingers to silently count to three before slamming his back into the door and scanning outside with his rifle. Mugsy and De Niro followed closely after him. The three saw a thin blood trail leading from just outside the room to the dark corridor.

"You want me to go after him?" asked Scipio.

"No," replied Mugsy. "We have no idea where those corridors lead."

"Terrell knows," replied De Niro. He walked back into the room and hollered, "All clear … come on out!"

Karla and Kevin appeared first. Karla was helping her brother keep weight off his injured leg.

Kevin waved off help from the others, "My sister and I can manage." He smiled through the pain, "Hell, I've been leaning on her my whole life."

Next, Tonio appeared with his arm around the shoulder of Terrell. De Niro waved them over.

"Terrell, we need you to direct us out of this basement, but first … what is that woman planning?"

Terrell looked from De Niro to Mugsy and Scipio before replying, "She's known as the White Widow."

"She's a British-born Islamic-convert terrorist, Cris," replied Mugsy.

"Her name is Samantha Lewthwaite," added Scipio. "She's the widow of the London 7/7 bomber Jermaine Lindsay. She became a member of Al Shabaab, and has been credited with masterminding four hundred murders, including the Kenyan university attack that left one hundred forty-eight dead."

Johnny-F was the last to walk out from behind the boilers, "She sounds like a monster."

"She's just a woman," replied De Niro, "a very deadly one."

"As far as the world intelligence agencies know, she's never even traveled to the United States," added Mugsy.

"Well, she's here now, and obviously planning something big," replied De Niro. He turned to Terrell, "You need to tell us everything you know, and quickly."

"We weren't told much," replied Terrell. "Just that we were being trained to execute … suicide bombings of ten different locations."

"Shit ... ten ...," replied Francis. "Where ...?"

"We weren't told. There are forty of us in all, four assigned to each location – one bomber, one handler, one driver, and one vest maker who could double for any of the others."

"Handler ..." Tonio inquired.

"A handler usually travels with the bomber," replied Mugsy. "He keeps the bomber motivated, guides him to the target, and, if the bomber chickens out, has the ability to remotely detonate."

There was a moment of silence as Terrell's intel sunk in.

"Terrell, how many ways are there out of this basement and up to the street?" asked De Niro.

"I only know of one."

"Don't tell me," replied Francis, "it lies on the other side of forty radicals, that nut of a woman, her husband ... and the gorilla that just tried to kill us."

"Actually, thirty-eight of them, considering I'm here and Teddy's gone." Terrell immediately regretted bringing up Teddy's name. He turned to Tonio in despair.

Tonio shook his head with a soft look which eased Terrell's grief.

Mugsy pulled the clip from his rifle, "We're also low on ammo."

De Niro tried to make a call, "John, I'm not getting reception, satellite or cell."

Francis tried his phone, "Mine is dead from the laser. Let me see yours, Cris."

De Niro handed it over.

Francis tapped on the screen for almost a minute. "Sat phones won't work indoors, especially this deep underground, shielded with reinforced cement and concrete. The same with cell phones, and the added problem that Detroit ranks tenth on the worst U.S. cities list for cell phone reception." Seeing the look on De Niro's face, he explained, "I read that on the flight here."

"So, we have to reach the street before we can call for help?"

"I'd say so, yeah."

De Niro exhaled audibly, "Well, let's saddle up and see how close we can get to the exit before we run into resistance.

"John, keep working on a way to communicate with the outside world. It may be our only hope of getting out of here alive."

"Will do. I have an idea, but I'm gonna need a couple of other cell phone batteries."

"Well, keep my phone. Karla ... Kevin how about donating yours too?"

Karla took her brother's phone and handed it over, along with hers.

"Mugsy and Scipio, you got point. Terrell, you'll guide them, but listen and remain behind them. We'll be right behind you," said De Niro.

Scipio winked at De Niro, "Roger that, boss."

As he passed De Niro, Scipio tapped him on the shoulder, "You're really getting the hang of the military jargon."

Mugsy was the next to pat him on the shoulder, "He should. He watches enough war movies."

Both men walked ahead and disappeared into the unlit corridor.

De Niro walked over to Kevin, "I think your sister could use a hand."

De Niro took Kevin's arm around his own shoulder to help him to walk. Karla supported her brother from the other side.

Tonio tapped Karla on her shoulder, "I'll take him, Karla. Do me a favor and try to keep an eye on Terrell."

"I'll do that," replied Karla.

CHAPTER 27

UNDERGROUND COMPOUND
BASEMENTS ALONG CHENE STREET
DETROIT, MICHIGAN
7:30 AM (LOCAL), MONDAY, JULY 04, 2016

Naheed and Malik sat on opposite ends of the table examining a map on a tablet computer as Khan burst into the meal room. He was bleeding from his arm.

"They've escaped."

Malik jumped to his feet, "What ... how?!"

"They got the vest off De Niro and placed it against the door."

"That's impossible," replied Malik. "The collar was made of titanium."

Khan became infuriated, "I saw the man with my own eyes. He was alive after the bomb exploded."

Naheed rose, "It seems these people are very resourceful and cunning. Where are they now?"

"We injured one of them. That should slow them down, but they may be only minutes behind me."

Malik began pacing and punching his hand, "Where are your men?"

"Both dead."

Naheed pointed to the blood dripping from Khan's arm, "And you?"

"A ricochet scraped me. It's a flesh wound."

Naheed nodded, "Okay. Quickly Khan, wake everyone. Take a detachment of twenty from the drivers and vest makers, and arm them. Position yourselves in the entryway, at the foot of the stairs leading out. They are not to reach the street even if it means sacrificing all twenty, including you. Is that understood?"

Khan nodded once, "Understood," and hurried out of the room.

Naheed stood with her arms crossed in thought.

Malik walked in front of her, "Naheed, what do we do if those twenty are killed? We will only have—"

She cut him off, "We will have a bomber and handler for each location."

"But ... who will drive?"

"I want you to make sure that at least one of each two-man team has a driver's license, or at least knows how to drive."

Malik brows raised, "Or at least knows how to drive ... Naheed, what if they get stopped by the police?!"

"Then you will tell them to detonate themselves, making sure to kill the policeman too," the aggravation was apparent in Naheed's tone.

Malik ignored her annoyance, "But, what if there aren't enough handlers to do the driving?"

Naheed stepped close to Malik. Her eyes met his with fury, "Then some of the bombers must drive!"

"Some of the bombers?! They are supposed to use the time in the cars praying!"

"They can pray as they drive!"

"Naheed ...!"

Naheed slashed her hand across her neck, "ENOUGH!!"

Malik ceased questioning her, venting his nervousness by exhaling loudly and blinking his eyes rapidly.

Naheed stepped back from him and turned away, "Once you choose the drivers for each team, send the teams to their vehicles. It's time we leave here. Instruct them to rendezvous at the mosque."

Her orders to evacuate calmed Malik down. His tone softened, "What will you be doing?"

"I'll go tell Nabil to pack his equipment. We'll load all of the vests into our SUV and I'll use the excess explosive to booby trap the stairwell, as well as the outside of the door."

"But, won't that trap Khan and the others down here?"

"I won't detonate the explosives until nine o'clock, when our bombers detonate themselves. Of course, if anyone attempts to open the door after we leave it will trigger them."

"Does Khan know?"

"I didn't tell him specifically, but he knows."

Malik stood silently for a moment.

"It has to be, Syed. Victory sometimes comes at great cost."

"I know. Khan is a good fighter and devout believer. He would consider it an honorable death."

Naheed walked up to him, placing her hands on his shoulders, and kissed his lips.

She nodded toward the door, "Go …."

* * * * *

Scipio crept to the intersection of the two corridors ahead of the rest and placed his back against the wall. He glanced back at Terrell.

Terrell pointed to the right.

Scipio nodded then waved for Mugsy Ricci and Terrell to join him.

"I hear movement."

"I hear it too," replied Mugsy. "Terrell, how far are we from the stairwell that leads to the exit?"

"It's down that corridor, to the right. At the end, you turn left into the entryway. It's a pretty large open area, right in front of the entrance to the stairwell."

John Francis joined them, "Guys, how close would you say we are to the exit?"

They looked to Terrell.

"I ain't good with measuring. Maybe a hundred feet to the stair-well, or so ...?"

"Why?" asked Mugsy.

"Cause, if we're close enough to the exit, I think I might be able to use the Ham transmitter built into my phone. But, I'll have to make a few adjustments, like linking cell phone batteries together, to give it enough power to reach a repeater station."

Mugsy nodded, "What do you need?"

"I need a place to work."

They looked at Terrell again.

"There's a room with a desk and a white board down the corridor to the left. The Widow used to use it as a classroom to train us."

"That'll do," replied Francis. He patted Mugsy and Scipio on their arms, "You two, hold down the fort so I can concentrate.

"Lead the way, Terrell."

De Niro was standing behind them. Francis smiled at him as he walked away.

De Niro joined Scipio and Mugsy, "Someone's got to look down that corridor and around the corner. See if Terrell's info is accurate."

"I'll go, boss," replied Scipio.

Scipio winked at Mugsy, "I guess you'll have to hold down the fort, Colonel Bowie."

The allusion didn't get past Mugsy, "Let's hope we fare better in our fort than Bowie did at the Alamo.

Mugsy turned to De Niro. He nodded over his shoulder at Kevin Matthews, "How's he doing?"

"I just checked the wound. I need to change the bandage, while John works. It's a good thing I had Woody train the boys and me in basic first aid."

Sergeant Ray "Woody" Woods was formally a Special Forces Medical Sergeant. Mugsy Ricci met Woody in Iraq when Woods saved his life, after a fierce firefight in Ramadi. When Ricci took over as President of The Watchman Agency, Woods was his first choice to become Chief Medical Officer for their para-military arm, ARCHANGEL.

Karla and Tonio approached, supporting Kevin Matthews on each side. Matthews grimaced in pain with each step. Karla tried to make light of the situation, as she kissed her brother's cheek, "I hope I have enough dress left to bandage your wound and remain decent."

De Niro took the shiv from Mugsy and cut a strip from the bottom of her dress, before tossing the makeshift knife back to him. He looked up and winked at her, "Do us a favor and try and stay out of sight of Johnny-F. If he sees this much leg, he won't be able to concentrate."

Scipio returned, "The young man got it right. The stairwell is about a hundred feet from where we're standing."

"Any sign of bad guys?" asked De Niro.

"Plenty, all heavily armed in that entryway area."

"How many?" asked Mugsy.

"More than a dozen, maybe two dozen, and they looked like they were digging in."

"Digging in," replied Karla, "you mean they're not heading our way?"

Scipio shook his head, "Not now they aren't. From what I could see, the big one was having the others turn over tables to protect them from fire in the corridor."

Tonio crossed his arms, "So, they're not gonna come looking for a fight, 'cause they know we gotta come to them to get out of here."

"That doesn't mean they won't send men our way, at some point," replied De Niro. "Mugsy and Scipio, stay here and act as our watchmen. The rest of us, let's get Kevin into the classroom. I'll change his bandage then rejoin you two."

Mugsy waited for them to enter the classroom before pulling the clip from the rifle in his hands. Scipio did the same.

"If they do come this way, we won't be able to hold them off for long."

Scipio peered down the corridor, "They'll come. When they do, let them get close. We might be able to grab the weapons of the first ones we down. I broke all the light bulbs in the corridor. It's narrow, which means their numerical superiority won't matter until they reach us here. Another thing that could help us … the walls are made of plaster and drywall. Both become a hazy choking dust cloud when bullets hit them, so a gunfight in that corridor will blind them."

"It'll blind us too, won't it?" asked De Niro.

"That's true, but they're the ones that have to traverse the length of the corridor. Advancing into a dark passage filled with a dust cloud won't help their aim. Meanwhile, we're firing from a stationary position at targets we know are heading toward us and with no cover. We just need the first in to get as close as possible so we can get their weapons."

"That might work if they send a handful. But if they come full force, we're done …," Mugsy nodded in the direction of the classroom, "and they're dead too."

Scipio shoved the clip back into his rifle, "Let's just hope Johnny-F doesn't spot Karla's legs."

CHAPTER 28

UNDERGROUND COMPOUND
BASEMENTS ALONG CHENE STREET
DETROIT, MICHIGAN
8:00 AM (LOCAL), MONDAY, JULY 04, 2016

Naheed set the last of the TATP charges on the basement door of the abandoned apartment complex. Khan stood with her.

"When I close these doors, no one may open them from inside."

Khan nodded without replying.

"You have your defenses set up?"

"Yes. We have manned barriers blocking entry from the west and north corridors."

"Very good." Khan's pensive expression was apparent to Naheed.

"Something else ...?"

"I continue to believe we should advance into the west corridor and attack full force now. Naheed, they should only have that one pistol and perhaps two of our assault rifles with limited ammunition and no way of resupply. We have the advantage."

"Do we? I would have thought the advantage was ours when we had five of them bound inside a locked room with a steel door. Or, when we caught their last two men and were carrying out their executions.

Khan scratched his beard.

"We cannot be sure of what these people are capable of doing. You seem confident of their weaponry and ammo, but I ask you, how were they able to cut through a titanium collar?

"And you feel certain they are in the west corridor. Why, because it's the shortest route here? What if they've doubled back and discover that we've bugged out? They could infiltrate from the north corridor while you attack with your men in the west corridor!"

Khan blinked without replying. The only visible sign of anger from being reprimanded by a white woman was the flaring of his nostrils.

"You are not to attack in full force, is that understood?"

Khan remained quiet until he realized that the White Widow was expecting an audible reply.

"I understand."

"Good," Naheed placed her hands on Khan's shoulders. Her sparking blue eyes met his black orbs, "We only need to keep them from escaping the basement until 9PM. Then you may plan your all-out assault, yeah?"

Khan nodded and started down the stairwell.

Naheed called after him, "Khan …!"

Khan stopped his descent, turned and looked up at her.

"Allahu Akbar! Tonight, we will strike terror into the hearts and minds of the infidels on their national holiday. We will give new meaning to the American's Independence Day!"

"Allahu Akbar." Khan watched as Naheed closed the basement door, severing the bright light and leaving him standing in darkness.

* * * * *

De Niro walked into the room they called the Classroom. Sitting on the floor, Karla was next to her brother Kevin. His head leaned against her shoulder. His skin was pale and his eyes were closed. On the opposite wall, Tonio and Terrell were sitting in chairs talking in low tones. De Niro could hear Terrell telling Tonio something about being a Muslim.

De Niro approached Johnny-F who was sitting behind a battered wooden desk tinkering with his cell phone. On the table, were the cell phones of Kevin, Karla, and Tonio, with their batteries removed.

"How's it coming, John?"

Francis held up what looked like a fountain pen, "I always carry this. Wasn't sure I was gonna get it back when that crazy woman made us drop our things into the bag. It's like the Swiss Army Knife of pens. Practically has every tool I need, except for a soldering iron … which, I think I should design."

"John …," De Niro nodded at his cell phone, "How is it coming?"

Francis huffed and went back to work, "It is coming along fine, but it will take some more time to complete. I'm trying to step up to twelve volts, while increasing the amperage by wiring the batteries together in a series-parallel connection. The problems are … I don't have a soldering iron, so I have to improvise, and the batteries aren't all the same."

"So, what …?"

"So, this whole thing could basically blow up in my face and then those nuts will come in here and behead all of us. That's generally what they do, isn't it?"

"I'll leave you to your work. Just try to hurry it up."

Karla met De Niro on his way out of the room.

"How's Kevin?"

"He's asleep. I wanted to thank you for all you did for him."

De Niro patted her arm.

"Mr. De Niro … Cris … are we going to get out of this? I mean, I know John is a tech genius, but these aren't exactly laboratory conditions."

De Niro led her to two chairs in the back of the room He nodded in the direction of Francis when they were seated.

"The first time I ever came out to Las Vegas was 1974. My dad and mom took me and allowed me to invite John too. In those days, there wasn't much for kids to do around the casinos except get in trouble, which we did … so John and I decided we'd go dune buggying out in the desert."

De Niro smiled at the memory, "I don't know where or how John found someone to rent two kids a dune buggy, but he did and off we went, with only a map and an extra can of gasoline.

"Well, we started out late morning and kept motoring farther and farther into the desert until around noon when we hit a rock that cracked the frame, turning the buggy into a hopeless pile of fiberglass and metal. That's when we realized we were completely alone somewhere in the desert with no way to call for help and too far to walk."

Karla glanced at Francis, "What did you do?"

"Me … I got on my knees and prayed. John was the one that realized the engine still worked. The only tools he found in the small trunk were a basic car repair kit and a rusted hacksaw. I had no idea at first what he was planning to do, but whatever it was, he had to work fast because we had very little water and no food or shelter.

"He began disassembling the dune buggy and hammering the parts into something that resembled a minibike frame. I thought he was suffering from heat stroke, but by nightfall he had mounted the engine onto the frame and attached two of the tires and off we went.

At first, we were hoping to make it back to the freeway, but once we got there, John decided to take us all the way to the hotel … where my parents were waiting furious."

Karla laughed.

De Niro rose from the seat and nodded in Francis's direction again, "Compared to building a minibike out of a dune buggy in the middle of the desert, this should be a breeze."

Karla watched De Niro leave the room then turned and watched Francis, who was talking to himself as he worked. She shook her head and smiled.

CHAPTER 29

Khan brooded as he paced back and forth near the barrier they erected at the entrance to the west corridor.

It is senseless to just wait while they formulate their plan to attack us. There is no other way out except past us, so it is only a matter of time. The White Widow is wrong to make us wait. She is correct ... they are very resourceful, but that is more reason to engage them now.

A look of resolve slowly emerged on his face as he stared at the dark passageway.

I will tell the White Widow they attacked us.

He called out to his second-in-command, "We have twenty men. They have six men, one woman, and one of their men is wounded. We are all armed with rifles with six clips each. I doubt they have a full clip between two rifles and a partially spent pistol."

Khan's second-in-command stood silently. He was a twenty-three year old Detroit orphan who was left at the mosque as a baby and was raised by clerics. He was given the Muslim name

Mohamed Ali. The boy had reached six-foot, four-inches, and over two-hundred, fifty pounds, by the time he was sixteen years old, which attracted Khan's attention to him. Khan personally trained him. Short on intellect, Khan chose him for his devout faith and loyalty.

"I will assign nine men for you to lead, Mohamed. You will find the infidels, attack and kill them all."

Mohamed loaded a round into the chamber of his AK-47, "Yes Khan."

Khan selected the nine and explained their mission. When Khan finished, Mohamed stepped in front of the young men and chambered a round in his AK-47.

Khan grabbed Mohamed's arms and looked up into his eyes, "Victory or do not return. Death to the infidels!"

"Death to the infidels!" mimicked Mohamed, as the others raised their rifles over their heads.

Khan smiled watching Mohamed pat each of the nine on their backs before following them into the dark west corridor.

＊ ＊ ＊ ＊ ＊

It was Scipio's turn to keep watch down the dark hallway. Behind him, Mugsy Ricci and De Niro sat with their backs to the wall of the connecting corridor.

Swiftly, Scipio snapped his head back and waved to the two, "We got company."

Mugsy and De Niro jumped to their feet as the deafening reports from assault rifles were instantly accompanied by chunks of the corridor walls exploding into fragments and dust.

Scipio crouched and hollered over the din, "Let them get close!"

A hailstorm of bullets streaked down the hall past the classroom, while still more chopped up the walls at all four corners of the intersection.

De Niro and Mugsy waited for a cue from Scipio as the gunfire grew louder. Their fingers twitched on their triggers.

With a subtle nod, Scipio twisted around the corner and began firing in single shots. De Niro and Mugsy did the same. Their first volleys dropped the two leading the charge, making the men directly behind hesitate, but a voice from behind them shouted, "Keep Going!"

Scipio made eye contact with De Niro and Mugsy. Once again, the three fired off single shots before ducking back behind the wall. Two more fell to the ground virtually on top of the first two. The pile of bodies in the narrow corridor combined with the growing gypsum cloud caused the advancing young men behind them to stop their advance. Coughs echoed from the West Corridor.

The same voice behind them shouted again, "Keep going!"

Another voice rang out, "They're cutting us down!"

Scipio pulled the clip from his rifle and showed it to De Niro and Mugsy, "I'm out."

Mugsy checked his, "I have two left."

"I gotta get to the dead ones' rifles," said Scipio.

De Niro tossed Scipio Mugsy's pistol, "There's one left in it."

Scipio motioned to Mugsy, "Let's do this." He rolled out lying prone, while Mugsy kneeled next to him. Both squeezed off single shots. Bullets zipped over their heads as two more fell.

* * * * *

The three in front of Mohamed panicked at the sight of bodies before them. They began retreating and firing wildly, adding to the gloom until Mohamed appeared behind them and physically shoved them forward.

One pleaded, "They are slaughtering us!"

Mohamed pointed his rifle, "Move or I will shoot you myself!"

The three paused long enough to look at one another in terror before advancing into the dusty haze with rifles blazing. By their third step, the head of the man in front exploded. The blood splattered on the faces of the remaining two. It stopped them both in their tracks. One screamed out in fury and kept shooting until he emptied his clip.

* * * * *

Mugsy pulled the trigger and heard the metallic clicking of an empty rifle. He rose from his knee and raced down the corridor, "Now Scip!"

Scipio jumped to his feet and followed him.

* * * * *

While one man turned and ran back in the direction of Mohamed, the other man who had emptied his clip, ejected it then pulled another from a sack around his waist. Before he could insert it, Mugsy tackled him.

Mohamed grabbed the man trying to run past him, "Where are you running?!"

The teen turned to Mohamed, but didn't reply. His blood-covered face and terror-filled eyes made Mohamed let go of him. He watched as the teen disappeared around the corner then turned to the noise of a struggle. The air was thick with a choking fog in the dark corridor. Mohamed tightened the grip on his rifle and headed toward the sound.

* * * * *

Scipio tossed Mugsy's pistol away and scrambled for a rifle still in the hands of one of the bodies on the floor. He grabbed it, but to his surprise, felt resistance. Scipio pointed the barrel away as bullets started spraying over his head.

* * * * *

After knocking the enraged young man to the floor, Mugsy made quick work of slashing his throat with the shiv. Spotting his rifle and full clip lying a few feet away, Mugsy started to crawl to them when he saw someone emerging from the haze. He froze next to the young man who was still making gurgling sounds and clutching his throat.

Mugsy remained still, unable to look anywhere except at the face of the young man whose throat he slashed. Instantly, a bullet was fired into the young man's head from above. He could see the legs of the man stepping closer. He couldn't tell whether the man was looking down the corridor, or at him.

The wait was over when Mugsy felt something hard tap him on the back of his head.

The son-of-a-bitch is poking me with his rifle to see if I'm still alive. Time to show him the error of his ways!

In a flurry, Mugsy twisted around, grabbed the barrel of the rifle and jerked it with as much force as he could muster. He managed to pull the rifle out of Mohamed's grasp, but the large man instantly kicked it, sending the weapon skidding away.

Mohamed reached down and clutched his massive hands around Mugsy's throat. Mugsy grabbed at Mohamed's fingers and tried to curl them back, but the young man was as strong as an ox. Mugsy began punching Mohamed in the face trying to break his hold, but that just made his fingers tighten even more.

* * * * *

The young man who retreated made it back to the barrier. He shouted to Khan, "They ambushed us!"

Khan grabbed his rifle and ran over, "Where is Mohamed?"

"He … sent me back to get you!"

"Is he alive?"

"Yes, back in the corridor."

"So, you left him alive and alone in the corridor?" Khan raised his rifle and put a hole in the young man's forehead. The others recoiled in silence.

Before racing down the corridor, Khan looked down and spit on the body, "A coward unworthy of paradise."

* * * * *

Scipio twisted the rifle back and forth eventually breaking it away from the man firing it. He turned the rifle and put two rounds in the back of the injured man's head then, wasting no time, he began stepping onto the pile of bodies to catch up to Mugsy.

* * * * *

Mugsy couldn't break Mohamed's strangle hold, even after smashing him in the face a dozen times. Blood streamed from his nose, but his eyes still glared with rage.

Mugsy felt himself weakening. He tried again to curl Mohamed's fingers back, but his grip was just too strong. Slowly, Mugsy's sight blurred and he went limp. Mohamed used even more brute force to lift Mugsy off his feet, by the throat.

* * * * *

Khan turned the corner just in time to see Mohamed lifting Mugsy. He called out to him, "Mohamed!"

Mohamed turned to look at his mentor.

* * * * *

Beyond the heap of bodies, Scipio rushed down the corridor until he saw Mugsy hanging limply in a large man's clutch. The man turned suddenly when someone shouted from behind. Scipio quickly took aim and pulled the trigger just as Mohamed turned to look at Khan.

* * * * *

Khan grinned with pride as he saw Mohamed turn to him while choking the life out of one of the infidels. His grin disappeared in an instant when the back of Mohamed's head exploded, splashing blood and brains onto the floor.

"NO!!"

Khan took aim, but before he could fire, a bullet slammed into his rifle, knocking it from his hands. He considered charging forward to avenge his young friend, but remembering the Widow's orders he retreated, disappearing around the corner.

Scipio could have dropped the bulky man but he ran out of ammo. Instead, he made his way over to Mugsy who had fallen to the floor unconscious. Scipio quickly snatched two more rifles and a couple pouches of clips from two other corpses, then went back, picked Mugsy up, and carried him fireman style, having to maneuver again over the mound of bloody dead.

De Niro met him half way, "Is he …?"

"He'll be alright, I think. Let's get him back to the Classroom."

* * * * *

Khan quickly returned to the corridor with five more men. This time, he had them all hang back as he scanned down the dark hallway with a flashlight. The air had cleared. He saw no one alive.

He pointed down the hall at his men, "Retrieve the weapons and ammo. Leave their bodies."

He walked over to Mohamed's body, knelt by it and said a prayer then stood up, "You were brave, my son. Your place in paradise is assured."

One of his men returned, "Khan, some of their rifles are gone."

Khan stared with hatred down the corridor, knowing he could not chance another attack. He and his men retreated to the entryway, leaving their fallen behind.

CHAPTER 30

UNDERGROUND COMPOUND
BASEMENTS ALONG CHENE STREET
DETROIT, MICHIGAN
11:00 AM (LOCAL), MONDAY, JULY 04, 2016

Mugsy sat up and rested his back on the floor of the Classroom, surrounded by De Niro, Karla, and Scipio.

De Niro took hold of his arms, "You okay, Mugs?"

Mugsy rubbed his throat, "Yeah, now that I'm free of that vice. That was one big, angry man." He looked over at Scipio, "Thanks."

Scipio patted his shoulder and turned to De Niro, "I better get back out there." He picked up one of the rifles and ammo bags and left the room.

Mugsy attempted to stand up, but De Niro guided him back down, "Take it easy for a bit."

"How'd we make out?"

"Scipio was able to grab two AKs and ammo poaches with four clips each, so we're better off than we were."

Mugsy shook his head, "All those dead misguided kids …."

"They're not exactly children," replied Karla, "and if they weren't dead, I'm sure we would be." Karla stood up and returned to her brother.

Mugsy looked at De Niro.

"She's upset about her brother. He needs to get to a hospital soon."

Mugsy nodded and stood up. It took him a moment to get his balance. He grabbed the other rifle and ammo belt.

De Niro held out his hand, "I'll go. You had your turn."

"I'm more useful out there," he nodded in the direction of Karla and Kevin, "and you're more useful in here."

He made it to the door when De Niro called out to him, "Mugs, we did what we had to do."

"I know Cris. It's hard to believe, though. We're in Detroit, not Somalia or Syria."

As he watched his brother-in-law leave the room, De Niro replied to himself, "It is hard to believe."

Francis called out to him, "Cris, would you come here?"

De Niro walked over to the desk and saw Francis holding up his cell phone with a wire running out the side connected to a small block of batteries being held together with rubber bands.

"I was able to step up the power without the batteries exploding or frying my phone, at least not yet, but there's another problem. I still don't think I'll have the power to reach a repeating tower, nor will this thing work for very long. So, I'm gonna have to see if I can connect directly with someone. That can be a crap shoot."

"Give it a shot, John."

"Alright." Francis took a few deep breaths as Tonio and Terrell joined them.

Francis tapped on the screen a few times, "I'm trying to find the best band. The good news is ... I was able to get our GPS coordinates. Alright ... here goes ...."

He turned up the external speaker on the phone. Faint radio

chatter broke through the white noise.

"Shit, someone's out there!" said Tonio.

Francis put his finger to his lips then depressed a button on the side of the phone, "Whiskey-Delta-Zero-Alpha-Kilo-X-ray, QST, I repeat QST."

He let the button up. Static returned, but no reply.

"What does QST mean?" asked Terrell.

"It's a general distress call to amateurs."

"Amateur what?"

"Ham radio," Tonio replied. He winked, "Mostly white people talking to white people on shortwave radios."

Terrell looked confused, "Why? In Detroit?"

"Not just white people," replied De Niro, "and there are Ham operators all over the world. It's like a hobby."

"Would everyone please shut up!" Francis gave everyone an angry look. "I can't hear as it is."

He tried again, "Whiskey-Delta-Zero-Alpha-Kilo-X-ray, QST, I repeat, QST."

Again only static came through the speakers, along with very faint, unintelligible voices."

Francis turned to the others, "This might take a while. I'm gonna have to noodle with the bands and frequencies."

"I'll put in a good word," said De Niro as he walked away.

Terrell and Tonio pulled up chairs.

"What did Mr. De Niro mean by putting in a good word?" asked Terrell.

"He means with the One above," replied Francis without looking up from his phone.

"You mean he's going to pray?"

Francis looked up at him, "He does that a lot, actually."

Francis and Tonio watched as Terrell stood up, "I used to too. Now seems like a good time to get back to it."

Francis winked at Tonio as Terrell walked away.

CHAPTER 31

Naheed opened the hatch and leaned into the back of the Suburban with Syed and the ten TAPP-packed suicide vests.

She called over one the handlers, "Go get a large sheet or towel from inside the mosque. There should be some in one of the closets. I want to cover these vests and keep the hot sun off them."

Syed walked over, "I stationed men at the front and back entrances, as well as a few on the side of the building, and one on the roof. The rest are inside the mosque. I told them to spend their time resting and praying. I wish the Imam was here to lead them in prayer."

"Good. Make sure you rotate them. It's going to be a very hot, humid day. I don't want them getting fatigued. Also, station a man outside this vehicle. No one is to be allowed to approach. And make sure the engine is run at regular intervals, with the air conditioner on. TAPP reacts badly to heat. I don't want us sending this SUV to the moon."

"Why don't we bring the vests into the mosque until it's time to deploy them?"

"Because I don't want them trapped inside in case the authorities somehow come upon us. Anyone comes to the door and we simply have the ones inside the mosque distract them while we drive the vests away."

"Should we check in with Khan?"

"I don't want anyone making or receiving calls. Is that clear?"

"I just thought—"

"I know, Syed. Khan understands and accepts his sacrifice. To honor him and the others, we should too."

Syed hesitated before crossing his arms and nodding.

Naheed walked up and kissed his lips, "You know what you must do if the others here are captured."

He looked away, "I know, but you must be my handler. I might need you to—"

She spun him around and kissed his lips again, "We will both do what needs to be done. Now, let's take one of the other vehicles and get some food to bring back here for everyone."

Naheed began walking toward the other SUVs, as the crackling of fireworks could be heard in the distance.

"I think all of the Middle Eastern restaurants will be closed today."

She turned with a smile, "I was thinking more about grilling … hotdogs and hamburgers, yeah? After all, it's the Fourth of July! We will celebrate like the Americans and then we will kill them. It will be a day of days!"

Syed smiled and followed her as the crackling became louder.

CHAPTER 32

Everyone inside the classroom was soaked in sweat as the humid, ninety-five-degree weather outside settled into the basement.

Kevin and Karla lay on the floor with their heads resting on each other. De Niro had to change his bandage again, as his blood continued to soak through.

Terrell and Tonio sat backwards on their chairs keeping their eyes on Johnny-F. They rested their heads on folded arms over the chair backs.

De Niro walked back into the room and over to the desk. Francis glanced up, wiping sweat from his forehead, "All quiet on the Western Front out there?"

"If they're as overheated as we are, no one's going to be attacking anyone until nightfall. The problem is … I think that's when they'll strike somewhere in the city. We have to get out of here before then. Are you making any progress?"

Francis stretched and yawned, "Sorry … it's the heat. And I keep thinking of the hotdogs and lemonade we're missing."

"Get a message out and I promise to host a barbeque in your honor back at the Estancia."

"I'll hold you to that. Meanwhile, I've made a few adjustments and added Scipio's battery to boost the power even more. I think I found a band and frequency that has chatter with enough signal power that'll give us the best shot of being heard. The thing is all of our batteries will be too drained after this try."

"Our prayers are useless unless we trust, isn't that right Terrell?"

"That's right, Mr. D." Terrell replied without lifting his head.

Francis rubbed his hands together, "Let's give this a whirl, then ...." He raised the volume and once again everyone heard white noise laced with distant garbled voices.

"Whiskey-Delta-Zero-Alpha-Kilo-X-ray, QST, I repeat, QST." Static.

"Whiskey-Delta-Zero-Alpha-Kilo-X-ray, QST, I repeat, QST."

This time they could hear a faint reply, "Whiskey-Delta-Zero-Alpha-Kilo-X-ray, this is November-Eight-Victor-Alpha-Foxtrot you are three by two by three, but your QST received. Go ahead, over."

Tonio and Terrell jumped out of their chairs, waking up Karla and Kevin.

"What does three by two by three mean?" asked Terrell.

It means my broadcast is readable with considerable difficulty with a very weak signal and a rough tone. In other words, they can hardly hear us."

Francis held his finger to his lips before replying, "November-Eight-Victor-Alpha-Foxtrot, this is Whiskey-Delta-Zero-Alpha-Kilo-X-ray we need an emergency message relayed via landline to seven-zero-two-three-nine-five-eight-eight-zero-zero. Do you copy?"

The voice came stronger through the speakers as Johnny-F

continued to tinker with his Ham radio app. "Whiskey-Delta-Zero-Alpha-Kilo-X-ray, this is November-Eight-Victor-Alpha-Foxtrot. My name is Frank. What's yours?"

Francis smiled, "They call me Johnny-F, Frank."

"Sounds like you're having a bad day, Johnny-F. Repeat that landline."

"Seven-zero-two-three-nine-five-eight-eight-zero-zero."

"That's Las Vegas, isn't it?"

"Roger that. We need a message passed onto our friends out there, stat."

"Go ahead, Johnny-F, I'm listening."

"Ask whoever answers to pass the message onto Vin Rigoni, Code Red, from Cris De Niro. Our latitude is four-two-dot-three-seven-one-eight-two-one-zero-four by longitude negative-eight-three-dot-zero-four-four-six-one-seven-five-seven. Did you copy that?"

"Vin Rigoni, Code Red, from Cris De Niro. Your latitude is four-two-dot-three-seven-one-eight-two-one-zero-four by longitude negative-eight-three-dot-zero-four-four-six-one-seven-five-seven, roger."

"Tell Vin we're trapped in a basement with a dozen hostiles blocking our exit. Tell him to mount Warbird and bring the cavalry a-sap."

The static returned, noticeably lower in volume.

Johnny-F's smile disappeared, "Frank, are you there?"

Static.

"Frank, do you read?"

Static.

"Come in, November-Eight-Victor-Alpha-Foxtrot. Do you read, over?"

The volume of the static was almost inaudible.

Johnny-F tossed his phone onto the table, sat back and rubbed his eyes, "Well boys and girls, that all she wrote."

"Do you think he heard enough to make the call?" asked De Niro.

"Well, he read back our GPS coordinates and the phone number for ARCHANGEL. Hopefully, Frank will come through, and who-ever's on duty manning the phone at the Coyote's Den isn't enjoying the Fourth festivities too much."

"None of my men would dare," replied Scipio who entered the room without anyone noticing. "They're all too damn scared of me."

"I'm scared of you and I'm not even one of your men," replied Francis.

De Niro took the rifle from Scipio and headed for the door, "I'll fill Mugsy in. Now all we can do is wait."

* * * * *

Frank Penderson tried several more times to reach Whiskey-Delta-Zero-Alpha-Kilo-X-ray, the one who said his name was Johnny-F, but he received no reply.

Penderson was a sixty-two-year-old former Army Special Forces Communications Sergeant who could tell the difference between a candy-ass civilian exaggerating a hangnail and a professional with a real problem.

He decided immediately that Johnny-F, whoever he was, was the real deal. He also recognized the other name ... Cris De Niro.

After typing Cris De Niro into his laptop's Google search, he verified what he thought he read somewhere. Cris De Niro owned a counter-terrorism agency and lived in Las Vegas, Nevada.

Frank put the yellow legal pad containing the notes from his conversation with Johnny-F on his knee, and reached for his cell phone.

He dialed the number and waited for someone to answer, "Hi. My name is Frank Penderson. I was asked by someone named Johnny-F to pass a message to a Vin Rigoni from Cris De Niro."

Penderson smiled when he heard the change in inflection as soon as he mentioned Cris De Niro's name.

"Yes sir, I can hold."

CHAPTER 33

"Here you go, gentlemen," Spiro Pescalitis, head of ARCH-ANGEL's Padael Squad set a tray down with an array of cake and pastries.

Karl De May, head of ARCHANGEL's Gabriel Squad was first to grab a donut, "I love red velvet!"

Vin Rigoni put two donuts and an apple strudel on a paper plate, "You can keep the red velvets. Just leave me the blueberry muffins."

Rigoni was head of ARCHANGEL's Michael Squad. He had out-ranked Pescalitis and De May in the Marines (Rigoni was a Chief Warrant Officer-5 (CWO5); Pescalitis and De May were CWO4s. He continued to outrank them in ARCHANGEL's hierarchy.

The three had been together since childhood. They grew up and went to school together in the Red Hook area of Brooklyn, New York, before all three joined the Marine Corps right out of high school.

Pescalitis poured coffee from a large metal insulated pot, "A new donut shop just opened on Green Valley Parkway. I think I bought them out of donuts. I dropped a big box off at Mr. De Niro's house for the party later, but saved this box for us."

A chime rang out from Rigoni's phone.

"Go ahead," said Rigoni, which was the command to connect the intercom transmission. Johnny-F had updated their Big-Brutha Data Management and Communications system to more effectively respond to vocal commands. The transmission was also automatically placed on speaker, detecting that Rigoni did not have earbuds, or the phone to his ear.

The male voice of the communications officer on duty replied, "Sir, there's an incoming call on the landline. A gentleman named Frank Penderson is asking to speak with you."

Rigoni looked at the others, "I don't know a Frank Penderson."

"Sir, he said that Johnny-F asked him to pass a message on, from Cris De Niro."

Pescalitis and De May walked over.

"Roger that. Patch the call to me."

"Yes sir."

"What's that all about?" asked De May.

"Why wouldn't Mr. D contact us via Double-B?" added Pescalitis.

Rigoni held his hand up to quiet them, "Mr. Penderson, this is Vin Rigoni. May I help you?"

"I hope you can," Penderson's voice bellowed from the speaker. I just received a landline relay request on the Ham radio from someone who called himself Johnny-F. He said to tell you Code Red, from Cris De Niro. Their latitude is four-two-dot-three-seven-one-eight-two-one-zero-four by longitude negative-eight-three-dot-zero-four-four-six-one-seven-five-seven. He also said to tell you that they are trapped in a basement with a dozen hostiles blocking their exit, and to tell you to mount the Warbird and bring the cavalry a-sap."

"Mr. Penderson, would you please hold on a moment?"

"I sure will."

Rigoni muted the phone call, "Spiro, try and contact Mr. D."

"I'm already on it. Big-Brutha is showing Mr. D, Mugsy, Johnny-F, and Karla all off grid."

"Contact their hotel rooms and also … reach out to Karla's brother, I think his name is Kevin. Karl, contact Duke O'Rourke and have him ready Warbird for takeoff within the hour. Tell him the destination is Detroit."

Rigoni hit an intercom button. Within seconds, the voice of Michael Squad's second-in-command and top sniper in all of ARCHANGEL, next to Scipio, "Gunny" Proctor came on, "Proctor …."

Many of the members of ARCHANGEL came from the U.S. military and still used their rank and nicknames from when they served. Only Cris De Niro called Proctor by his given name, Tim.

"Guns, we just got a Code Red. Assemble Michael, full combat gear. Have them meet us at Warbird a-sap. We lift off within the hour."

"Roger that."

Rigoni took the call off mute, "Mr. Penderson, are you still in communications with Johnny-F?"

"Negative," replied Penderson, which gave Rigoni the impression he served also in the military.

"Is there anything else you can tell us, Sir?"

"Yes," replied Penderson. I checked those coordinates. They are in a part of town that has basically been decimated. The area is no longer patrolled by the police, and if you're thinking of calling them in to help, forget it. I don't think they'd take a call to that part of town seriously, especially not on the Fourth of July."

"I understand. That's okay. We'll handle it ourselves."

"If I recall, the flight time from Las Vegas to Detroit is about four hours. Your friends sound like they're in a real pickle. I hope they last long enough for you to get here."

"A code red takes our travel time into consideration," replied Rigoni. It also means they want us to handle this without the authorities."

"Interesting," replied Penderson. "Not one of our Army codes. You sound like you served. What branch?"

"Marines …."

"That explains it."

"It's not a Marine code either. It's our own."

"Your own …? Well, I read about Mr. De Niro, so at least I know you're the good guys. I'll tell you what I'll do. I remain at my station here listening for your Johnny-F, just in case."

"I appreciate that, Mr. Penderson."

"Call me Frank."

"Call me Vin, Frank, and like I said, we sincerely appreciate all of your assistance."

"That's okay," replied Penderson, "we hammers have to look out for one another."

Rigoni hung up as Pescalitis began, "Rigs, I contacted their hotel rooms and spoke to the hotel manager. Apparently, they ordered room service last night and haven't been heard from since."

"Did you try Karla's brother?"

Pescalitis nodded, "No answer."

"Alright, contact Michelle Wang at The Watchman and bring her up to speed. I gotta go and tell Cris's boys we won't be making the party."

"Are you gonna tell them anything else?"

Rigoni thought about it for a moment, "You know, by the time my kids became teenagers they were so used to my being away for reasons unknown that they stopped concerning themselves. I think it's pretty much the same way for Richard and Louis too."

Pescalitis stepped up to him, "Rigs, don't you think you should tell them?"

"No, I don't, not until I have something to tell them."

Pescalitis blinked then nodded and grabbed a donut before leaving the room.

Rigoni grabbed a blueberry muffin and followed him out.

CHAPTER 34

Naheed sat with the handlers at a picnic table that was set up in the mosque's parking lot. Some were eating and drinking while others, like her, were relaxing and listening to Arab Detroit Radio playing through a laptop.

She opened one eye and watched as Syed exited the back door of the mosque and made a beeline for her. She closed her eyes as he approached.

"Naheed, we should not have left the Imam's body that way. There are people we can trust that I can call—"

"No calls."

"But Naheed, he is a holy man. We cannot just—"

She opened her eyes, "Syed sit …."

The others watched as he hesitated before obeying the order.

She sat up, "The Imam himself would not want us to jeopardize our mission so close to our victory."

Syed frowned and looked away, "Truly, what victory can we have with the Imam's body rotting in the back of his car."

Naheed leaned in toward him, "Syed, the wound we will inflict on the great Satan will be severe. More severe than the body count from the blasts, we will strip them of their freedom on the very day they commemorate it. Never again will they be able to celebrate without fear. We will replace their freedom with fear."

Syed remained silent. Naheed allowed him his silence as she rubbed his back and noticed his eyes reddening.

"You know I am prepared to sacrifice my life for this great victory. I just thought …," Syed swallowed hard, "it would have been wonderful for the Imam and Khan to have witnessed it."

Naheed turned his face with her hand and kissed his cheek, "First, we will only sacrifice ourselves as a last measure, and as for the Imam and Khan … they will both wake up in paradise knowing their sacrifices were not in vain.

"We have already shown the Americans they are not safe in their tall buildings or on their military bases, workplaces, or clubs. Now, we will show them that they are not safe on their holidays either."

Syed grinned as Naheed placed her nose against his. Her eyes sparkled with glee, "Think of it, my love, we have turned their airports into a nightmare, now, with their obsession with political correct foolishness, they frisk fat white grandmothers while allowing our fighters into the country by the dozens."

Syed's grin became a broad smile.

"And look at this city … the once-great Detroit, home of American auto manufacturers, now it looks like an atomic bomb fell on it. The moral decay and corruptness of this country has eaten away its luster, leaving it a barren wasteland. This city is only the first major victim."

Naheed stood up and raised her voice so the others could hear, "Their bloated military and handcuffed law enforcement cannot protect them, nor can their crooked politicians. Our mission tonight will show them we are here and we can strike them even in their heartland!"

She turned up the volume of the music. Then took Syed by his hands, raised him to his feet and waved the others to join them dancing, "Tonight, we take their independence!"

CHAPTER 35

Colonel James "Duke" O'Rourke, USMC, retired and now in charge of Cris De Niro's fleet of aircraft brought the mega-jet to a halt. He removed his headset and began shutdown procedures with his co-pilot Captain Douglas "Charger" Miller, USAF, retired.

Vin Rigoni poked his head into the cockpit, "We all set with the FBO?"

"Affirmative, Charger contacted them in flight." O'Rourke pointed out the window, "We have this entire remote corner of the lot to ourselves. And as you can see, we're currently their only customer."

"That's a sad state of affairs," added Charger as he continued to throw switches, "a major city and no private aircraft visiting for the Fourth of July?"

Rigoni patted Charger's shoulder, "Motown ain't what it used to be. If it's okay with you Colonel, we're going to start unloading our equipment and personnel."

Duke unfastened his seatbelt and, at 6'4", had to crouch as he stood, "Charger and I can lend a hand. Then, what do you want us to do?"

"Just have Warbird re-fueled and keep the nosey bodies away. I'm gonna leave a couple of men onboard in the CC." Rigoni referred to the main cabin considered command and control.

"Roger that."

O'Rourke followed Rigoni through the Forward Cabin and into the high-tech Command and Control Cabin. The "CC" looked like the bridge of a starship, with monitors and electronics of all kinds built into sleek mahogany cabinets. The cabinets themselves were built into the cabin-separating walls and fuselage, allowing a round mahogany Command Center table to occupy the center of the enormous space.

Rear of the CC were separate cabins for Cris De Niro, two senior executive cabins, and one large general personnel cabin that could accommodate twenty-four. All the cabins were equipped with large multi-functional seats that could convert into beds, along with bathrooms, desks, entertainment centers equipped with plasma TVs and Big-Brutha terminals. Rear of the cabins was a large galley and dining room, and fully-equipped gym.

Cris De Niro paid just over $200 million for the Boeing 747-8F, custom-designed to his specifications, and then let Johnny-F install another $100 million of state-of-the-art technology into it. De Niro's sons christened it "Warbird," in honor of their dad's love for the Star Trek series.

Inside the CC, Spiro Pescalitis, Karl De May, Gunny Proctor and four other members of ARCHANGEL's Michael squad were already manning consoles around the Command Center.

Rigoni took his place at the circular table. O'Rourke stood behind him.

"Let's get a recon-drone airborne."

"Aye-aye," replied Pescalitis as he tapped his control monitor. Several of the screens lining the walls changed to a high-def color image of a mini-drone coming to life in the cargo-area belly of Warbird.

The various drones created by Johnny-F for ARCHANGEL were designed to look like different types of birds. Recon-drones looked like hawks, while Attack-drones looked like eagles. There were also Carrier-drones that looked like gulls, and a variety of surveillance drones that resembled everything from owls to robins to humming-birds.

Everyone watched as the hawk on the screen opened its eyes revealing two ruby red night-vision, thermal, infrared, telescopic cameras. The cameras could both broadcast and record whatever they targeted.

Pescalitis tapped another button on his control monitor opening a small hatch on the belly of the plane. The Recon-drone, with the designation RD-1, spread its wings and began flapping them, lifting itself off from its perch and gracefully exiting Warbird through the open hatch. The monitors now changed to RD-1's perspective as it quickly soared to one-hundred-fifty feet.

"I'm sending it to the coordinates we were given," Pescalitis tapped another button on his screen, "now."

Instantly, RD-1 banked and headed northeast. On the bottom right of each monitor, a mileage tick-off appeared. It read, "20.9 miles and was rapidly counting down by tenths.

"It should take RD-1 about twenty minutes to arrive overhead the target coordinates," said Pescalitis.

"Very good," replied Rigoni. "In the meantime, De May, deplane the SUVs and get them loaded."

De May nodded and headed aft.

"Gunny, did you get the schematics to the building at those coordinates?"

Gunny Proctor tapped the screen in front of him, changing the monitors around the Command Center's workstations to a 3-D blueprint. He used his finger to zoom inside the building, "As far as I could tell, all the buildings on this street have been vacant for at least three years. This particular one was a furniture store, once upon a time."

O'Rourke studied the rendering over Rigoni's shoulder, "Our people could be held in any one of them."

"That's possible." replied Rigoni. "But my bet would be in the basement. These buildings are completely gutted and crumbling with no electricity, water, or gas." He brought up a satellite image from Google. "On top of being extremely unsound, on a hot, humid day like today, the heat and odor must be stifling inside. Basements are naturally cooler and could offer no line-of-sight from street-level."

"From the looks of the street, they couldn't hide our people inside that rat trap," replied Pescalitis. "Take a look. The building in question is partially collapsed. They must be in the basement."

Rigoni studied the Google map street-view that Pescalitis put up. O'Rourke continued looking over his shoulder, "It's like looking at a street in Hiroshima right after we bombed it."

Rigoni looked over to Proctor, "Whaddaya think, Guns?"

"From the looks of the area so far, we'll be spotted from a mile away if they have anyone guarding the front. On the other hand, the overgrown fields and burned-out buildings offer a clear field of fire."

"Then, let's wait until RD-1 is overhead before we decide on a course of action."

Proctor and Pescalitis both nodded.

Rigoni stood up, "But we don't have to wait here. Let's get moving to the target. We can monitor RD-1's progress from our vehicles. I don't want to get too close, so let's rendezvous …," he touched the map on his screen which placed a red marker on everyone else's map, "there, about five blocks west."

De May returned, "Our wheels are all set."

Rigoni nodded, "Saddle up gentlemen."

CHAPTER 36

Covered in sweat, De Niro's head bobbed as he sat in a chair inside the Classroom.

I'm nodding off. I better check on the others.

Standing, he immediately felt light-headed and had to get his bearings before looking around the room.

Johnny-F was still sitting behind the desk, with his head resting on his arms. Terrell and Tonio were sitting on the floor next to the desk with their heads leaning against one another's.

De Niro walked to the back of the room and squatted next to Kevin Matthews. Karla was sitting next to her brother, on the floor, with his head on her lap. She was the only other person awake in the room.

"How is he?"

Karla stroked her brother's hair, "He's sleeping, but at times he starts to shiver uncontrollably."

De Niro checked the make-shift bandage, "At least his blood coagulated and the bleeding has stopped."

"Probably because he's so dehydrated. We all are. Cris, do you think John's message got to ARCHANGEL? If we don't get Kevin to a hospital soon … I'm afraid …."

De Niro put his hand on her shoulder, "Don't lose hope, Karla. Our people will come for us and we'll get Kevin to the hospital. If he wakes up just keep him from moving. We don't want that wound to start bleeding again."

She nodded.

"I'm gonna check on Mugsy and Scipio."

De Niro went to the door and peered down the corridor. All he saw, and now could smell, were the bodies piled on one another. He crouched and hurried down the corridor to the junction where he found Scipio and Mugsy sitting on the floor with their rifles in their laps.

"How are you guys holding up?"

"I-H-T-F-P," replied Scipio.

De Niro looked confused.

"It stands for 'I Have Truly Found Paradise,' translated, 'I Hate This Friggin' Place.'"

De Niro smiled.

Mugsy nodded toward the Classroom, "How are our people holding up?"

"They hate this friggin place too. Kevin is stable. The bleeding stopped, at least for now. What about our friends near the exit?"

"Not a peep from them in a while," replied Scipio. "They have to be as hot and bothered as we are."

"Karla just asked if I thought John's message got to ARCHAN-GEL. I told her not to lose hope. Was I just telling her the truth, or what she needed to hear?"

Mugsy and Scipio looked at each other, then Scipio checked

his watch, "If his message did get through, they probably would've landed a little while ago and are making their way here."

"And if his message didn't get through, what's our Plan B?"

"Let's give them another hour," said Mugsy. "If they don't get here by then, the three of us can mosey down that corridor, like the Earp brothers and Doc Holliday, and have our own little gunfight at the O.K. Corral."

"As long as I get to be Wyatt," replied Scipio. "Mr. D. can be Doc."

De Niro took a seat next to Mugsy, "If we get out of here, I'm never going to watch that movie the same way again."

* * * * *

Sitting backwards, with his chin resting on the back of an aluminum folding chair, Khan scanned the room. Spotting the guard standing at the stairwell entrance with his eyes closed, he walked over to him and smacked him in the side of the head, "Wake up!"

The rest in the room jolted.

The young man jumped to attention, "I wasn't sleeping … I was praying."

"Pray with your eyes open! That goes for the rest of you!"

Khan checked his watch, "We only need to remain here less than three hours more. Until then, no one sleeps, understood?"

They replied almost in unison, "Yes Khan!"

CHAPTER 37

**CORNER OF RUSSELL STREET & EAST FERRY STREET
DETROIT, MICHIGAN
6:20 PM (LOCAL), MONDAY, JULY 04, 2016**

Two black raven Cadillac Escalade ESVs pulled to a stop, at the corner of the deserted street. Sitting in the row behind the front seats of the first SUV, Rigoni hit a button that lowered a monitor from a center console. Seated next to him, Pescalitis touched a button on his Big-Brutha cell phone and the overhead monitor came to life with the camera feed from RD-1. The recon-drone hovered over a partially-collapsed white building.

Rigoni examined the screen closely, "Doesn't look like there are any guards on the streets … or anyone else for that matter. In fact, not a person or vehicle in any direction, as far as RD-1 can see."

"No sign of cameras anywhere either," added Pescalitis. "They must be pretty sure no one knows they're there."

"Pescy, can you zoom in and scan the perimeter?" asked Proctor, from behind Rigoni.

Pescalitis used his cellphone to make RD-1 zoom and scan around the building.

"Wait, what's that, in the back?" asked Rigoni. "Spiro, hold it there and zoom in more." Rigoni pointed to a dark rectangular area in the back of the building.

Pescalitis tapped his screen and the cameras on RD-1 zoomed in tight.

"Looks like a door," replied Proctor.

"Yeah, but what's on it?" asked Pescalitis.

Rigoni stared at the image closely, "Can't make it out, but that door looks much cleaner than the rest of the building.

"Alright, Pescy, send RD-1 to the front of the building and make it hover while we get going. Unless any of you gentlemen disagree, I don't see any reason why we can't just pull up in front."

No one replied.

Rigoni tapped the driver's shoulder, "Okay, take East Ferry straight to Chene then turn left and pull up right in front. I'll signal our tail vehicle."

The sleek, armored SUVs pulled away from the curb in tandem.

* * * * *

The SUVs rolled to a stop in front of the dilapidated building. Before their engines went silent, doors flew open, and men wearing black body armor exited from both sides of the vehicles. By the time they made it to the rear of the SUVs, the hatches were open.

Rigoni pressed a button to the right of the hatch which--in quick succession—folded and moved forward all of the back seats, and then opened double-enclosures underneath revealing a large utility compartment. Rigoni began handing rifles and ammo bags to each man, while De May did the same at the second SUV.

Once everyone was armed, Rigoni pulled his balaclava over his face, compelling the others to do the same. Rigoni pointed between the vehicles, "One man remains here. Check comms …."

One by one, each man depressed a button then spoke naturally into their Big-Brutha encrypted communications system. "Mike-1 … Mike-2 …."

The "Mikes were members of Michael Squad, beginning with Rigoni as squad leader, or "Mike-1. Pescalitis was "Gabe-1," short for Gabriel squad leader, and De May was "Pad-1," short for Padael squad leader. They usually only used their call signs when in a combat situation, though Rigoni, Pescalitis, and De May rarely used theirs when addressing each other.

"Spiro, take two men up the street and around the corner to the top of the alley … approach from there."

"Roger that. Mike-5 and Mike-6, you're with me."

"Mike-5, roger."

"Mike-6, roger."

Rigoni drew a circle in the air with his finger then pointed down the small overgrown space to the right of the building before leading them in, indicating for all to follow.

"Karl, bring up the rear."

"Roger that."

Rigoni and the men behind him scanned the overgrowth, sometimes poking the barrels of their rifles into it. They reached the alley in the back and waited until they saw Pescalitis and his two men approaching from the other end. They converged at the basement door.

Rigoni pointed around them, "Karl, set up a perimeter."

De May pointed to three spots and immediately Mike-4, Mike-5, and Mike-6 took up defensive positions facing the alley into a field behind the building. He pointed to a fourth spot and Mike-3 took a position facing into the overgrown lot.

Rigoni lifted his balaclava as he examined the door, "Pescy, take a look at this."

Pescalitis raised his black mask and took a moment to examine the cylinders taped and wired to the door, "Looks like Mother of Satan, TATP."

"Can you disarm it?"

Pescalitis took tools from his utility belt, "Sure, if it doesn't blow up in my face. Frankly, I'm surprised it hasn't already detonated from the heat of the Sun. This stuff isn't called Mother of Satan for nothing. Rigs … have everyone step way-the-hell back. I mean like twenty feet, at least."

Rigoni waved everyone back. They watched as Pescalitis used long-nose pliers, wire cutters, and a screwdriver to remove the explosives from the door. Walking slowly and softly, he carried the taped cylinders down the alley and into an abandoned shack.

He exited the shack wiping sweat from his forehead and rejoined Rigoni at the basement door.

"That didn't take very long."

"That one wasn't rigged with any sophistication, no booby-traps, like it was meant to keep people in. Oh, but you should know, it was wired in series."

"So, what are you saying … more explosives on the other side of the door?"

"It's possible. Only way to be sure—"

"Is to open the door … alright, everyone back. I got this."

Rigoni waited for everyone to back away again before turning the knob. He thought about inching the door open then decided that was more nerve-wracking than opening it faster. So, he tugged on the knob and pulled the door open about six inches. The door creaked but nothing else happened. Rigoni waited a few moments in case someone inside might have heard the creak, then opened the door all the way as quietly as he could.

He pulled his balaclava back over his face looking down the dark stairwell and waved the others over.

"Spiro, you take the rear. De May, Gunny, you're with me."

Slowly and silently, they descended the cement stairs.

CHAPTER 38

UNDERGROUND COMPOUND
BASEMENTS ALONG CHENE STREET
DETROIT, MICHIGAN
7:00 PM (LOCAL), MONDAY, JULY 04, 2016

After being scolded by Khan, the guard at the entrance to the stairwell stood rigidly at attention. He was more concerned with Khan seeing him close his eyes than with anyone breaking in. That fear made him miss the creak of the back door and the men now sneaking down the dark stairwell.

But years of training in Iraq and Syria before joining Syed in Detroit, sharpened Khan's senses. From across the room, he looked up when he thought he heard a noise come from the stairwell.

Khan looked over at the guard who was standing at attention, but he didn't seem to hear it. Khan kept his eyes on him though.

After a minute, Khan scratched his head. Something was making the hairs on the back of his neck stand up. He didn't know what, but his instinct was to grab his rifle whenever he felt that way. Even though none of the others reacted, Khan felt tension rising in the room. He looked to the west corridor then walked over, past his men stationed behind the barricade and checked down the dark hall. He saw no one alive, and remained there a moment scratching his chin.

* * * * *

Rigoni pointed to De May, then pointed at the guard who had his back to them.

De May nodded and took out his Marine-issued Ka-Bar knife.

Rigoni counted down with his fingers, three … two … one …

In one fluid motion, De May stepped behind the guard, placing his muscular forearm around the man's neck and quickly tugged the man into the darkness of the stairwell. Before the guard knew what was happening, De May stabbed him in the jugular vein with his free hand. The guard instantly went limp. De May laid the body down quietly.

Though Rigoni and the others had their rifles pointed, no one inside the room reacted. Rigoni looked back at Pescalitis who shrugged his shoulders.

Next, Rigoni signaled to Proctor. Proctor immediately pulled out a small circular mirror that rotated on a long telescoping metal rod and extended it until they could see into the room.

"Eleven tangos."

Rigoni nodded and waited for Proctor to retract and stow the mirror before beginning another countdown with his fingers, three … two … one ….

* * * * *

Khan shook his head trying to rid himself of the antsy feeling that had come over him. He turned to walk back into the entryway when he noticed the guard at the stairwell was missing. His training dictated he investigate, but his instincts told him to run and hide. He listened to his instincts, not a moment too soon.

Khan pointed at the stairwell and hollered to his men to attack, just as Rigoni, Pescalitis, De May, and Gunny Proctor burst into the room firing. He disappeared into the west corridor as bullets riddled the barricade.

* * * * *

One by one, Rigoni, De May, Pescalitis, and Gunny Proctor took aim and dropped the hostiles in the room, many before they even reached for their weapons. In less than a minute, ten young black men were lying dead on the floor scattered about the room.

Rigoni waved lazily over his head, "Secure the room."

De May and Gunny Proctor marched to the far end checking for signs of movement. There was none.

De May stepped around a barricade and glanced down the dark west corridor, "Rigs, you need to see this."

Rigoni joined him and looked down the corridor, "Bodies …."

Rigoni lifted his balaclava and watched Pescalitis examine the bodies in the entryway.

Pescalitis wiped his fingers across the forehead of one of the corpses then showed Rigoni.

"These guys were sweating like pigs. It's hot down here. I bet they've been stationed here for hours."

"Which probably explains why they were so ill-prepared for our arrival," replied Proctor.

Pescalitis counted the bodies to himself, "Rigs, didn't you say eleven tangos? There are only ten bodies here."

Rigoni pulled his balaclava back over his face rotating his finger over his head, "Everyone, on me."

Slowly, they entered the west corridor, lightly kicking the corpses as they reached them. Approaching the junction, they brought their Israeli-designed X-95 bull pup assault rifles to their shoulders.

Rigoni held his hand up and made a fist, then, in succession, pointed to the left and right junctions. The four men stood in two rows as Rigoni counted down with his fingers again.

Three … two …

Before he could drop the last finger, he was looking down the barrel of an AK-47.

"What took you guys so long?" asked a sweat-soaked Scipio.

Behind Scipio stepped Mugsy Ricci, armed with another AK-47, and Cris De Niro armed with a pistol.

De Niro tucked the pistol into his belt and offered his hand to the four, "Excluding Scipio, I can speak for all of us … we're just glad you finally came."

Mugsy nodded down the corridor, "Anyone hurt?"

"Just the bad guys," replied Rigoni as he pulled his balaclava off. "Are there anymore down these corridors?"

"We're not sure," replied Mugsy, "but we doubt it. The bulk of them pulled out hours ago and left that contingent behind to keep us here."

"One problem. We counted eleven tangos when we infiltrated from the stairwell, but we only downed ten. Number eleven couldn't have made it into the stairwell or the other corridor, so he had to come this way."

"No one past us, here," replied Scipio. "Did you check the bodies in the corridor?"

"We gave them a kick, but to be honest, the bodies stink." Rigoni turned to Pescalitis, "You and De May, check them again. Number eleven has to be hiding among them, so be careful."

Rigoni waited for the two to head back toward the pile of bodies before turning back to De Niro, Mugsy, and Scipio, "What's crazy is the door was wired with explosives on the outside. So, even their own weren't getting out of here without blowing themselves to smithereens. The blast would've created an avalanche that would've trapped everyone down here for good."

"That means whatever they're planning topside is worth the lives of all the men down here," replied De Niro. "Listen, we have to get Kevin to the hospital. He caught a round in the leg."

Pescalitis and De May returned. Both were cringing. Pescalitis coughed, "Those bodies are rotting in this heat something awful! We checked. If anyone's hiding amidst that rotting flesh, he'd be dead from the smell."

"Maybe you counted wrong, Rigs" replied Mugsy.

Rigoni peered down the corridor again, "Maybe." He grabbed Pescalitis's arm, "Run up to street-level and ready one of the SUVs to take Mr. Matthews to the hospital."

He turned to De May and Proctor, "Mr. D, will show you to Mr. Matthews. Help him into the SUV and be easy with him."

De Niro led De May and Proctor to the Classroom.

Rigoni rejoined Mugsy and Scipio and thumbed over his shoulder, "Looks like you had a hell of a battle."

"They charged down the hall like they were invincible," replied Scipio. "That was a mistake."

"We didn't see any of them moving or making sounds. They smell dead but should we check to be sure?"

"They weren't all dead when we downed them, but their moaning stopped hours ago," replied Mugsy. "We don't have time to check now. We'll call the local authorities as soon as we're out of here."

"Make sure you tell them to call in the bomb squad first. The walls of the stairwell are still wired with TATP and there's another explosive device in a shack out back."

Johnny-F came charging out of the Classroom. He ran out and threw his arms around Rigoni, "I never thought I'd be so happy to see your ginny mug."

Tonio and Terrell were the next out of the room. They were followed by De Niro, with his arm around Karla's waist, and then De May and Proctor on each side of Kevin Matthews, practically carrying him.

Mugsy and Scipio allowed everyone to walk ahead of them. They took their time, holding their noses, and stepping over the bodies. Mugsy and Scipio followed, but Scipio stopped at the end of the corridor and looked back.

Mugsy headed into the entryway before sticking his head back into the west corridor, "You coming, Scip?"

Scipio continued to stand there looking back at the bodies.

Mugsy joined him, "Something wrong?"

"Not sure. I just don't remember the pile that way."

"What way?"

"It seems … bigger, higher, somehow."

"You know corpses swell in this kind of heat."

Scipio took a few steps back into the corridor.

"Scip … we gotta roll."

He stared another moment then turned and joined Mugsy, both hurrying out of the entryway and up the stairwell.

The west corridor was once again dark and silent. It remained that way for a few minutes before the pile of bodies began to move. From underneath, Khan crawled out and stood up. He wiped the death off him then picked up his rifle and headed after them.

CHAPTER 39

Khan exited the basement door and quickly snuck into the overgrowth on the side of the building. Carefully, he crept as closely as he could without being seen or heard. He watched as the wounded one was being loaded into one of two black SUVs then made a call.

He spoke barely over a whisper, "Naheed … Khan. Men came and killed all our fighters. I alone survived. I'm spying them now outside. They freed the prisoners."

Naheed's voice came through Khan's earbud, "Do they know our location?"

"I'm trying to listen to them now …."

* * * * *

De Niro opened the door to the rear SUV and let De May and Proctor help Kevin Matthews get in. Karla went around and got in next to him.

Mugsy walked over, "Cris, how about you drive them to the hospital? Detroit Receiving is only about five minutes from here."

De Niro hesitated.

Karla detected his hesitation and leaned over for them to see her, "I can drive my brother."

"I don't want you driving," replied De Niro.

"I don't want to be a man down, Cris."

"I'm not a man?"

Scipio joined them, "No, you're not. You're the boss. And like we keep telling you, you're the only one that isn't expendable."

De Niro grinned, "Since I'm the boss, it also means I can do what I want."

Francis joined them, "I'll drive her … I mean him … I mean … I'll drive them."

Scipio patted Francis's back, "We're sure you would."

Mugsy shook his head, "We need you John."

De Niro raised his brow, "So, you need him, but not me?"

"Gentlemen," the pained voice came from Kevin Matthews, "would you like me to drive?"

No one replied.

Tonio walked over with Terrell, "How about Terrell and I drive my friend and his sister to the hospital, while y'all go and take care of business."

De Niro looked at Mugsy who paused before nodding.

Tonio jogged to the driver's door, "No worries. T and I got this!"

De Niro saw blood running from under the bandage on Kevin Matthews' leg. He knelt next to him, "Wait … let me fix his bandage."

* * * * *

"Naheed, quickly, dispatch a vehicle. Have it meet me at the top of the alley on Palmer. Tell them to hurry! They are splitting up."

"One of our SUVs is on the way with two of our men. Khan, you must prevent them from reaching the hospital!"

"I understand. It will be done."

"Do the others know our location?"

"I did not hear them mention anything about your location, but they have walked closer to the lead vehicle now, out of earshot."

"Are you armed?"

"Yes, with a rifle."

"Can you not shoot them?"

"They are too scattered, I could not get them all. Better if I go after the ones going to the hospital. You will have to deal with the others if they make it to you."

"Understood."

Khan heard Naheed disconnect then quietly backed himself out of the overgrowth and headed back into the alley. A dark blue Chevy Suburban raced to a stop just as he reached the street, around the corner. A man jumped out of the front passenger seat, carrying an assault rifle and held the door for Khan to get in. The driver waited for Khan to close the front passenger door then got in behind him before taking off from the curb.

* * * * *

Naheed stuffed her cell phone into the front pocket of her jeans, "Syed, it's time! She started typing on her laptop, "I'm sending the locations to the handlers now. Get the bombers suited up now … quickly!"

Syed ran over and grabbed her by her arms turning her to him, "What has happened?"

"You must move quickly!"

"I said … what has happened?"

"Khan called. The prisoners were liberated by a team of—"

"I knew it!" Syed cut her off. "I told you we shouldn't—"

"Syed … enough!" Naheed grabbed him by his arms. "Khan wasn't sure if they're headed here. We must deploy the bomb teams now." She began typing again, "And Syed … bring a vest for yourself."

Syed stood motionless.

Naheed turned her eyes up at him. She finished typing, closed her laptop then turned and faced him again, "Syed, we must be prepared in case something happens to the rest."

He remained motionless.

She kissed his lips softly, "If it is Allah's will, we will join the Imam in paradise today. Whatever his will, we must not fail."

Syed nodded.

She kissed his lips again, "Now go and get everyone to their vehicles, take one for us, and meet me in front of the mosque."

Naheed watched as Syed raced across the parking lot.

CHAPTER 40

CHENE STREET
DETROIT, MICHIGAN
7:45 PM (LOCAL), MONDAY, JULY 04, 2016

"From what Terrell told us there were a total of ten bomb teams," said De Niro. "If we assume a team per location, we have ten locations."

"Shouldn't we be calling the cops?" asked Francis.

"And tell them what? We have a strong suspicion that terrorists are planning to attack up to ten locations in the Detroit area? They'll ask where and we'll say, we don't know." They'll ask when and we'll say, we don't know. Then they'll want to question us, which will prevent us from doing anything."

"At least they'll be on alert."

"John, they're already on alert," replied Mugsy. "It's the Fourth of July."

Francis nodded then exhaled audibly, "Then what can we do?"

All eyes were on De Niro as he grabbed Scipio's phone from his hand, "My battery is dead." Scipio and Mugsy watched as he brought up a map, "Mugsy's right. It's the Fourth of July … what if they're planning to attack Fourth of July festivities?"

"Fourth of July festivities have been going on all day," replied

Francis. "There's a baseball game, beach events, barbecues and parties all over the city, and they've had hours to hit them."

"Negative," replied Rigoni. "We've been monitoring local and national news and there's been no reported attacks."

"I think they've been waiting … for this …," De Niro tapped the screen and let them see a webpage with the heading, "Top Fireworks Displays in Detroit."

"Fireworks displays usually start around 9 PM," replied Mugsy.

"Which means they might still be staging somewhere," added Scipio, as he checked his watch. "But they'll be hitting the road soon, if they haven't already."

De Niro tapped the screen, "That's exactly what I think they're doing, and I bet I know where …." They looked at the location he marked on the screen - Faisal Islam Mosque. "It's ideal. They know it, the authorities and people leave it alone, it's large enough to stage four dozen people, and it's not far … five minutes away."

Mugsy opened the passenger doors to the SUV, "I'm having RD-1 sent to the mosque. Pile in, gentlemen."

Rigoni, De May, Pescalitis, Gunny Proctor, and Scipio got in the back, while Mugsy got in the driver's seat.

De Niro stopped Francis, "John, stay here with Michael Squad and contact Michelle. Have her coordinate with the FBI and bring them up to speed. When they get here, you can take them into the basement."

"I'd prefer never to go back down there again, thank you very much."

De Niro patted his shoulder, "Fine, then just show them the door and don't forget to show them the shack where Pescalitis put the explosives."

De Niro got into the passenger seat and Francis closed the door for him, "Be careful Cris. Remember to stand behind the rest of these knuckleheads."

Francis stepped back as the SUV lurched from the curb.

CHAPTER 41

The light turned red. Tonio came to a halt and turned in his seat, "How you doing?"

The pain was evident on Kevin Matthews' face, "Can't wait to get this lead out of my leg."

"How far is the hospital?" asked Karla.

"Less than five minutes," Tonio turned back in his seat and noticed headlights approaching from the north on Russell Street.

He could make out a dark Chevy Suburban with three men inside. The light changed, forcing the Suburban to stop as Tonio crossed the intersection. The man sitting in the passenger seat tried to conceal his face, but Tonio recognized him.

"Shit …," he floored the accelerator, "our friend is back, hold on!"

Tonio looked in the rear-view mirror and saw the Suburban giving chase.

Karla looked out the back window, "I think one of them has a rifle!"

Karla screamed as a bullet crashed through the back window and slammed into the headrest of the seat behind her brother.

"Get your head down, woman!" shouted Tonio as he began zigzagging, then turned right so abruptly they momentarily rode up on two wheels.

Kevin Matthews grabbed his leg and winced in pain as he peered out the window, "Tonio, isn't the hospital in the other direction?"

"We ain't going to the hospital."

Tonio looked in the rear-view mirror again and saw the Suburban making the same dangerous turn as he just made.

"That mo-fo behind us will shoot our asses the moment we slow down."

He raced past the sign that read "To Route 94."

"Where are we going?" asked Karla.

"When in trouble … head for the 'hood."

* * * * *

The driver saw the sign for Route 94 as he raced past, "He is heading for the highway!"

Khan loaded another clip into his rifle, "Stay with him. If you lose him, you die."

* * * * *

Tonio continued to zigzag from lane to lane and sometimes used the shoulders on each side of the highway to dodge traffic. Still, the Suburban remained behind him.

Tonio spoke into the rearview mirror, "No phone … no gun. Two things no self-respecting Detroiter should ever leave home without."

Karla looked out through the broken back window, "They're still behind us … they're gonna catch us!"

Tonio floored the accelerator and turned sharply across three lanes toward the exit ramp. The SUV jumped the curb, barely missing a light pole, and began tearing up the grass embankment. Tonio slammed the brakes. The SUV lurched to a stop just a foot away from a tree.

Tonio looked over his shoulder, "Where'd they go? We lose 'em?"

* * * * *

The driver tried the same maneuver as Tonio did, not realizing there was a dark blue Jaguar sedan next to him. The Suburban slammed into the side of the car forcing them both off of the highway and onto the grassy shoulder past the exit.

The man in the Jaguar rolled his window down and began shouting, "You stupid bastard! What the hell is the matter with you?!"

Khan's passenger door was slammed against the Jaguar driver's door. Khan opened his window and slammed the butt of his rifle into the driver's face. The man crashed onto the passenger seat motionless, with blood pouring from his nose.

Khan pointed the rifle at his driver, "Go around him!"

The driver stepped on the accelerator, as sparks shot out from metal rubbing against metal between the two vehicles. The Suburban turned sharply until it was pointing straight at the Escalade about one hundred yards away with only the exit ramp separating them.

Khan aimed his rifle out the window, "Go!"

* * * * *

Karla looked at her brother as he grimaced in pain. Blood was running down his leg.

"We have to get Kevin to the hospital!"

Tonio spotted the Suburban racing toward them. Switching into reverse and flooring it, the tires kicked up grass and dirt all around them.

"Stay down!"

Switching into drive, Tonio floored the accelerator and raced over the grassy knoll until he reached the circular exit ramp. The tires screeched as they touched the pavement. Behind them, the Suburban did the same thing.

"Why'd you get off the highway?" asked Karla.

When Tonio didn't reply, Kevin Matthews strained to look out the window, "He's heading for Seven Mile."

"Seven Mile ... why are you taking us to that hellish part of town?"

Tonio didn't stop as he turned right onto Gratiot Avenue. He looked in the rearview at Karla, "'Cause that's my turf."

"You're bloods—"

The thudding of bullets piercing the rear quarter panel cut her off.

Tonio floored the accelerator again, "Just gotta get there ...."

The two SUVs swerved in and out of traffic as they raced south along Gratiot Avenue through the Eastpointe area until they reached Seven Mile East. There, Tonio turned left and headed east until he reached his old stomping grounds, the Heilmann Recreation Center, in East Detroit.

Reaching the old park, he jumped the curb and raced across the field where he played football as a boy, then crossed Maddelein

Street and jumped the curb again, stopping inside an oval parking lot outside the Fisher Magnet Upper Academy middle school.

The Suburban was close behind.

Tonio unbuckled his seat belt and turned, "You two, stay in the car and stay down." He turned off the engine and got out.

Karla unbuckled and sat on the floor next to her brother. She looked up at him as she tended to his bandage, "Where is he going?"

Kevin Matthews blinked slowly as he looked out the window, "He's going to introduce ISIS to old school, East Detroit."

* * * * *

Khan held his hand up, "Stop here." The SUV rolled to a halt. Khan and the two men got out, all three toting AK-47s. They ducked when they heard explosions all around them. Fireworks of all types were lighting up the sky and crackling on the ground, in every direction.

"What's the matter, you never heard fireworks before?" Tonio stood with his hands crossed in front of him.

Khan and his men looked around. From every direction, people of color of all ages, shapes, and sizes stepped into the light of the parking lot.

A voice called out, "That you, Shah?"

Tonio grinned, "Yes sir, how you be, Jimbo?"

Four men walked up to Tonio and threw their arms around him. The gold tooth of the largest one, Jimbo, sparkled with every rocket that burst overhead.

Jimbo nodded to Khan and his men, "Who the chumps with the choppers?"

"They why I'm here. Seems they think East Detroit is Beirut or some shit."

Khan and his men raised their rifles. In that moment, they felt gun barrels pressing against the backs of their heads.

Tonio led the others over to them. He stood nose to nose with Khan his men disarmed Khan's.

"This one here ... murdered my son. And he didn't just murder him. He ... cut my son's head ...," Tonio's voice broke down.

Jimbo rubbed the back of Tonio's neck with his massive hand, as he raised his voice to the crowd around them, "All y'all who ain't with my crew, get outta here now!"

The people standing around quickly dispersed and disappeared until only a dozen men, armed with pistols, were left.

Karla got out of the SUV, went around and helped her brother out.

Jimbo pulled a large stiletto from his pocket and handed it to Tonio.

Tonio pressed the button springing the six-inch blade from the handle and placed it under Khan's throat, "Tell me brother, do Muslims believe in an eye for an eye?"

Khan sneered.

"Tonio ... don't!" cried Kevin Matthews as Karla helped him walk over.

Tonio kept staring into Khan's eyes, "I told you both not to get out!"

"If you kill him, it'll be cold-blooded murder!"

"You saw what he did to Teddy!" Tonio pushed his nose against Khan's, "He ain't a man. He ain't even a dog!"

"Killing him won't bring Teddy back! Listen to me!"

Tonio nodded to Jimbo, "Keep them back."

Jimbo turned toward Karla and Kevin and raised his hands in the air. Khan saw the pistol tucked into the back of Jimbo's pants. In one quick motion, he pulled it and shot him.

Instantly, Tonio swung his arm and rammed all six inches of the blade into Khan's belly, pulled it out, then shoved the blade straight up under Khan's chin.

Khan's eyes met Tonio's again as he collapsed to his knees.

"I hope to see my boy again, but y'all definitely going to hell."

Khan fell facedown to the ground.

Tonio bent down next to Jimbo, now lying on his stomach, grabbing his butt.

"Jimbo, where you hit?"

"He shot my ass. That mo-fo shot my ass!"

Tonio smiled, "Shiitt … and I thought he might've hurt you. Brother, it'd take a bazooka to penetrate that fat ass."

Laughter broke out.

"That ain't funny, homeboy. This shit hurts! Somebody call an ambulance!"

"Make that two ambulances," added Kevin Matthews as he started slipping out of his sister's arms.

Tonio rushed over and supported him, "Let's get you back in the SUV."

"I'll sit in it, but brother, I ain't going anywhere with you at the wheel again!"

Tonio turned, "If you boys don't mind, sit the other two on the floor with their hands on their heads, and if they move, cap their asses until someone comes to get them."

Fireworks began lighting up the skies over their heads. Karla got off the line with Michelle Wang, "Michelle said she'll contact the Feds to come get those two. She looked up and forced a tired smile,

"Now, this is what I call Independence Day."

CHAPTER 42

Kneeling on the roof of a Mason lodge abandoned long ago, Mugsy tapped the communication button as he looked through binoculars, "Gunny, what's your location?"

Lying prone, Gunny Proctor replied, "On alpha LOA."

The LOA or "limit of advance" was generally the closest point an attacking force could reach before being detected by the enemy. Scipio had sent Proctor to the same spot where he and Tonio had been, in the overgrowth around the train tracks, across the street from the mosque.

"Status ...?"

Proctor looked through the Nightforce NXS 8-32x56 scope attached to his .300 Winchester Magnum sniper rifle. He had begun utilizing the .300 Win Mag to honor the memory of American Sniper, Chris Kyle. The .300 Win Mag was Kyle's favorite rifle.

"I have a clear firing lane to the front of the building, but limited to the back."

Mugsy tapped his comm again, "Scip, what's your location?"

Scipio, Rigoni, Pescalitis, and De May were kneeling behind

a wooden perimeter fence that stretched out from both sides of a one-hundred-foot gravel driveway leading to the back of the mosque. Kneeling behind Scipio was Pescalitis. On the other side of the driveway were Rigoni and De May.

Scipio nodded to Rigoni and tapped his comm, "On bravo LOA, but we're too far back to do any good. There's a shuttle bus parked in the grass in front of an inner fence that would bring us about fifty feet closer."

Mugsy handed the binoculars to De Niro, "Can you see what he's talking about?"

De Niro put the binoculars to his eyes and tapped the night vision button, "We can see the fence and just make out the front of the shuttle bus."

Mugsy tapped his comm, "Gunny … thoughts?"

"I can see the top of the shuttle bus. The exterior of that fence he's talking about cuts off my field of vision."

De Niro scanned the front of the mosque, "No one out front.

"Let's see what RD-1 sees," Mugsy tapped into the feed from RD-1's camera. "Confirmed, no hostiles out front."

Mugsy replied, "Okay, Scip, move up to that bus, if you can."

Proctor scanned back toward the mosque, "Hold it. We've got movement … hostiles pouring out the back of the building."

* * * * *

Syed was the first to walk out the back door, followed by nine drivers. He watched as each headed to their designated vehicles and started the engines.

Naheed walked out the back door and joined him. She looked out toward the street then turned impatiently to Syed, "Those people could get here at any moment. What's taking so long?"

"They were all praying. Without the Imam, many had become anxious, especially the bombers."

The bombers and handlers began exiting out the back door. Syed ran to the SUV with the suicide vests in back, opened the hatch, and began handing them out to each bomber.

Naheed looked across the street toward the train tracks. She couldn't see anyone, but she had an uneasy feeling she couldn't shake ever since Khan called her. She called to Syed, "Hurry!"

* * * * *

Scipio waved his hand. Rigoni and De May took off in a crouched position until they reached the back of the shuttle bus. Then Rigoni waved his hand and Scipio and Pescalitis joined them.

Scipio peered around the back of the bus, "We still can't see anything from here. I'm gonna peek around the corner of the fence."

Crawling, Scipio hustled to the end of the driveway and twisted his head around the broken, wooden picket fence. The lighting was dim, but he could make out a line of young men leading to the back of an SUV.

He whispered to himself, "What the heck are they doing—" but cut himself off when he saw Syed handing out what looked like large padded vests. His worst fears were confirmed when he saw one young man putting the vest on under his shirt.

Scipio raised his Tavor X-95 bullpup assault rifle, took aim and fired two shots in close succession.

* * * * *

Syed reached into the SUV and took out the second vest, being careful not to drop it. He turned to hand it to the second bomber in line when he spotted movement near the driveway. He could make out a figure in black holding a rifle and immediately took off running toward Naheed, who was still standing near the back door. Syed was three-feet away when he heard two shots before being propelled into the air, as a result of the explosion behind him.

* * * * *

A millisecond after Scipio squeezed the trigger, the young man wearing the suicide vest burst into a white ball of flame and a millisecond after that all the vests, except for the one Syed had in his hands, exploded inside the back of the SUV. The ferocity of the blasts bounced the fifty-eight-hundred-pound vehicle into the air and flipped it over, long-ways.

The other eight bombers that were lined up in back were now lying motionless on the ground. The blast knocked Scipio to the ground too.

Gunny Proctor watched the spectacle through his scope, "Holy shit!" He tapped his comm, "Scipio, come in."

Rigoni and De May helped Scipio to his feet and back behind the fence. Pescalitis stood in front of them with his rifle drawn and spoke over his shoulder, "What the hell just happened?"

Scipio brushed dirt off his pants and ignored the question, "Spiro, there's another way out of that back parking lot. I want you to block the exit with our SUV. Rigs, give him the keys."

Rigoni handed Pescalitis the key fob to the SUV. Pescalitis took off running.

Proctor's voice broke through again, "Scipio, do you read, over."

Scipio tapped his comm, "I'm okay."

"What happened?" The voice belonged to Mugsy.

"They were beginning to divvy out suicide vests. I shot the first one I saw and all of them went up."

"Are you sure it was all of them?" asked Mugsy through the comm.

Scipio glanced at Rigoni then tapped his comm, "Negative … no way to be sure."

* * * * *

"Mugs, there's no one in front of the mosque," said De Niro. "We need to get down from here and take a closer look."

"Cris there's almost five hundred feet of barren land between this building and the front of the mosque. That's over a football-sized killing field if they spot us."

De Niro reached over the edge of the one-story building and dropped himself down. Mugsy shook his head and followed him. They went around the back of the building and started down a battered path that cut through the open field between them and the mosque.

"Now what?" asked Mugsy.

"Now we see who's faster," replied De Niro with a wink. Holding a rifle, De Niro took off running. Mugsy gave chase.

* * * * *

Syed was blown off his feet. He landed hard on top of Naheed with his back singed while still holding the suicide vest. Thick, white smoke enveloped them.

"Get off me," hollered Naheed.

Syed arose to his knees. Getting to her feet, Naheed looked around then nodded to the back door of the mosque, "Take the vest inside. Open the weapons lockers for the others and get us weapons, then wait for me inside the Imam's office."

Syed looked up at her, "Naheed ... it wasn't my fault."

Naheed scanned the surroundings then looked down at him and nodded, "I know. Go."

Syed got to his feet and headed for the back door.

Naheed looked at the burning and dismembered bodies sprawled on the ground but was more concerned with the exploded vests, "Such a waste."

She looked past the overturned SUV at the eighteen handlers and drivers who had gotten out of their vehicles. She could see fear on their faces.

She waved them over, "Come!"

As they ran over, she pointed to the back door of the mosque, "Go in. Syed is opening the weapons lockers. Arm yourselves and meet me inside the back door."

As the smoke began to dissipate, Naheed waited for the last to enter the building before following them in.

* * * * *

Gunny Proctor looked for a target, but the smoke continued to conceal most of the parking lot. He tapped his comm, "I can't see a thing ... gotta wait for the cloud to lift. I can't provide cover until it does."

"Roger that," replied Scipio.

Proctor continued to scan the lot. As the smoke thinned the head of a female came into view. He took aim, but before he could get a shot the woman disappeared behind a roaming plume. With his finger on the trigger, Proctor waited with anticipation for the plume to dissipate. Once it did, there was no one there.

He tapped his comm, "The smoke's finally gone, but so are the hostiles. A female vanished before I could drop her, and now I don't see a soul alive in the parking lot."

* * * * *

Scipio returned to his previous position at the end of the fence where the gravel driveway met the parking lot. He looked for himself then tapped his comm, "They must have gone into the mosque. We have to assume they have a weapons stash inside."

"Orders for me?" asked Proctor through the comm.

Scipio looked in the direction of Proctor's location, across the street, "Remain there. Take down anyone that leaves the mosque, either side."

"Roger that."

A moment later, Proctor's voice broke through the comm again, "Scip, I have two armed individuals approaching the front of the mosque on foot, from the west … wait, it's Mr. D and the Captain."

Scipio stepped out onto the path and looked through his binoculars then tapped his comm, "Mugsy, where the hell are you going?"

* * * * *

De Niro and Mugsy crossed the street and took up a position at the front corner of a house directly adjacent to the mosque's smaller, front parking lot.

Mugsy tapped his comm, "We can't be sure all the vests were destroyed, so we can't let anyone out of the mosque until help arrives. Cris just called Michelle. She's contacting Detroit SWAT and the bomb squad now."

De Niro tapped Mugsy's arm, "Michelle said she finally got to them. They said their ETA is about fifteen minutes."

Mugsy continued, "Okay, everyone … the cavalry said their ETA is one-five minutes. Until then, we need to keep the hostiles contained inside the building. Shoot anyone that so much as sticks their head out of that mosque."

Scipio replied, "Understood," followed by Rigoni, De May, and Pescalitis, in close succession with, "Roger," and then Proctor's, "Roger that."

De Niro looked at his watch, "Eight-fifteen. They should be here by eight-thirty."

He peered around the corner of the house then scanned the night sky. Fireworks were illuminating the horizons in all directions.

"Something tells me they're not going to wait long before they try something."

Mugsy loaded another clip into his rifle, "I got the same feeling."

CHAPTER 43

Naheed stood at the back door as the fighters returned, armed with AK-47s.

"Listen to me. We can still strike the infidels tonight. You must not allow anyone to enter the mosque for the next thirty minutes. And I want you to breed fear in them. Shoot anyone you see outside. Anyone you see, you shoot!

"After that, you may try to escape from here or remain defending the mosque and become martyrs with Syed and myself. We will be inside the Imam's office. We have one vest left. We will rig the vest to explode upon opening the office door, but we will need thirty minutes to rig it and destroy any records the Imam might have locked away."

She looked from one frightened face to another, "Remember, the fates of your families depend on your success here tonight."

Naheed waited for that to sink in, before continuing, "Now, you will split up into two teams, handlers, take up positions at the front entrance, and drivers, here at the back."

Naheed watched, concealing a grin as the eighteen complied by splitting up into two groups of nine.

Naheed patted some of the drivers on their shoulders, "Fight well ... Allah be with you, and bring us victory!"

* * * * *

Scipio stationed Rigoni, De May, and Pescalitis to his right, along the tattered wooden fence with two meters between each other.

Pescalitis's voice broke through the comm, "Anyone, wanna take bets on whether they try to break out the front or back?"

"And what if they just stay inside," replied Rigoni.

"I'll give five-for-one they don't," replied Pescalitis.

"At least we don't have to storm the place," replied De May. "Just keep 'em in sounds good to me."

* * * * *

Mugsy peeked around the corner of the house, "Either they're gonna turn this into a Waco scenario or they're deciding whether to surrender." He stepped back from the corner, "My money is on surrender. That mosque isn't a compound like Waco. They probably have very little food in there, and once SWAT arrives, they can shut off their water and electricity. It's gonna be a hot night."

De Niro took his place and tilted his head around the corner. The report of an AK-47 crackled, as a 7.62x39mm round sliced a piece of paneling off the wall of the house, three inches over De Niro's head.

De Niro fell backward and looked up at Mugsy, "How much money do you have on you? Because you just lost it."

Scipio's voice came through the comm, "Was that rifle fire?"

Mugsy replied, "Affirmative. Someone inside just took a pot shot at Cris's head."

"He okay?"

"He's smiling, partly because they missed and partly because I just lost a bet."

"Roger that."

Mugsy helped De Niro to his feet, and brushed debris from the wall off his shoulder, "From now on, I'll do the peeking."

De Niro cleaned the rest off with his hands, "I don't think they want to be peeked at."

* * * * *

Naheed walked into the Imam's office then closed and locked the door behind her. Syed was sitting in the Imam's chair. He was staring at the last suicide vest lying on the desk.

Naheed walked over, "Do you have a weapon for me?"

Syed hesitated. Maintaining a stare, he handed her a pistol.

Naheed tucked the pistol into her waist, "Syed, there is no time for contemplation. You must keep your faith strong, as the Imam did."

"That is easy for you to say," he replied without looking up. "You won't be wearing the vest."

Naheed turned his chair to make him face her, "I won't be wearing the vest, but I'll probably be dead shortly after I witness your glorious sacrifice."

He looked up at her.

She knelt before him, put her lips on his and let them linger, "We both knew it could come to this. Now, it's time we take our place among the heroes of Islam. Our sacrifices will inspire legions of new followers to the true faith."

He stared into her eyes, "I wish I had your courage."

She took the detonator from the table and held it out, "You just need to trust me. I will have courage for both of us."

She stood up, "Help me move the desk."

Syed stood and grabbed the side of the desk opposite her. Together, they moved the desk forward revealing a small trap door.

Naheed lifted a brass latch and pulled the door open then stepped down a few rungs of an iron ladder, "The Imam had this tunnel dug when the mosque was built. He only told me of it a week ago, in case something went wrong. Hand me the vest."

Syed grabbed the vest from the desk and handed it to her. She disappeared with it, then heard her voice echoed, "Come."

Syed stepped down the ladder to find Naheed holding two flashlights. She handed him one then grabbed keys off a small metal hook screwed into the raw wood-lined tunnel wall.

"You take the vest. Let's go, this way."

She started walking down the narrow passage.

Syed picked up the vest, put it on, and then followed her.

CHAPTER 44

Cris De Niro and Mugsy Ricci watched as a towering matte black vehicle with "DETROIT POLICE" stenciled on the side, known as "The Bear" turned and lumbered to a stop directly in front of the entrance to the mosque.

De Niro waved his hands frantically at the driver to get him to pull up farther, but it was too late. AK-47 rounds began ricocheting off the heavily-armored Bear in all directions. The driver immediately pulled forward until the small house De Niro and Mugsy were utilizing as a vantage point blocked the line of fire to the large vehicle.

A tall, burly man, wearing black tactical body armor, a black uniform, black boots, and a black baseball cap jumped out of the passenger seat. Immediately, he began deploying fifteen similarly-clad officers before heading over to De Niro and Mugsy.

He offered his hand, "I'm Lt. Barren. You must be Mr. De Niro."

De Niro shook his hand, "This is Mugsy Ricci, President of The Watchman Agency."

"You're the folks that saved Las Vegas a few years ago."

"At a price," replied De Niro.

Lt. Barren nodded in understanding, "What do we have here?"

"There were about forty armed Islamic radicals," replied Mugsy, "pretty much Detroit locals trained here. It appears we came upon their plot to use suicide bombers to attack multiple locations in the city.

"One of our men shot one of their suicide vests in the back parking lot, igniting the rest. The blast took out about half of them. The rest took shelter inside the mosque."

Lt. Barren stepped to the side of the house.

"I wouldn't do that," said De Niro. "Peaking around the side can get you shot at, take it from me."

Lt. Barren nodded, "Thanks. Anything else you can offer?"

"They seem to be mostly armed with AK-47s and they haven't attempted any form of communication with us," replied Mugsy. "There are only two ways in or out of that mosque that we know of, the front and back. We have men stationed at the back. We haven't seen anyone enter or leave since the blast."

Hearing the faint high-pitched whine of RD-1, Lt. Barren looked up, "What's that?"

"That is one of our reconnaissance drones," replied Mugsy.

Lt. Barren nodded then offered his hand again, "Thank you, gentlemen, you've been very helpful. We'll take it from here. Once my men take up position at the back, you can pull your men," he nodded up to the sky, "and equipment out."

De Niro and Mugsy watched as six SWAT team members set out from behind The Bear. The moment they came into view of the front of the mosque bullets rang out driving them back.

Mugsy tapped his comm, "Scip … SWAT's here but they're held up on our side of the building."

"Understood," replied Scipio with the sound of gunfire coming from his end. "They opened fire at us a few minutes ago. Looks like they're shooting at anything that moves."

"Roger that. Sit tight. A Lieutenant Barren is in charge of the SWAT team. As soon as his men make it to your position, you stand relieved. Then grab our vehicle and meet us at Klein and Far Streets."

"Roger that."

Lt. Barren walked back over, "I'm having half my men take our vehicle and drive around the block to your men."

"Good idea," replied De Niro.

* * * * *

Naheed led Syed through a tight cobbled-out tunnel until they reached an iron ladder at the end of it. She climbed up then entered a combination into a pad lock to open the trap door. Syed followed her, emerging into a one-car garage. Parked in front of the trap door was a late model, tan, Chevy SUV.

Naheed headed to the garage door then turned to Syed, "It's time. Put the vest on then get in the driver's seat, but don't start the engine yet. I want to check outside first."

Syed hesitated. Naheed could see the sweat dripping from Syed's brow.

Naheed approached him and placed her forehead on his, "Trust me, my love. Paradise awaits us both."

Naheed waited for him to get into the SUV before lying on the floor and opening the garage just enough to peek out. She saw a few sets of black booted legs walking back and forth on the sidewalk.

She shut the garage door and made a call on her cell, "It is Naheed. We just received intel that the infidels are surrounding the mosque."

Seeing that Syed was listening with growing tension on his face, she turned her back. After giving the order, she turned back to Syed, "It is imperative they follow my instructions to the letter. They are to begin in three minutes. Is that clear?"

Naheed slipped the cell phone into her pocket and walked over to the driver's door. Syed lowered the window.

"Get ready. Our fighters are about to cause a diversion to allow us to escape. As soon as we hear it, I'll open the garage door while you start the engine. The moment I get in, take off, but don't speed. Turn right out of the driveway, so we don't attract their attention."

Syed nodded at the garage door, "Who is out there?"

"Men in military gear, probably the Detroit SWAT team."

"Our fighters won't be able to resist them for long."

"No, they won't, but it will be long enough for us to escape. I am familiar with the tactical reactions of para-military units like the American SWAT teams. If all goes well, their attention will be drawn to our fighters, and we can slip away undetected."

Syed wiped sweat off his forehead with his forearm then nodded.

Naheed's eyes sparkled with confidence, "We are one, Syed. Our success is their success. Our victory is their victory."

* * * * *

"We've got movement," Mugsy waved De Niro and Lt. Barren to join him at the corner of the house. The doors of the mosque opened.

Lt. Barren put a bullhorn to his mouth, "To the individuals inside the mosque. This is Lt. Barren of Detroit SWAT. You are surrounded. Come out with your hands on your head and you will not be injured."

Mugsy looked through his binoculars, "Nothing yet."

De Niro placed his hand on Lt. Barren's shoulder, "Lieutenant, with respect, the men still inside were about to don suicide vests when we came upon them. They won't surrender."

Lt. Barren returned a look of contemplation broken by Mugsy's voice, "They're coming out. Two just emerged with hands on their heads. Their walking this way."

A voice then crackled from Lt. Barren's radio, "Sir, two individuals just emerged from the back door with their hands on their heads. They're heading right for us."

Mugsy held up his hand, prompting Lt. Barren to reply, "Stand by."

Mugsy tapped his finger, "Gunny, scan the two that just walked out, with your scope."

Gunny Proctor replied, "Roger."

Looking between De Niro and Lt. Barren, Mugsy waited a moment before replying, "Gunny, do you see any signs of suicide vests or weapons?"

There was a slight pause, before Proctor's one-word reply, "Negative."

"You have a sniper out there?" asked Lt. Barren.

"We do," replied Mugsy. "He's a few hundred yards south, in the field across the street."

Lt. Barren patted Mugsy's shoulder, "We got it from here." The lieutenant turned and spoke into his walkie-talkie, "Let them advance until they're out of the line of fire, then use caution when--"

Lt. Barren cut himself off when he saw the men from the mosque stop walking.

A second later, he heard the voice of his man at the back of the mosque crackle from the walkie-talkie, "Sir, they stopped walking."

Mugsy turned to De Niro and Barren, "What the hell …?"

De Niro peered around the house, "Both stopped walking at the same time … that's coordinated."

Lt. Barren replied into his radio, "Order them forward."

He put the bullhorn back to his mouth, "This is Lt. Barren. You, from the mosque. You are to continue to walk straight ahead until you are out of the parking lot."

They watched as neither man moved.

"I'm telling you, Lieutenant," said De Niro, "these people don't surrender."

Mugsy raised his hand, "One just drew a knife!"

They watched as one of the two men pulled a knife from the back of his pants and raised it above his head.

Lt. Barren grinned, "I guess no one told them never to bring a knife to a gunfight."

Mugsy turned to Barren, "Lieutenant, with your permission, our sniper can put a round in his arm."

"Negative," replied Barren, "he's no threat to us with a knife. Let's see if I can talk to—"

"Allahu Akbar!!" One of the three young African-American's cried out the familiar Arabic phrase with a Detroit accent, cutting Barren off.

Suddenly, the man lowered the blade to his own throat and slit it. Instantly, he collapsed to the ground clutching his cut throat while blood spurted from the deep wound.

Barren's radio crackled to life again, "Sir, one of their men back here just slit his own throat with a knife he had concealed!"

Lt. Barren made eye contact with De Niro before hollering a

command into his radio, "Do NOT approach him! Stand your ground!" Barren held his arm up to give the same command to the men with him. He spoke again into his radio, "Have paramedics dispatched immediately. Fill them in and tell them not to park on this block or to leave their vehicles until I give the order."

Another voice came from his radio, "Lieutenant, two news trucks just pulled up."

"Shit," cried Barren, "that's all we need, these nuts committing hara-kiri on the evening news." He replied into his radio, "Keep them back. Set up a perimeter—"

"Lieutenant," exclaimed Mugsy, "you better take a look!"

The three watched as the second man produced a knife from behind him and raised it over his head, in the same way. A moment later, his man at the back of the building reported the same thing.

Barren turned to Mugsy, "Tell your man to put a round in his arm."

Before Mugsy could tap his comm, voices shouted out from inside the mosque, followed by a stream of young men all armed with AK-47s running out the door. They fanned out into the parking lot as they exited the building.

Barren's man in back reported the same thing happening there.

De Niro watched as Barren's SWAT team took cover and raised their weapons.

"They must be crazy. They have no cover!" Barren spoke into the bullhorn, "All of you drop your weapons now or you will be fired upon!"

Barren hadn't lowered the bullhorn before bullets flew in every direction, including knocking the vinyl siding off of the wall of the house just inches away from him.

Bullets crashed through the windows at the back of the house and zipped over De Niro's head in front. Mugsy waved at him and shouted over the din of gunfire, "Get back and stay down!"

De Niro ducked and moved backwards toward the stoop leading to the small wooden porch of the house. As the sounds of gunfire became deafening, brightness from above and behind De Niro caught his attention. He looked up to see Fourth of July fireworks exploding in the air, adding to the chaos.

De Niro's eyes were drawn to the glowing embers falling from the sky. Their multi-colored trails led his gaze to fall upon the garage door ten feet away, next to the house. The door was opening and Chevy SUV was emerging.

De Niro stepped toward the vehicle, but it raced past him then accelerating up the street before he could see who was inside. He watched the SUV disappear around the corner then turned to the others. Everyone else was returning fire or ducking for cover. No one else seemed to notice.

He rubbed his chin, Either, whoever that was might've just heard the gunfire and wanted to get the hell out of Dodge, or ….

He turned and saw that the garage door was still open. With the gun battle blazing behind him, De Niro stared at the open garage door trying to piece together events.

You're sitting in your house. Gunfire erupts, bullets crash through your window, you want to escape, so you head to your garage ….

De Niro rubbed his chin.

The garage isn't attached to the house, so how did they get from the house to the garage? Not from the front door, or I would have noticed; or the back door, because the back faces the mosque. No way anyone would step out in the direction of gunfire.

De Niro saw a side door entrance to the garage. With the sound of automatic rifle fire echoing from the other side of the house, he stepped out far enough to see if there was a side door exit from the house.

No side door, so how did you get in the garage? We've been here awhile, so I doubt you entered that sweltering garage before we got here.

His curiosity piqued, De Niro approached the dimly-lit garage and entered. Just a few feet in, he saw the trap door. Exhibiting the carelessness that Mugsy and the rest of his team warned him against, he hurried over and dropped down, reemerging with his finger pointed directly at the mosque.

Racing down the street in their dark SUV, Scipio screeched to a halt in front of the driveway and jumped out, just as De Niro ran out of the garage.

Before Scipio could ask, De Niro held his hand up and tapped his comm, "Spiro, its Cris. Is RD-1 still overhead?"

"Affirmative. It's hovering over the back of that house."

"A late model Chevy SUV just left the garage next to the house a few minutes ago, heading … northeast, at least to start. See if you can find it with RD-1."

"That won't be easy, boss, with all the fireworks."

"Do your best." De Niro pointed to the SUV, raced over and jumped into the passenger seat, "Scipio and I are will drive north-east. We'll follow RD-1's GPS as we watch her video feed. I'll let you know if we spot the vehicle."

"Roger that."

Scipio buckled into the driver's seat and took off from the curb as he and De Niro could barely make out the small drone passing over them taking the lead.

"This is Riggy," Rigoni's voice broke through their earbuds,

"Heard your comm with Spiro, we just saw a late model Chevy SUV pass by on Mt. Elliott Street, heading south. De May thinks it turned left on Conant Street."

"Cris, where the hell are you," Mugsy's voice cut in.

"Hold on a sec, Mugs. Roger that, Rigs. Did you get that Spiro?"

"Affirmative, vectoring RD-1 now."

Scipio turned down Mt. Elliott and floored the accelerator, roaring past Rigoni and the rest as he turned on Conant.

De Niro tapped his comm, "Mugs, I saw someone leave the garage next to the house. Inside the garage is a tunnel I believe leads to the mosque. You better check it out. Meanwhile, Spiro is trying to find the vehicle with RD-1, while Scipio and I do the same on the ground."

"Roger that."

"What's your status?"

"Most of the tangos that came out of the mosque have been put down, but there's still a few who made it to cover and they're putting up a fight."

De Niro shook his head, "Understood, but you need to check out that tunnel and be careful."

"Roger that. You be careful too."

Scipio winked, "I know he meant that 'you' for both of us."

"Boss, I think we might've spotted him," interrupted Pescalitis. "Roll back the feed and check out the SUV that made the right turn onto Harper Avenue."

De Niro swiped his finger across his Big-Brutha and replayed the last twenty seconds of the RD-1's video feed. He saw the familiar vehicle turning.

"That looks like it. Whoever it is might be heading for the ninety-four. How fast can RD-1 fly again?"

"Not fast enough. You better get on their tail before she loses contact at the highway."

Scipio turned on Harper Avenue and gunned the engine, "On it!"

"Positive confirmation," said Pescalitis, "RD-1 spotted the Chevy SUV getting on the ninety-four, heading westbound, about a half-mile ahead of you."

Scipio raced up the entrance ramp and onto the highway, jumping into the left lane as quickly as he could. Traffic was relatively light. Within minutes, he and De Niro made visual contact with the vehicle.

"Hang back," said De Niro. "Let's hope they don't know we're on their tail."

Scipio slowed down, "Should we try and contact SWAT or Detroit police?"

"They could be monitoring police frequencies, for all we know. Let's just see where they're heading."

"And when we find out, what then? Do you even have a gun?"

De Niro grinned and shook his head, "Good ol' Mugsy didn't think I needed one since I was with him."

Scipio returned a smile, "The real reason is ... he knows you're capable of doing things like jumping in an SUV and chasing after terrorists."

"All the more reason I should be armed."

CHAPTER 45

SOUTHFIELD FREEWAY
2.25 MILES EAST OF GREENFIELD VILLAGE
DEARBORN, MICHIGAN
9:15 PM (LOCAL), MONDAY, JULY 04, 2016

Naheed smiled as she read headlines from a news feed on her cell phone, "Terrorist cell surrounded at Detroit Mosque … siege continues as casualties are reported. Allah is good to us, Syed! Not only did our fighters allow us to escape, but their battle continues to divert attention away from us."

Syed wiped sweat from his brow, "Does it say how many have died?"

Naheed looked up at him, "It does not, but obviously not all of them. Their battle is being broadcast live to the entire world. Our brothers and sisters everywhere are seeing their bravery, and soon they will see our victory."

Naheed switched to a map program. She pointed, "This is the exit."

Syed put on the blinker and looked in the rearview mirror, "Traffic has picked up."

Naheed continued to study the map, "Perhaps more infidels that will die at our hands. As soon as you get off, be ready to turn right, into the parking lot of a bank. We'll leave this vehicle there."

"How far are we from the target?"

Naheed tapped her Uber app, "Just over two miles. There are houses on the next street. I'm requesting a car pick us up in front of one of them. If the FBI is ever able to trace us back to the ride, they will waste even more time investigating the owners of those homes.

Syed melded into the exiting traffic. With a line of cars ahead and behind him on the exit ramp, he turned into the parking lot of the bank.

* * * * *

Scipio exhaled audibly, "Light traffic the whole way then they choose the exit with the most traffic."

De Niro was looking at a map on Big-Brutha, "We're in Dearborn, getting off at the Oakwood exit. It's a major thoroughfare--"

Traffic suddenly came to a crawl in front of them. Scipio hit the brakes, "Cris, I don't see them. Do you?"

The traffic picked up speed in front of them, but stopped again because of a light at the intersection.

Scipio tightened his grip on the steering wheel, "We lost them."

De Niro, studied Google maps. "The fireworks show at The Henry Ford Museum is right down the road a couple of miles. That explains the traffic and that's where our friends must be heading. Hang a right at the intersection."

Scipio waited for traffic to pass then shot out and turned right, just ahead of Naheed and Syed as they walked out of the bank parking lot.

* * * * *

It took just five minutes for an Uber driver to pull up. Naheed and Syed hopped in and the car took off.

CHAPTER 46

THE HENRY FORD MUSEUM
GREENFIELD VILLAGE
DEARBORN, MICHIGAN
9:45 PM (LOCAL), MONDAY, JULY 04, 2016

Scipio followed a line of vehicles into the immense parking lot. Overhead, the night sky illuminated with multiple bursts of multi-colored light.

Scipio shook his head, "This place is humongous. There's no way we'll be able to find them here … if they are here."

De Niro kept his eyes moving, "Follow the signs to Fire Work Station. If I were them, I'd time my attack at the conclusion of the fireworks show … which should be in less than fifteen minutes."

"With a crowd this size, we probably won't get parking within a mile of the display."

"I'm not sure about that. I know a lot of folks who hate to stay until the end of anything. They just have to beat the traffic."

Scipio glanced at De Niro, "You mean, like you do every time we go to see a UNLV Rebels game?"

De Niro ignored the gibe, "Drop me off as close as you can to the entrance. I'll make my way up toward the front of the crowd and see if I can spot them from there. Meantime, park the car and hang toward the back. It's our only shot."

"And just how are we supposed to spot them?"

De Niro winked, "Look for the two people not looking up."

* * * * *

A red, four-door Toyota Camry pulled to a stop just outside the closest parking lot adjacent to the grassy field in front of Fire Work Station.

The Uber driver turned to the man and woman sitting in the back seat, "This is about as close as I can get you."

The driver saw the sweat on Syed's forehead.

"You feeling okay? The heat's been getting to lots of people to-day."

Without speaking, Syed and Naheed got out and waited for the car to pull away.

Naheed took Syed by his shoulders, "It's time." She nodded behind him, "Take that path and continue straight until you reach the grass, and remember, walk casually until you reach the center of the most crowded spot."

Syed could barely nod, paralyzed by fear.

Naheed massaged his shoulders gently, "Relax Syed. Be sure to reach the spot by nine fifty-five. That's about the time the final fireworks barrage will be ignited. Keep your eyes on your watch. When you see nine fifty-eight, that would be the optimal time."

Again, Syed nodded, this time a little more relaxed.

Naheed kissed him on his left cheek and then his right, "That spot will be holy ground. It will be the place you embark for heaven."

Syed stared at her for a moment, "And what of you? Will you be alright?"

This time she kissed his lips, "I'll remain here. In the chaos of that moment, I'll try to slip away. If I cannot … don't worry about me. Now go and Allah be with you."

Syed turned and headed for the path.

Naheed looked around the parking lot. Only a few cars were leaving and less were pulling in. She couldn't help smiling.

Those who are here will remain until the finale. It will be their finale too.

* * * * *

With every parking spot in sight taken, Scipio thought about pulling the SUV onto a knoll, but he reconsidered when he saw police, both on horseback and foot, patrolling all around him. That left him with no choice but to park at the far end of the immense lot, farthest from the fireworks display.

He got out looking at a map on his Big-Brutha phone and started jogging. He checked the time, "Nine-fifty and I gotta be a quarter mile away."

* * * * *

De Niro entered the grassy area and looked around. A knot grew in his stomach from the size of the crowd. There were thousands of people sprawled out in an area equal to two football fields. Fire Work Station, the staging area for the fireworks show was on the opposite side of the rectangular field. Making matters more difficult the field was unlit. The only light illuminating the throng in front of him was from the multi-colored bursts in the sky, and the only sounds were from their explosions.

De Niro tapped his comm, "Scip, I'm at the grass. I'm gonna make my way to the front, so I can look at faces instead of backs."

De Niro heard Scipio's reply of, "Roger that," as he looked up to Heaven and said a silent prayer.

* * * * *

Syed checked his watch as he entered the grassy area through a narrow security checkpoint that no one was manning. Sweat dripped into his eye stinging it. He wiped it away then tried again. His watch read nine fifty-four.

He looked up at the sky for a moment, but was numb to the grandeur of the aerial display. He let his eyes trace down to the point of origin of each ordinance. They all seemed to shoot up in the air from a hundred-fifty-foot grandstand on the other side of the field. He made a mental calculation of where he thought the exact center of the crowd would be, about a soccer field away and directly centered with the grandstand.

Syed started off in that direction by bumping into, and almost knocking to the ground, an overweight African-American woman who was walking with an equally overweight African-American man.

The man grabbed Syed by his arm, "You need to watch where you're walking, son!"

Syed ripped his arm free and reached into his pocket for the cell phone trigger, showing it to the man. A small crowd gathered around them.

The large man knotted his brows in confusion, "Now, what you gonna do … call the po-lice?"

"That boy ain't right," said the lady as she tugged on her man's arm. "Leave him alone, Tyrone."

The man pointed at Syed's face, "You lucky I gotta take a pee or I'd shove that phone up your ass, son."

Syed's chest was heaving as he watched the couple walk away. People chuckled at the sight of him holding the cell phone in front of him like it was a weapon. Syed shoved the phone-trigger back into his pocket and hurried ahead.

* * * * *

Naheed meandered through the narrow parking lot as she waited for the minutes to pass. The lot only had two rows of diagonal parking spaces, and with the lot being the closest to the grassy area, every spot was taken.

Seeing she would have to traverse a long distance to exit the Village grounds, she thought briefly about trying to steal a vehicle to make her getaway, but quickly dismissed the thought. There were too many things that could go wrong. There were police roaming everywhere and she couldn't break a window for fear of an alarm going off. And though she learned to hot wire older vehicles, certain models were more difficult than others. Then, there was the possibility of unexpected traffic or the owner realizing the theft and immediately alerting the police.

By her reckoning, it was about a half-mile to the closest exit. Walking at a quick pace she estimated it would take her about ten minutes to reach it. In that time, the police inside the Village would be able to coordinate with outside units to close the exits, but she had a plan for that. It was based on her ability to blend in with Caucasians and her acting ability. Those were two things that had saved her from capture many times.

She checked her watch.

Nine fifty-five. Syed should have reached the target.

* * * * *

Scipio checked the time as he crossed from the larger parking lot to the closer, smaller one.

Nine-fifty-five.

He tapped his comm as he picked up the pace, "Cris, I had to park in another zip code. I haven't even reached the grass yet. Where are you?"

"I made my way to the front of the crowd--"

The small man dressed in black noticed a woman generally matching the description he was given of the White Widow standing in the small parking lot.

Scipio stopped in his tracks, placing his hand to his ear, pretending to talk into a cell phone, "Okay, well I'll keep looking for you, but first I have to find the grass. I'll call you back."

Scipio heard De Niro ask, "Something wrong?" as he approached the woman standing by herself in the dark lot. When he was close enough he noticed a cell phone in her hand. He could tell she was aware of his approach, yet she avoided looking at him.

He closed the last few feet with a smile on his face, "Excuse me, dumb question, where exactly is the grassy area where everyone is watching the show? I had to park so far away, I got turned around."

The woman pointed without looking at him.

I gotta get her to turn around and say something.

"I should've known. Just follow the bombs bursting in air, right?"

Scipio waited for an answer. Receiving none, he continued, "The big finale is supposed to happen in a few minutes. Aren't you gonna stay for it?"

Scipio stepped around to face her. Finally, she looked at him with an annoyed expression.

He maintained his smile as he recollected, The White Widow's description … big blue eyes.

"I guess this is as good a place as any to watch from."

"I thought I heard you speaking to a friend. Shouldn't you be looking for him or her?"

And I've heard that British-accented voice. It's her.

Scipio chuckled, "You heard that, did you? You're right. I should call him."

Scipio reached into his pocket with one hand while simultaneously grabbing her thumb with the other, the one over the phone trigger. He shook her hand until the phone fell to the ground. He picked it up and placed it in his pocket.

Still holding her by the thumb, he bent her arm behind her and pointed his pistol at her temple, "Gig's up, lady. Where's your friend?"

Naheed winced in pain as Scipio continued to bend her thumb backwards, "I said, where's your friend?"

"What friend?"

"Your friend wearing the jacket that goes boom."

"I don't know what you're talking about."

Scipio checked the time on his Big-Brutha phone.

Nine fifty-seven.

He picked up the phone trigger. Still holding her thumb, he pushed her in the direction of the path leading to the grassy area.

Naheed struggled with him, "Where are you taking me?"

"We're gonna see if we can find your friend. I'm sure he's somewhere on the grass."

She laughed, "You know, if we find him, he'll be the last person you see."

Scipio pushed her to a slow jog, "Actually, he'll be the last person you see. I'll be standing behind you."

* * * * *

Syed walked between two long lines of beach chairs, directly centered with the grandstand. The chairs were filled with people looking up at the fireworks display, while children surrounded them, the youngest holding sparklers. There were coolers filled with beer and soda, and a few small grills with hotdogs still sitting on them. He stopped and stood in the midst of a particularly dense area. No one seemed to notice him, as the intensity of the display started to increase.

He checked his watch and watched it turn nine-fifty seven. Reaching into his pocket, he took hold of the phone trigger, closed his eyes, and began silently counting down.

CHAPTER 47

GRASS FIELD
THE HENRY FORD MUSEUM
GREENFIELD VILLAGE
DEARBORN, MICHIGAN
9:57 PM (LOCAL), MONDAY, JULY 04, 2016

De Niro made his way to the front of the crowd. A line of police and private security stood at ease facing the crowd, forming a perimeter around the firework's staging area.

A heavy-set, bearded man wearing a high school baseball shirt with "Coach Dave" imprinted on the front pocket approached him. He was wearing a large backpack and carrying and even larger duffel bag. He had to speak up over the noise of the explosions overhead, "Looking for any fireworks?"

De Niro glanced up then back to scanning the crowd, "I think I found them, thanks."

"I meant stuff for you to shoot off afterwards. I still got a bunch of good stuff left, everything from M80s, to mortars, to ten-ball, sky thunder, super big roman candles."

"Roman candles …," De Niro remembered them from his childhood in Ridgewood, New York.

"Yeah," the man held one out, "they're handheld tubes that fire starburst projectiles from one side."

De Niro ignored the man as he heard Scipio speak into his ear-bud, "Cris, I found the girl, but the guy isn't with her, and she won't give him up."

De Niro checked the time.

Nine fifty-seven.

He tapped his comm, unconcerned with the bearded man, "So he's here somewhere. I'll check from the front."

"I'm bringing her up from the rear. I'll look as I go, but Cris, we're not gonna be able to stop him. Watch yourself."

The bearded man realized De Niro was speaking to someone on a comm and put his hands up, palms facing out, "Are you a cop? I was only kidding about the fireworks."

De Niro looked over the man's shoulder. The most crowded area was right in front of him and at least fifty yards deep with people.

The bearded man began backing away but De Niro motioned for him to stop, "Coach Dave, right?"

Confused, the man nodded, "Do we know each other?"

De Niro pointed to the man's shirt and winked, "Do you have the fireworks on you?"

Still not sure whether he was in trouble or not, the man tapped the duffel bag, "I got everything with me."

De Niro reached into his pocket and handed the man a roll of hundred dollar bills, "I'll take everything you got."

Staring wide-eyed at the money, the man took it, dropped the duffel bag, and began counting with a look of elated shock on his face.

De Niro dropped to his knees and quickly unzipped the bag.

The man looked down at him, "Whatta ya doing?! You better be a cop, 'cause there's a line of cops right behind you!"

De Niro ignored him as he rifled through the duffel bag, "Where's the roman candles?!"

The man took his backpack off, unzipped it and reached in, keeping his eyes on the procession of law enforcement right behind them looking up to the sky awaiting the finale. He took two roman candles and showed them to De Niro.

De Niro grabbed them, "Light one."

"Are you, crazy?! You can keep the bags!" The man backed off then lumbered away.

Quickly, De Niro scanned the people standing close by until he spotted a long-haired twenty-something smoking a cigarette. He hurried over to him concealing the roman candles, "Hey man, you got a light?"

The guy reached into his pocket and tossed him a cheap lighter.

Here goes nothing. If I was him, I'd be right in the middle ….

De Niro held one roman candle in his left hand and tucked the other under his arm pit. He struck a flame and lit the fuse then aimed over the heads at the center of the crowd. A few people in front of him backed away when they saw the sparks begin to spit out the end of the tube.

The first starburst ejected from the end, its flame sailed just above the center throng. Instantly, people began scattering in all directions. Some adults ran and grabbed their children, while others ducked and covered themselves.

De Niro started jogging into the parting crowd, as charge after charge shot out. He aimed the projectiles to slam into the grass where the crowd had thinned, inducing the people who had cowered to run. The final bursts of bright colors caused the desired chaos De Niro hoped for, as virtually everyone in the field began dashing for cover. Their stampedes were hindered by all the chairs and debris scattered around. People fell over them and were knocked to the ground.

The first roman candle went idle. Its end ebbed into a small flame. De Niro looked over his shoulder at the police and security as they were making their way toward him. The uniformed men drew their pistols but appeared unsure of what to do next.

They don't want to shoot with all these people running around. Good thing for me!

De Niro turned back to see a solitary figure wearing a bulky jacket standing alone, illuminated only by the strobe effect of fireworks in the air, and seemingly unaware of the chaos all around him.

That's ... what was his name ... Syed!

* * * * *

Syed decided to spend the final sixty seconds silently counting to calm his mind and shut out everything he heard around him. When sixty seconds were up, he opened his eyes and realized he was standing alone.

It took him a moment to grasp that there were embers of fireworks all around him still glowing in the grass. He looked up to see if they were from an errant mortar. Lowering his eyes, he caught a glimpse of a man standing thirty feet away peering at him. He wasn't sure, but the man looked familiar, very familiar.

Syed blinked in confusion then remembered his objective. Surveying around him, he saw people running from the field in every direction.

Clutching the phone trigger, he considered for a moment whether to detonate himself right there, but then caught sight of a throng amassing behind him in the distance.

They're heading for the entrance I used. It won't allow more than a few to pass through at a time.

He let go of the trigger and checked his watch. It read nine fifty-nine.

He heard a voice call out to him, "Don't move!" He recognized the voice. It was the infidel, Cris De Niro.

The fireworks suddenly ceased and darkness enveloped the field. Instantly, Syed began walking as hurriedly as he dared in the direction of the escaping throng.

* * * * *

De Niro watched the crowd disburse, except for Syed who remained standing in place. He glanced back to see the two policemen approaching with their pistols drawn. Quickly, he turned back in the direction of Syed and hollered, "Don't move!"

Hearing De Niro shout, the policemen stopped a few feet to his left and right assuming firing positions. The larger of the two did the talking, "Drop what's in your hands and interlock your fingers behind your head!"

De Niro didn't face either of them, keeping his eyes on Syed, "Officers, that man out there is wearing a suicide vest."

The officers looked out beyond De Niro, as darkness suddenly blanketed the field.

Turning on his flashlight and holding it under his pistol, the same officer repeated his order, "I said drop what's in your hand … now … and interlock your fingers behind your head!"

Ignoring the command, De Niro dipped his head and spoke to his phone, "Double-B, what time is it?"

Bewildered, the officers remained in their firing positions when a muffled, calm, male voice replied, "The time is ten o'clock in the evening, central standard time.

Instantaneously, the grandstand erupted in deafening sound and blinding light, as the entire row of mortars simultaneously fired their final salvos into the air. Within seconds, plumes of multi-colored pyrotechnics irradiated the night sky and everything on the ground within a quarter mile, including the field, the evacuating crowd, and Syed, who was walking hurriedly in their direction.

The policemen lurched and ducked at the sound of the thundering blasts. It took a moment for them to regain their composure and raise their pistols again, only to realize that De Niro was no longer standing between them. Scanning with their flashlights farther out into the field, they spotted De Niro running away at full sprint.

"He's heading for the exit!" Pistols in hand, they took off in pursuit.

* * * * *

Frustrated at the slow pace he had to maintain, Syed lost ground to the evacuating mass ahead of him. Naheed had engrained in him just how volatile TATP was, and how sensitive it was to agitation of any kind, so he had to remain walking. Thoughts of regret began filling his mind.

Why did I not detonate myself when I was back there in the crowd? I should not have closed my eyes!

He looked around.

Why did Naheed not detonate me?

Those thoughts disappeared, and his frustration turned to

nervous excitement when he saw a crowd forming at the narrow security checkpoint. Syed carefully picked up his pace, considering the growing throng his ticket to Paradise.

* * * * *

De Niro ran as fast as his legs could carry him. He closed the distance to Syed to under thirty feet, but could tell he wouldn't be able to reach him in time.

He slowed to a jog and tapped his comm, "Scip!"

"Cris, where are you?"

"No time to explain. Are you near the Security Checkpoint?"

"Roger that. We're coming up on it now."

De Niro didn't miss that he said "we," but there was no time to inquire.

"Scipio, it's the one we told you about, Syed. He's heading that way. No way to stop him. He'll detonate as soon as he reaches the throng. Get those people to take shelter now!"

Increasing his pace to a full dash, De Niro didn't wait for a reply.

* * * * *

Gazing at the large crowd clogged on the far side of the Security Checkpoint, Scipio realized the dilemma he was facing. There would be no way for him to both warn the crowd and maintain custody of Naheed. From the urgency in De Niro's voice, his choice was clear.

Scipio shoved Naheed, knocking her to the ground then raced past her slicing through bunches of frightened people. In front of two uniformed police officers directing the human traffic, he jumped up onto one of the perimeter tables to see over the crowd and into the field, but his vision was limited to the illuminated area nearest the checkpoint. He couldn't see anyone resembling Syed, and there was no way for him to know how close he was.

Ahead of Scipio was a mass of scared people doing their best to compress themselves into single-file lines. Scipio tried unsuccessfully to get everyone's attention by shouting to them, so he drew his pistol and fired four shots into a large trash bin at his feet. The two policemen knelt and drew their pistols, while some of the women screamed in terror as he held up his hand and shouted, "I'm with the FBI! Do exactly as I say! A bomb is about to go off in the field! Everyone, turn the tables around you on their sides and get down behind them! Do it now!

Scipio watched for a moment as no one moved. Finally, the two policemen grabbed one of the tables and started turning it over. They repeated Scipio's orders and the people nearest the checkpoint began helping while passing the word back to the people behind them.

Knowing he'd most likely never spot Syed, Scipio jumped down and began helping.

* * * * *

Near the checkpoint, Syed heard the gunshots and someone shouting something, but he didn't hear what was said. He knew it had to be something about him when he saw the people turning the tables over. His nostrils flared and he picked up his pace even more.

They are too late!

* * * * *

De Niro heard four shots and hoped they were fired by Scipio.
That's my cue … If I'm gonna do something, it has to be now!
He had less than a minute to consider his options.

If I can't catch up to him, I'll have to try and detonate him remotely, before he reaches those people.

Pulling the lighter from his pocket, De Niro dropped to the
ground and lit the remaining roman candle. As soon as the fuse
ignited, he heard the voice of the large policeman from behind him,
"Don't move!"

Approaching De Niro with caution, the two officers stepped
around him on each side with their guns pointing at his head. They
made it to within a foot of De Niro when they saw the fuse disappear into the long tube he was holding.

"Get down!" cried De Niro.

After hesitating for only a split second, both fell onto their bel-
lies, as the first fireball erupted from the end of the tube. The fiery
mixture of bentonite, lifting charge, pyrotechnic star, black powder,
and delay charge hurled over the right shoulder of Syed, exploding
when it hit one of the tables.

The bigger cop shouted, "What the hell are you doing?!"

De Niro adjusted his aim, "Brace yourself!"

The officers looked up just in time to see a second fireball explode from the tube.

* * * * *

Syed flinched when the fiery orb soared over his shoulder. It
almost knocked him off his feet, passing so close he felt the heat on
his neck. The explosion illuminated everything in front of him. He

could see that not everyone made it behind the tables. Just twenty feet from him, people were lying on the ground, some huddled next to others, some alone, some lying flat, and others curled up in fetal positions.

His mind became focused on only one thing – reaching them. Regaining his balance and clutching the phone trigger securely in his hand, Syed took off running, no longer considering the danger of prematurely setting off the bomb.

Just a few meters closer and it won't matter where I detonate, Allah be praised!

Syed saw brightness overtaking him even before he triggered the bomb. Continuing to run as fast as he was able, he smiled.

I must be entering Paradise! It is beautiful!!

The thump on his back wiped the smile from his face.

* * * * *

Naheed got to her feet, at first, not knowing what just happened. She saw the man who had overtaken her running ahead and disappearing into the exiting crowd. Then it occurred to her.

It must be Syed!

After looking for police, Naheed decided to check the field before making her escape. She had to know what happened to Syed, so she made her way to the fence and looked in. There, she saw why Scipio let her go.

Four shots rang out. She watched as he began ordering the others to take cover.

But, where is Syed? He must be close by!

She couldn't see anything beyond the security checkpoint area as the field was covered in darkness.

Naheed cursed to herself as she continued to check all around for police.

I'm in danger of being caught every second I linger here, but Syed must be close. Why else would he let me go?

Naheed's attention was drawn to the sound of screams erupting from the area near the now turned-over tables. They were followed closely by a streak of light slamming into one of the tables closest to the field.

The streak erupted into a bright explosion of light, illuminating the entire area. Naheed could clearly see people lying on the ground, on both sides of the tables. She looked out to the field, in the direction of the streak of light, and saw a solitary figure about fifty meters away from the checkpoint. Her eyes glittered when she realized who it was.

Syed!

Naheed's moment of exuberance became one of horror when she saw a second streak of light suddenly erupt out of the darkness from a point some meters behind Syed. The streak seemed to slice a white line through the gloom. Helplessly, Naheed watched as the line came to an end, slamming into Syed's back.

Less than a second passed before Syed took on the appearance of the Sun. Naheed had to shut her eyes tightly and turn away from the brightness of the flash. A split second passed before the boom of the explosion reached her ears.

Naheed grabbed hold of the fence in anticipation. At first, her heart raced with excitement seeing nothing but stillness and smoke, accompanied by dead quiet as the echoes of the mighty blast faded.

Her heart sank as she watched people emerge from behind the tables, many of them heading out into the field to check on those lying in the field. She couldn't believe her eyes as-one after another-all the people lying in the field got to their feet. Some were wailing in pain, others were silent from shock, but none appeared to have life-threatening injuries or mutilations.

Naheed's heart filled with anger.

Total failure! All the effort and time and money ... wasted!

She rubbed her temples to try to relieve the pounding headache growing from her inability to process her first failure.

Staring at Syed's smoldering remains, her thoughts changed.

I didn't fail, that fool failed!

And then she spotted him. Naheed's face contorted into a wolf-like snarl, as she glared down at the small man dressed in black as he sprung up from behind one of the overturned tables. Her hands tightened into claws pressing against the wire mesh of the cyclone fence.

That man is to blame! He will die by my hand!

Filled with fury, Naheed withdrew her fingers from the fence and headed with intent along the outer perimeter toward the security checkpoint. A few feet from the end, nonchalantly, she picked up a discarded beer bottle from the dirt. There were a number of them lying under a sign that read "Bringing bottles onto the field during the fireworks show is prohibited."

Maintaining her brisk walking pace, she effortlessly broke the bottle on the end of the fence then turned onto the path leading down to the field. Naheed quickly glanced at the jagged weapon she was now holding.

It took her a moment to relocate the man responsible.

He will regret letting me go!

Scipio had moved out into the field and was now helping a bloody, dazed woman to her feet.

The farther down the path Naheed walked, the more congested it became. Terrified and wounded people were walking like zombies in all directions. The air smelled like a mixture of grilled hotdogs, hamburgers, chicken, exploded fireworks, and ironically, the mildly-pleasant, acetone-laced odor of ignited TATP.

Reaching midway through the line of overturned tables, Naheed spotted two police officers walking in her direction on either side of a man with a familiar face.

Cris De Niro ….

Naheed stopped in her tracks and watched as the small man dressed in black ran over to them.

Of course, … that one must work for Cris De Niro!

As if he knew she was there, the one dressed in black suddenly twisted his head and looked in her direction. Naheed turned around quickly only to see a battery of police converging on the entrance, at the security checkpoint.

Shit!

Naheed let the shard from the bottle fall out of her hand as she weaved herself into the exiting throng of traumatized locals. She passed two groups of police and paramedics who offered her assistance, one at the security checkpoint entrance and another at a triage staging area in the adjacent small parking lot. She turned them down with a simple shake of her head before finally making her way out the main entrance to the park.

As paramedic vehicles and fire engines roared past her on the street, Naheed looked back in the direction of the field once more. Her rage receded with a thought that brought a haughty grin.

His death wasn't worth my life.

Naheed decided to put some distance between her and the growing mayhem at the park. She walked several blocks before calling Uber and waited the eight minutes standing in the shadow cast from a Christian church. The name on the sign said, "The Church of Our Savior."

She shook her head. The irony didn't escape her.

Getting into the front passenger seat the world's most infamous female terrorist casually escaped from the scene, into the night.

CHAPTER 48

ROOM 303
UNIVERSITY OF MICHIGAN HOSPITALS AND HEALTH CENTERS
ANN ARBOR, MICHIGAN
1:30 PM (LOCAL), TUESDAY, JULY 05, 2016

Checking the hall to make sure doctors or nurses were not heading toward the room, Mugsy Ricci closed the door and opened his attaché. He withdrew three of five champagne flutes, a next-gen cork remover, and a $6,700 bottle of Armand de Brignac Brut Gold Champagne.

He pressed the stainless-steel champagne opener onto the cork, gave it a slight twist, and effortlessly ejected the cork from the bottle. The popping sound was barely audible.

Ricci filled the tall glasses midway with the pricey bubbly and handed served Karla and her brother, as Kevin gingerly sat up in his hospital bed with his leg wrapped in bandages.

"I thought Tonio and Terrell were coming?"

"They came early this morning. Tonio said he had 'other important matters to attend to' this afternoon, whatever that means."

Ricci motioned to Karla with his glass, "Time to contact the Keystone Cops."

Karla smiled as she tapped the communications app on her

Big-Brutha then held it so Ricci and Kevin could also see. Within seconds, the screen came alive with images of Johnny-F, Rigoni, De May, Pescalitis, and Gunny Proctor aboard Warbird. They gathered together so the camera could capture all of them. Karla and Kevin could see they too were holding identical flutes of champagne.

Karla shook her head with a smile, "You haven't left the ground yet, but I see the party has started."

Johnny-F held up a clone of the bottle Mugsy just opened, "Actually, our benevolent leader left Mugsy and me explicit instructions to open these ridiculously expensive bottles, so we can all toast to the success of Project New Detroit!"

Vin Rigoni jumped in, "How's your leg, Kevin?"

"It's fine … something I've been trying to tell everyone around here—"

"The doctor said he lost close to two pints of blood and was going into to shock when he arrived," Karla interjected.

"Which reminds me," Kevin took over again, I wanted to thank Mr. De Niro. The doctor told me the way he bandaged my leg saved my life. Is he there?"

"I'm afraid not," replied Johnny-F. "He had other important matters to attend to, but he instructed me to lead the toast …."

Kevin Mathews looked at his sister and Mugsy, "Again, with the 'other important matters?'"

Johnny-F raised his glass. Everyone on both sides of the video call followed.

"To Kevin's leg healing so he can take the helm of a fully-funded Project New Detroit!"

The men behind him hollered, "Hear, hear!"

Ricci and Karla echoed them, "Hear, hear!"

Karla leaned in and kissed her brother's cheek before everyone emptied their glasses.

A quiet moment went by while they savored the elegant champagne.

"Mm-mmm, now that was a taste of Heaven," Kevin Matthews held up his glass and motioned to Mugsy for a refill. Johnny-F did the same.

Matthews' tone turned sincere, "I want to thank all of you. None of this would be possible without the risks you took, and the efforts you made. And I especially want thank my sister Karla for introducing me to Cris De Niro."

He paused then raised his glass, "To Cris De Niro!"

Once again, everyone hollered, "Hear, hear," before emptying their glasses.

Karla said good-bye to the men aboard Warbird before signing off.

Mugsy looked at the time on his Big-Brutha, "Karla, we better get a move on if we want to catch the Delta non-stop to Arlington. It departs at two-fifty-six."

Karla nodded then looked down at her brother, "Do you promise to obey the doctor? If she says 'you should stay overnight,' no arguments, got it, little brother?"

"I got it, sis. Now, go already, so I can get started convincing her that it's in her best interest to discharge me."

Karla put her hands on her hips, "And how is that in her best interest?"

A grin appeared on her brother's face, "Because then I can take her to a nice romantic dinner this evening. Did ya notice she's a beautiful lady, and she wasn't wearing a wedding ring?"

The three erupted in laughter.

* * * * *

Johnny-F looked around the main cabin then headed into the forward cabin where he found Scipio sitting in front of a bank of monitors. He stepped up behind him, poured another flute of champagne and handed it to him, while he studied the feeds on the screens.

Scipio broke out of deep thought, took the glass and tapped it against Francis's, "Thanks, what's the occasion?"

"Let's see, we toasted to Karla's brother, to the success of Project New Detroit, and to our illustrious leader."

Scipio raised his glass, "Cool," then downed it in one gulp and handed the empty flute back to Francis.

Johnny-F leaned in to study the screens closer, "You know you just guzzled about $300 worth of champagne."

Before Scipio could respond, Francis pointed to the screens, "What exactly are we looking at?"

Scipio leaned back and stretched, "Feeds from the airport, bus station, train station, ferry station, and a few highway traffic cams. Basically, a waste of time."

"You're looking for that woman?"

Scipio rubbed his eyes, "That woman, who just happens to be the world's most notorious female terrorist. The infamous White Widow ... I had her in my grasp and I let go."

"From what you told us, you had to let her go or a lot of people would've died."

Scipio got up from his chair as Duke O'Rourke and Charger Miller joined them. They remained quiet, but had heard the conversation as they walked in.

Scipio nodded to them then replied to Francis, "That's the thing.

I let her go to try and save a bunch of people, but she's out there now, free to murder a whole bunch more. For all we know, her next attack will jeopardize ten times the amount of people as this one … or even a hundred or thousand times more."

No one replied.

Scipio took the bottle from Francis, took a swig, then handed it to O'Rourke who did the same before handing it to Miller.

Scipio winked with a sarcastic grin, "I should've heeded the age-old adage, 'a terrorist in hand is worth two in the bush.'"

"Nonsense," Duke spoke up. "You did what you had to do. You made a choice. You chose to save lives now. Besides, there's no guarantee she'll even be able to plan another attack. This one obviously didn't work out too well. Her terrorist superiors might not be too happy about that. And who knows, she might be caught before leaving the country."

Scipio turned his back to the others and began staring at the screens before answering without turning around, "She'll escape and she'll plan another act of terrorism. I'll just have to stop her before she murders anyone else."

O'Rourke glanced at Francis who just shook his head.

Miller broke the silence, "Anyone know when Cris is getting back? Our gas tanks are topped off and we're ready to fly. I want to get home in time for tonight's day-after Fourth of July barbecue at Cris's house."

"Who planned that?" asked Francis.

"Duke and I just got an invite from Cris's sons, Richard and Louis."

"I got one too," added Scipio. He winked at the pilots, "Didn't you, John?"

Francis tapped on his phone a number of times, "Uh … hmm …

the smtp server must be lagging. I'm sure my invite is coming."

Scipio put his arm around the über-tech genius's shoulder, "Don't worry about it. You can be my date tonight."

CHAPTER 49

Terrell sat on the stoop outside his grandmother's home. Tonio stood in front of him speaking into his cell phone, "Okay, we're here."

Briggs slipped the phone into his pocket, "That was Mr. D. He said he's on his way to the airport, but he wants to give you something before he leaves, so he's coming here first."

Terrell looked up with his brow raised, "Give me something? Mr. D is coming here, now?"

Tonio took a seat next to the young man and put his arm around his shoulder, "T … I wasn't supposed to tell you about any of this yet. Mr. D made me promise to wait until after he left—"

"Tell me what? What's goin' on?"

"Mr. D is setting up a college scholarship fund in Teddy's name, the 'Ted Brown College Fund.' It'll be tied to Project New Detroit."

Tonio took a flyer from his pocket and read from it, "Let's see … the fund will pay full tuition and room and board for up to ten scholarship recipients per year to attend any university in the State of Michigan. To be awarded, the recipient must live in Detroit, agree to complete a four-year college degree as a full-time student, while also agreeing to intern with one of the companies that'll be based in P-N-D.

"At the end of the internship and upon graduation, the recipient could be offered a full-time position with the company."

Terrell nodded his head deeply, "That's … cool, very cool. A scholarship fund named after Teddy. He would've like that."

Terrell thought a moment, "But why couldn't you share that with me, until after Mr. D left?"

Tonio's eyes sparkled as his lips stretched into a wide smile, "'Cause Mr. D and I are the only Trustees. He put me in charge of selecting the recipients and I told him I've already selected the first recipient."

Terrell stared back then shot to his feet as it sunk in, "Me …? I'm the first recipient? You're choosing me?!"

Tonio belly-laughed.

Terrell paced back in forth with nervous excitement, "I should go tell Grandmom! Wait … what if I can't handle the classes, or keep up my grades? Heck, I can't even get to the classes with Detroit's crappy public transit system."

Tonio stood up and stretched, "Well, making the grades is on you, son. I know you can do it or I wouldn't have considered rewarding you the scholarship. You're a hardworking, smart young man when you want to be."

The sound of a car approaching grew louder. Tonio waved his arm for Terrell to follow him to the curb.

"As to getting to classes, I think Mr. D has a solution."

On cue, De Niro pulled in front of them driving a brand new, billet silver Chrysler 300. He jumped out and tossed the keys to

Tonio as he walked around the car.

Tonio handed the keys back to him, "Sorry Mr. D, I had to tell him about the scholarship before you left. This honor also has to go to you."

Terrell put his hand out. De Niro extended his intending to shake it, but Terrell used his grip to pull De Niro close, "I don't know what to say, Mr. D, except … thank you! And I won't let you down."

"I know you won't, son." De Niro looked over his shoulder at Tonio and nodded at the car."

Tonio folded his arms, trying to maintain a straight face, "I didn't tell him about that yet."

"You might as well."

Terrell broke from De Niro and turned to Tonio, "Tell me what? Something else?"

"Mr. D wanted it to look like it was coming from me, but—"

Tonio was cut off as De Niro tossed him the keys. Tonio handed them to Terrell, "These are yours, so you can get to your classes on time."

Terrell's eyes locked on the keys in his hands. He was speechless.

"The car is all yours, son," said De Niro. "The title is in your name, paid in full, including insurance and registration."

Tonio's eyes met De Niro's, as they saw Terrell wiping tears from his.

"I don't know what to say. I can't thank you enough …."

Gently, De Niro laid his hand on the back of Terrell's neck, "Don't thank me, thank God."

That made Terrell look up, smile, and nod.

"Thank you, Father God!"

De Niro patted his back, "Now, if you don't mind, how about

testing your new wheels by dropping me off at the airport. I have a plane full of knuckleheads probably drinking me out of house and home waiting for me."

De Niro got in the back seat and Tonio got in the front, as Terrell ran around to the driver's side and started the car.

"Hooey ... that sounds like one sweet engine," said Tonio.

De Niro smiled with pride, "Five-point-seven-liter, V8, HEMI® MDS VVT engine. Only the best for our young apprentice."

Terrell put the car in gear and left the curb in a lurch.

Tonio mock-braced himself placing his hand on the dashboard in front of him, "I forgot to tell you one more requirement of the scholarship recipients. They can't kill the Trustees."

The car filled with laughter.

CHAPTER 50

De Niro picked up an empty champagne bottle from the table, as Scipio stood with his arms crossed, his eyes jumping from one monitor to the other.

De Niro dangled the bottle in front of Scipio's face, "I see Johnny-F chose from the bottom row of our onboard stock."

Scipio took the bottle and turned, "That's what you get for leaving that knucklehead in charge of anything."

"Dare I ask how many bottles were part of the victory celebration?"

Scipio raised his brow with a grin, "Since I downed an entire bottle, I think I'll exercise my fifth amendment right."

It was De Niro's turn to raise a brow.

"If it matters, it was a really good vintage … and we toasted to your health."

"No wonder John's been evading me ever since I came aboard." De Niro glanced at the monitors, "Any progress?"

Scipio leaned down and typed onto a keyboard in front of the screens then stood up straight again, "Negative. I just set the system to record these feeds until midnight. I'll review the tape when I get back to the Coyote's Den."

"What good will that do?"

"Probably no good." Scipio grabbed one of his elbows and pushed it up to stretch, then exhaled audibly, "We already alerted the Feds. They have a region-wide APB out for her now, but something tells me the White Widow will elude capture."

Scipio walked past De Niro and took a seat at the forward-most table. De Niro followed and sat opposite him. Both men strapped themselves in, as the whine from Warbird's turbines increased initiating their taxi roll.

Scipio raised the window screen and gazed out the portal, "Since I can't stay to help find her, the least I can do is review those feeds, especially since I'm the person who got the best look at her."

De Niro knew the remark was pointed at him, "The FBI made it plain Scip ... they appreciated your offer, but didn't need your assistance."

Scipio muted a chuckle, "My infamous reputation lives on."

De Niro closed his eyes and interlocked his fingers, resting his palms on his stomach, "Who knows, maybe you'll spot her on the recording. Then you can enjoy telling them 'I told you so.'"

Scipio glanced at De Niro and decided to do the same, lowering the window shade, and closing his eyes, "Or maybe I won't tell them anything at all."

The interior of Warbird fell quiet as the large aircraft ascended into the bright afternoon sky. In the forward Ops Cabin, monitors continued to cycle through the various feeds Scipio set to be recorded.

On the leftmost monitor, the one cycling camera views from each of the terminals at Detroit Metropolitan Airport, a woman dressed in flight attendant's wardrobe flashed onto the screen. The stately blonde was leaving a bathroom rolling an overnight bag behind her and mixing into a small group of people, in the General Aviation Terminal. Within seconds, she had walked from view.

* * * * *

Naheed strode assertively, but not briskly, trying her best not to look up or conspicuously away from the security cameras she spotted out of the corner of her eyes. She headed directly out of one of the windowed doors leading to the tarmac and then to the largest private aircraft parked outside, A Bombardier Global 8000. The impressive aircraft was scheduled to fly eight automotive executives to London, non-stop.

London was where Naheed wanted to go. She had planned her escape months before. Regardless of whether the operation was successful or not, Naheed wanted to return to England, because of her ability to blend in and disappear. She chose the method of transport – private jet – because of the ultra—lax customs and security of private flights, especially lax for the crews working private flights.

Naheed researched uniforms worn by private jet flight attendants and purchased one, complete with the appropriate name badge. The British-born terrorist was about to assume yet another alias.

Naheed slowed her pace to call an Algerian computer hacker living in Paris, named Karim.

Like other young Muslim extremists with computer skills, Karim contracted his services to various terrorist organizations. Karim had performed several jobs for the White Widow in the past, including hacking into and altering a Norwegian cargo line's secured ship's manifest; shutting down a Kenyan police station's security camera surveillance system; and most-recently, adding Naheed's alias to the Detroit Department of Motor Vehicles driver's license database.

This time she tasked Karim with sending an email to masquerade as an inter-corporate email from the company that booked the flight attendant for this London flight.

Naheed watched the pilot, co-pilot, and a female flight attendant climb the steps to the jet, as she spoke into her phone, "Is it done?"

Karim's voice was one of an early-twenties geek, fast-talking and almost incomprehensible to Naheed because of his street-French-Arabic accent.

"Yes, of course, of course. It was easy."

"What's the attendant's name?"

"Pauline Appleby, a silly British name. And your name is Donna Andrews."

"You made sure the email is an exact duplicate?"

"You think I'm a stupid man?"

Naheed ignored him, "And you made sure the email looks like it was sent from the company, correct?"

Naheed heard laughter, "No, I did a shitty job. You will definitely be caught!"

Naheed, now Donna Andrews, had no time or patience for an impudent Algerian punk, "Karim, I have given your address and the addresses of your mother, sister, and girlfriend to my associates in Paris. If I don't contact them from London after touchdown of this flight, they are instructed to find you and your family and slit your throats. I won't ask again."

The laughter ceased and the call fell silent.

Finally, Karim spoke slower and with a sheepish tone, "I assure you, it's an exact duplicate of real thing. Lady, you, tell your friends … leave me and my people alone."

"You better be right, dear boy."

The White Widow put her phone away as she climbed the steps and entered the cabin of the magnificent jet.

She was confronted first by the flight attendant. She offered her hand, "Hi, you must be Ms. Appleby?"

The flight attendant smiled, "And you must be Ms. Andrews. How about you call me Pauline and I call you—"

"Donna," Naheed smiled. "Nice to meet you, Pauline."

"Same here Donna. I was notified by our illustrious boss this morning that I'm supposed to show you the ropes."

Naheed bit her lower lip, "I hope you don't mind. I mean, I know it was rather short notice. I sort of begged to be trained on this flight."

The senior flight attendant winked, "Definitely not because of my legendary reputation. Missing home, are we?"

"Guilty. But I'm sure I'll be spreading the word of your reputation, after this flight. That is, if you can put up with my rookie mistakes."

The pilot appeared from the cockpit, "And who have we here?"

Appleby replied, "Captain Maury Wells, this is flight attendant-in-training Donna Andrews. Donna will be joining us for this flight to soak up all of my in-flight knowhow and experience."

Captain Wells took Naheed's hand in his, "Well isn't that nice. Very nice to meet you Mrs. … or is it Ms. …?"

Appleby removed Naheed's hand from the Captain's, "Lesson one, my dear, never trust a pilot, except on take-offs and landings."

The co-pilot appeared behind the pilot and tipped his cap.

Appleby turned Naheed and guided her away. She spoke loud enough for both men to hear, "Lesson two, don't trust any man who earns his living in a cock pit."

The pilots' laughter filled the cabin.

The White Widow began welcoming passengers onto the jet, all middle-aged American men, a few flirting with her from the moment they stepped aboard. She secretly delighted in serving the American pigs wine and food and putting up with their flirting, while escaping capture right under their noses.

Within minutes, the passengers were seated and Naheed was helping Pauline secure the cabin door. She took one last look outside before the door was closed.

Thinking about the American who had almost captured her, she waited for Appleby to walk away before whispering to herself lines from one of her favorite plays.

"Go hence, to have more talk of these sad things. Some shall be pardon'd, and some punished ...."

The White Widow flashed a spiteful grin and added, "But not today."

###

AUTHOR'S FINAL NOTE

Reports: Dearborn cleric radicalized London attacker

Detroit News staff and wire reports Published 11:57 a.m. ET June 5, 2017

A Dearborn cleric popular among Islamic State extremists helped radicalize one of the terror suspects in the London attacks that killed seven people Saturday, according to reports.

According to the Telegraph, a former friend of one of the three dead suspects claimed one of the attackers had been radicalized while watching Dearborn cleric Ahmad Musa Jibril's YouTube videos and said he contacted authorities after becoming concerned over his friend's extremist views.

The friend, who was not identified at the request of police, told the BBC's Asian Network: "We spoke about a particular attack that happened and like most radicals he had a justification for anything and everything and that day I realized I needed to contact the authorities."

He added: "He used to listen to a lot of Musa Jibril. I have heard some of this stuff and it's very radical. I am surprised this stuff is still on YouTube and is easily accessible. I phoned the anti-terror hotline. I spoke to the gentleman. I told him about our conversation and why I think he was radicalized."

The suspected attacker was not arrested and was allowed to keep his passport. "I did my bit, I know a lot of other people did their bit, but the authorities did not do their bit," the friend said.

British police arrested a dozen people Sunday in a widening terrorism investigation after attackers using a van and large knives turned a balmy evening of nightlife into a bloodbath and killed seven people in the heart of London. Three of the suspects died in the attacks. The Islamic State group claimed responsibility.

A 2014 report by the London-based International Center of the Study for Radicalization and Political Violence described Jibril, 46, a popular Palestinian-American cleric born in Dearborn and another Western-based cleric, Musa Cerantonio, as "important figures whose political, moral and spiritual messages are considered attractive to a number of foreign fighters" and cited their following on social media.

"Their popularity is also reflected on Twitter, where they are followed by 60 and 23 percent of foreign fighters respectively, and is particularly strong among groups like ISIS, whose members provide a majority of their likes and follows."

The report added: "None of this should suggest that either individual is a member of ISIS or Jabhat al-Nusrah, nor should it be taken as indicating that they are involved in facilitating the recruitment of foreign fighters."

In 2005, Ahmad Jibril and his father, Musa Abdallah Jibril, 66, were convicted on 42 counts of an indictment charging them with bank fraud, conspiracy, money laundering and other counts. Ahmad Jibril was sentenced to 5 years and 10 months in prison; his father, to 4 years and 10 months. Federal authorities accused the Jibrils of buying 13 homes and two apartment buildings in Metro Detroit since 1988 and insuring them for far more than they were worth. They were accused of defrauding six local banks of more than $250,000.

The government produced a 'Supplemental Sentencing Memorandum' that stated that a family photo album seized during the investigation contained 'photos of Ahmad as a teenager dressed as a mujahid… (and) photos of very young children holding apparently real firearms, "playing" at holding each other hostage and aiming the weapons at each other's heads,' according to the report by International Center of the Study for Radicalization and Political Violence.

The memorandum also revealed that Ahmad Musa Jibril was running a radical Salafi website (AlSalayfoon.com) at the time of his arrest that "contained a library of fanatically anti-American sermons by militant Islamic clerics, in English and in Arabic."

They also found that he had sent a fax to CNN in 1996 claiming responsibility for the Khobar Towers bombing in Saudi Arabia, warning "[t]here will be a series of bombings that will follow no matter how many lives of ours are taken."

In March 2015, a federal judge in Detroit ordered Jibril to testify about his finances, days before his supervised probation was set to expire.

During a hearing in U.S. District Court, Chief Judge Gerald Rosen ordered Jibril to testify under oath about the source of his income. Jibril cited his Fifth Amendment right against self-incrimination.

During the 2015 court proceedings, Jibril's attorney Rita Chastang said "there is no evidence he is hiding assets."

The Saturday assault unfolded over a few terrifying minutes, starting when a rented van veered off the road and barreled into pedestrians on busy London Bridge. Three men then got out of the vehicle with large knives and attacked people at bars and restaurants in nearby Borough Market until they were shot dead by police.

"They went: 'This is for Allah,' and they had a woman on the floor. They were stabbing her," witness Gerard Vowls said.

Florin Morariu, a Romanian chef who works in the Bread Ahead bakery, said he saw people running and some fainting. Then two people approached another person and "began to stick the knife in … and then I froze and I didn't know what to do."

He said he managed to get near one attacker and "hit him around the head" with a bread basket.

"There was a car with a loudspeaker saying 'go, go' and they (police) threw a grenade. ... and then I ran," he said.

London police said officers killed the attackers within eight minutes of arriving at the scene. Eight officers fired some 50 rounds, said Assistant Commissioner Mark Rowley, the force's head of counterterrorism.

Islamic State's statement Sunday from its Aamaq news agency claimed the group's "fighters" were responsible, according to the SITE Intelligence Group.

The Author

Gerard de Marigny is an American novelist and screenplay writer. He is currently beginning work on WHITE WIDOW (ARCHANGEL: Mission Logs #3), and the novella JOSHUA'S COUNTRY. Both books are also scheduled for release in 2017.

Since his 2011 inaugural publication of THE WATCHMAN OF EPHRAIM (CRIS DE NIRO, Book 1), Mr. de Marigny has independently published five CRIS DE NIRO novels and two ARCHANGEL novellas. These literary works are set in the days and years following September 11, 2001 when a non-governmental based counter-terrorism firm is formed to respond to crises born from a variety of modern geopolitical events.

The series of books resonate with espionage, sub-genre fiction readers from around the world. The books have become Amazon best sellers in eight countries and Gerard has over 200,000 fan followers from across the world.

Prior to his writing career, Gerard worked in the financial services industry, and prior to that, he wrote, recorded and produced music for other artists, for television and was a member of the rock band, Americade. He is a graduate of Penn State University. Gerard and his wife Lisa live in the foothills of Las Vegas, Nevada with their four sons, Jared, Ryan, Jordan, and Noah.

Follow Gerard de Marigny

Author's Website: www.GerarddeMarigny.com
Facebook: www.facebook.com/Gerarddem
Twitter: www.twitter.com/GerarddeMarigny
Publisher's Website: www.JarRyJorNoPublishing.com
Contact Gerard de Marigny
mailto:g@GerarddeMarigny.com

Also by Gerard de Marigny

NOW AVAILABLE

IN EBOOK, PAPERBACK, AUDIOBOOK* FORMATS!

(*Audiobook editions available only for Books 1-3)

CRIS DE NIRO

Also by Gerard de Marigny

NOW AVAILABLE

IN EBOOK AND PAPERBACK

ARCHANGEL

COMING SOON!

NEW *ARCHANGEL!*

WHITE WIDOW
Mission Log #3

From Master Storyteller
Gerard de Marigny